DEATH OF A TOTAL WASHOUT

"Too bad about Cluett. What was it? Pneumonia?"

Tillie shook his head. "He was shot."

"*Shot?*" A line-of-duty death was the last thing Sigrid expected for Michael Cluett.

"Last night," said Tillie, pleased to have captured her complete attention. "They found him early this morning, just three blocks from his house in Manhattan Beach."

"What happened? Who shot him?"

"Unknown. Off-duty, though. Eberstadt talked to a guy over with the Six-Four and he said they've got a diver working around the footbridge that goes across the bay to Emmons Avenue."

Tillie gave an involuntary shiver at the thought of diving into Sheepshead Bay today.

Sigrid walked out into the squad room, trailed by Tillie, who speculated aloud on the chances of those divers finding anything more than rusty crab traps and broken beer bottles. . . .

BY MARGARET MARON

PAST
IMPERFECT

MARGARET MARON

BANTAM BOOKS
NEW YORK LONDON TORONTO SYDNEY AUCKLAND

PAST IMPERFECT

A Bantam Crime Line Book / published in association with Doubleday

PUBLISHING HISTORY
Doubleday edition published February 1991
Bantam edition / May 1992

ISBN 0-553-29546-2

Published simultaneously in the United States and Canada

Bantam Books are published by Bantam Books, a division of Bantam Doubleday Dell Publishing Group, Inc. Its trademark, consisting of the words "Bantam Books" and the portrayal of a rooster, is Registered in U.S. Patent and Trademark Office and in other countries. Marca Registrada. Bantam Books, 666 Fifth Avenue, New York, New York 10103.

PRINTED IN THE UNITED STATES OF AMERICA

RAD   0 9 8 7 6 5 4 3 2 1

For Toby and Margaret Maron Quaranto,
who have proved over the years that water may
indeed be as thick as blood.

My thanks to Carolyn Wheat, Jean Quaranto, Priscilla Ridgway, and Susan Bonanni for their help with certain technical details.

PAST
IMPERFECT

Chapter
1

The Urban Renewal Society on a raw January night was basically no different from a dozen other middle-class bars that dotted lower Manhattan. There was the same smell of booze and tobacco mingled with damp woolen overcoats, the same gleaming mirrors and glass shelves of multihued bottles behind a long oak bar, the same small square tables at the front and larger round ones at the rear, the same smoky blues drifting in and out between voices, laughter, the tinkle of ice on glass.

Many New York bars, though, used pulldown steel mesh to protect against break-ins. The Urban Renewal Society's barred door had once secured a holding cell in a now-vanished precinct station. Some bars had pictures of prize fighters on their walls; others, depending on their clientele, displayed prominent politicians, movie stars, or TV celebrities. The Urban Renewal Society catered unabashedly to cops and its walls were a rogues' gallery of uniformed police officers. Scrawled across the pictures were words of affectionate derision: "To Sal and Mike, who now have a license to steal." Or "To Mike—good luck keeping Sal's hand out of the till!" These were interspersed with signed photographs of four of the last six police commissioners plus one elegantly tailored inspector now retired from Scotland Yard, an impassive-looking Navaho Tribal Police officer, and a beautiful blonde SBI agent from North Carolina.

Amid old-fashioned handcuffs, nightsticks, whistles, and other police paraphernalia from bygone days, the two ex-cops who owned the place had hung a somber wooden plaque with the names and badge numbers of former customers, men and women both, who'd been killed in the line of duty.

Over the cash register hung a twenty-dollar bill, a twenty tendered for a round of drinks on opening day and framed for good luck because it was the first bill to slide across the gleaming new bar.

Counterfeit, of course.

"—another Miller Lite for the returning hero and me," said Matt Eberstadt, who was just sober enough to remember he was supposed to avoid extra calories. "And gin and tonic for the new millionaire."

The barman was devoid of curiosity and merely repeated the big detective's order, "Two Miller Lites, one GT, what else?"

"Scotch for the Gold Dust Twins, a Molson for the dear departing, and—and—" He blinked beerily at the thin gray-eyed woman who sat opposite him at Urban Renewal's largest rear table. "And bourbon and Coke for the lieutenant!" he finished with a triumphant grin.

"Jeez, Eberstadt," grumbled Bernie Peters, fishing in his glass for the slice of lime as the waiter headed back toward the bar. "If I'd wanted the whole world to know about my win, I'd have rented that moving sign at Times Square."

Eberstadt's rumpled face registered hurt and Jim Lowry, whose sandy brown hair was nowhere near the gold of the woman seated beside him, said, "Aw, come on, Bernie. Tell us how much. You can trust us. We're family."

"Sure, sure," Peters jeered.

"Leave him alone," said the blonde as a mischievous dimple flashed in her smooth cheek. "He's afraid we'll tell the little wife. Afraid she'll spend it all again."

"And am I wrong?" Bernie Peters leaned around Eberstadt's bulky figure to confront the young detective face-to-face. A very attractive face, too, but Bernie usually reacted to her needling too automatically to register Elaine Albee's blonde prettiness anymore.

"Look what happened last month," he complained. "I win three hundred and she buys Christmas presents for the kids like it was three thousand. If I tell her I won nineteen—"

He caught himself and leaned back in the leather-padded oak chair.

"Nineteen *hundred*?" Tillie was seated on Peters's left and his round face, thinner now and still pale after his long hospital stay, was as wistful as his voice.

Detective Peters looked from one openly curious colleague to another before giving a rueful, hands-up shrug. "Nineteen thousand."

"Holy Mother of Mary!" sighed Mick Cluett.

"Before taxes," Peters warned, though a sheepish grin spread over his pleasantly homely features.

A flash of naked envy swept around the table, then their indrawn breaths and raised eyebrows turned to congratulations, laughter, and offers to sell him gold mines, Florida swamplands, and halvsies in a used Lamborghini Elaine Albee had been drooling over since mid-December.

"You could drive it all week and I'd just use it on the weekends," she said generously.

"Forget it," Peters told her. "I'm getting a mini-van. Taking delivery on it this weekend."

The barman returned with their drinks and a fresh bowl of popcorn, and Matt Eberstadt passed the check over to his newly flush partner.

"See what I mean?" Peters took it like a good sport, but he shook his head as he drew out his wallet. "You guys are worse than Pam."

"You're really not going to tell her?" asked Elaine Albee.

"I'll tell her. I just won't tell her how much." He fixed them with an earnest look. "And you gotta promise not to either, okay? Now that she's back working part-time, she thinks our money troubles are over. I'll give her a thousand to blow on the house, but if she knew the real figure—"

Normally Lieutenant Sigrid Harald didn't let Bernie Peters's patronizing attitude toward his wife annoy her. If it were left to her, none of them would know anything of each other's private affairs; but tonight, she'd had just enough bourbon to loosen her usual constraint.

"Won't she find out when you file your tax returns?" she asked coolly.

"Pam?" The younger man snorted. "Tax forms give her a headache. She signs where I tell her to and says she'll bake me a cake with a file in it if the IRS ever runs me in."

As the others laughed and continued to pelt Peters with suggestions for new investments and pleas to borrow his lucky coin when next they bought their own lottery tickets, Lieutenant Harald sipped her fresh drink and considered the empty chair on her right, next to Tillie's. Captain McKinnon should have been here by now. She glanced at her watch surreptitiously and wondered if she could just make a few pro forma remarks and leave.

Although no longer as awkward in social situations as she'd been even a year ago, the lieutenant still wasn't comfortable at these off-duty gatherings. She was genuinely glad that Tillie had finally returned to full duty after his near-fatal encounter with a bomb back in October, and she was equally glad to be sending Mick Cluett back to Brooklyn to finish out the forty years he was determined—against all logic—to serve; but as far as she was concerned, a brisk handshake in the office would have been sufficiently demonstrative for both events.

Unfortunately, Elaine Albee's spontaneous let's-have-a-party had popped out in Captain McKinnon's hearing and their big gruff boss had said, "Good idea, Albee. Set it up and we'll be there, right, Harald?"

"Certainly, sir," she'd answered neutrally.

For some reason, Captain McKinnon seemed to value Michael Cluett, a sag-bellied old-timer who, in Sigrid Harald's opinion, should have been encouraged to retire ten years ago. Instead of specialing in some young go-get-'em when Tillie's accident left them shorthanded, McKinnon had specifically requested Cluett's services and had even growled at Sigrid when she told him baldly that it would take three Cluetts to replace one Tillie.

"Has he refused a direct order?" snapped McKinnon

"No, sir."

"Does he do what you ask him?"

"Yes, sir."

"Then I don't see what you've got to gripe about, Harald."

"Because that's all he does, Captain—exactly what's ordered or asked. No initiative, no drive."

"If you can't motivate your people, Lieutenant—"

"*My* people are busting their butts to cover Cluett's," Sigrid had said icily.

"Well, maybe you should take a page out of their notebook." Anger stiffening every muscle of his large frame, he'd stood up then to show that their interview was over. "Get off Cluett's case, Harald, and maybe you could learn something from him."

This from a man who expected a hundred and ten percent from the rest of his subordinates?

At first, Sigrid had thought it was because Cluett was one of the veterans from McKinnon's days as a rookie, but she'd never heard the captain reminisce about the good old days. In fact, it was only a few short months since her discovery that McKinnon and her own father had once been partners and close friends—a friendship that ended when Leif Harald was gunned down in the line of duty when she was quite young. McKinnon had spoken of him but once and then only after she'd stumbled over the connection by accident.

And he certainly didn't seem to find much time for Cluett. Although he'd counseled—in point of fact, *ordered* —patience and understanding, Sigrid had seen him cut the older man short whenever Cluett wandered from cases in hand and began to talk of bygone times.

Almost as if he were afraid of what Cluett might remember?

She lifted her eyes from the glass of bourbon in her hand and found that Cluett had stopped following the banter of the younger detectives on the other side and had turned his heavy body toward her. His mouth was crammed with popcorn and more spilled from his other hand as he held out the bowl to her. She took a few of the salty kernels and passed the bowl along to Tillie.

Cluett washed the last of his popcorn down with a long swallow of beer and continued to gaze at her until she could no longer avoid his stare.

"So!" she said, forcing a cheerful note since this was the last time she'd ever have to deal with him. "It's back to the Six-Four for you?"

"Back to Sheepshead Bay," he nodded. He leaned back in the chair beside her. His watery eyes were drink-glazed now and a grain of popcorn added a fresh spot of grease to the yellow V-necked sweater that protruded over his girth beneath a gray jacket that was at least one size too tight. His words seemed more for his own ears than hers and were barely distinguishable above a Mel Torme standard that provided a mellow background for the voices of their colleagues.

"No more old Mickey Cluett to kick around, treat like dirt."

Sigrid stiffened.

"Yeah, you're your daddy's daughter. A couple of times I wondered. He was such a hell of a guy and you—" The old detective took another swig of his Molson and wiped his mouth with the back of his hand. "But yeah, Leif Harald could look at you with that same go-screw-yourself look. Freeze a man's balls. If he still had any."

"See here, Cluett—"

"Aw, what the hell," he said wearily. He found the

kernel of popcorn on the overhanging ledge of his belly and rolled it between a meaty thumb and forefinger. "Forget it. Shouldn't of said nothing. Sorry."

He lapsed into beery silence as Mel Torme's velvet fog segued into the opening chords of Peggy Lee's "It Never Entered My Mind."

Across the table, Elaine Albee gurgled with laughter at something Bernie Peters had said; and beyond them, a sixsome of civilian workers clinked their full glasses in raucous toast.

Sigrid lifted her own glass, grateful that none of the others seemed to have heard Cluett. Unfortunately, the older man's resentful apology made him turn maudlin.

"We were working outta the old One-Six when you were born. Me and Leif and Mac. Even bounced you on my knee a time or two. Now here you are a lieutenant and Mac's a captain and I'm just a detective second class. If your daddy hadn't got his self killed, maybe he'd be your captain now 'stead of Mac."

Sigrid saw Tillie begin to tune in on Mick Cluett's inebriated maunderings and she tried to shut them off. "That was a long time ago," she began.

Cluett gave a defeated wave of his thick hand. "Yeah, yeah, and you don't want to hear. Don't blame you. Who wants to hear that her daddy's own partner was—"

Suddenly Captain McKinnon loomed up behind him and clasped him on the shoulder in heavy familiarity. With a loud scraping noise, he pulled out the chair between Tillie and Sigrid and his gruff voice cut through the bluesy music, blanketing all conversation. "Sorry I'm late, people. This round's on me."

Chapter 2

Three weeks later they learned that Mick Cluett had missed his forty years on the force by exactly sixty-one days.

January had given way to February, which promptly inflicted its usual misery on the city. As snow and sleet alternated with bone-chilling rains, the concrete canyons of lower Manhattan did their annual imitation of a wind tunnel designed to test some gigantic arctic flying device. Lieutenant Harald's face was numb with cold when she returned to headquarters after a late lunch that day and punched the elevator button.

Despite fleece-lined boots, her toes felt frozen and a heavy camel hair coat hadn't prevented a lump of ice from settling between her shoulder blades, which was probably why it took her so long to pick up on the elevator chatter.

Every day another officer seemed to come down with flu, bronchitis, or that debilitating misery known as walking pneumonia; so when she overheard a hoarse-voiced computer clerk speak of a wreath for poor old Mickey Cluett, Sigrid assumed that his out-of-shape cardiovascular system hadn't been able to fight off winter's germs.

One of the Police Administrative Aides sneezed and

another P.A.A. blew her reddened nose dispiritedly. "They'll be taking up a collection for my wreath next," she said as the elevator creaked to a stop.

Sigrid escaped from their virus-ridden company and made it back to her own office without being sneezed upon a second time. As she sorted through the messages on her desk, Detective Tildon joined her, his round face solemn.

"Did you hear about Mick Cluett, Lieutenant?"

"That he died? Yes, I gathered," she replied, trying to read a name someone had scrawled on a message notice. "Is this Eberstadt's handwriting? If he's not going to write legibly, he ought to print everything. Too bad about Cluett. What was it? Pneumonia?"

"You didn't hear?" Tillie's mild blue eyes shifted from the memo to her face. "He was killed. Shot."

"*Shot?*" A line-of-duty death was the last thing she expected for Michael Cluett.

"Last night," said Tillie, pleased to have captured her complete attention. "They found him early this morning, just three blocks from his house in Manhattan Beach."

Knowing his superior's hazy grasp of geography in the outer boroughs, he elucidated, "That's the Sheepshead Bay area—east end of Coney Island."

"What happened? Who shot him?"

"Unknown. Off-duty, though. Eberstadt talked to a guy over with the Six-Four and he said they don't have much yet, but he heard they've got a diver working around the footbridge that goes across the bay to Emmons Avenue."

Tillie gave an involuntary shiver at the thought of diving into Sheepshead Bay today.

In her rookie year, Sigrid had briefly toyed with the idea of volunteering for diver training. Swimming was still her only concession to physical exercise for its own sake and she swam four or five times a week year-round, but that was in heated enclosed pools. Having to go into any of the icy waters surrounding New York—even when protected by a wet suit—was definitely not high on her list of how to spend a February afternoon.

She walked out into the squad room, trailed by Tillie, who speculated aloud on the chances of those divers finding anything more than rusty crab traps and broken beer bottles.

As Sigrid passed the coffee maker, Dinah Urbanska stepped back to make room and a box of artificial sweeteners went flying.

Urbanska had made detective only six months ago. A powerfully built young woman, five eight, a hundred forty pounds, with golden brown hair that she kept knotted on the top of her head, Urbanska had proved her dedication, intelligence, and physical endurance with seven years of patrol work before coming to the Twelfth. But she was like a coltish palomino in the squad room. Cups leaped from her hands and upended on someone else's desk; at her touch, books slid off shelves, staplers flew apart and reports jumbled. One of her cases, fortunately a minor one, had been thrown out of court because she screwed up a key bit of evidence.

Red-faced, she picked up the packets of sweetener. "It was awful about Detective Cluett," she said, and Sigrid recalled that the younger woman had worked a couple of cases with the old officer.

"My friend in the Six-Four thinks they might have a witness," said Matt Eberstadt, looking up from his desk. He handed the lieutenant a report he'd just finished and sheepishly deciphered the message he'd taken for her earlier.

"An eyewitness?" Bernie Peters leaned back in his chair at the adjoining desk. His voice was still hoarse from his own bout with bronchitis. "You didn't tell us they had a witness."

Eberstadt rubbed the bald spot in front of his rapidly disappearing hairline and shrugged. "Vinnie didn't know any details—he's not working the case—he just knows they're acting like whoever did it might've thrown the gun in the bay there. Somebody heard a splash. That's why they called in divers."

"Probably turn out to be a beer bottle," said Sam Hentz.

Hentz was something of a problem for Sigrid. A dapper, almost natty dresser, he was a thoroughgoing professional who had expected to get her job and thought she'd only been promoted in because of her sex. He was even more chauvinistic than Bernie Peters, though more subtle in expressing it. When Hentz's regular partner retired and Sigrid paired him with Dinah Urbanska, she expected the fledgling detective to come back clawed and shredded.

So far, it hadn't happened. Urbanska's clumsiness drove everyone else up the wall; but for some quixotic reason, Sam Hentz had endless patience with her. He was a good teacher, too, one who took time to explain the details, thereby giving her a chance to develop her own investigator's skills. To Sigrid's surprise, the temporary arrangement seemed apt to become permanent.

Most of the time, Hentz remained as aloof as before, but today the violent irony of Cluett's end drew him into their conversation.

They batted it around a few minutes more as Jim Lowry returned from court and Elaine Albee drifted back from Records, where she'd been researching some aspects of a current case. Lowry hadn't heard of Cluett's death and had to be brought up to speed, while Albee had picked up a few extra details from a record clerk whose aunt was a friend of Mick Cluett's next-door neighbor. The young blonde officer smoothed the crease in her russet corduroy slacks as she perched on the edge of Eberstadt's desk to share the clerk's aunt's account.

"She said Cluett went out to walk the dog and when he didn't come back right away, his wife got mad and went on to bed without waiting up for him. Jeanie's aunt's friend said that walking the dog was Cluett's excuse for slipping over to his favorite bar a couple of nights a week. The dog woke Cluett's wife an hour or two later, scratching at the back door and whining, and she got up to let it in, but she was still mad so she didn't worry about him till she got up this morning and realized that he'd never come home.

"She called her daughter over on Ocean Avenue to ask if he'd spent the night there—that's what he did if he got especially bombed—and she'd just hung up the receiver when someone from the Six-Four rang her doorbell and gave her the bad news."

"Poor lady," Tillie said soberly. His own wife had gone through something similar back in October and she'd told him how it felt to pick up a telephone and hear someone from the department tell you your husband's hurt. Marian's caller had been mercifully terse, the whole message delivered in seconds, yet it'd seemed to her that all eternity had been compressed in that brief instant between hearing that there'd been an incident—her immediate, time-stopping certainty that Tillie was dead—and then hearing that he was in a hospital, still alive.

Marian Tildon had gotten lucky. Irene Cluett hadn't.

"In the midst of life, we are in death," intoned Eberstadt, whose own wife was religious.

It was something to think about, they agreed.

Nevertheless, none of them felt personally touched by the older detective's death, even though they'd each worked with him a time or two in the three months he was there. He'd been specialed in as a temporary substitute while Tillie recovered from a bomb that exploded next to him at a cribbage tournament, and he was like someone from a different era, from a time when the police force was mostly Irish and seniority had really made staying on the job worthwhile for lower-echelon men like Mickey Cluett.

There had been speculative murmurs as to why Captain McKinnon would accept Cluett even temporarily; and at first, the general feeling was that Mickey Cluett must have a rabbi near the top, someone too powerful for McKinnon to buck. But when the man arrived with a beer gut that had been years in the making, a wide face, hard blue eyes surrounded by puffy bags, and big hands that ended in broadly spatulate fingers—"From sitting on his hands too long," the trim Sam Hentz had quipped—it was clear that he was merely a place holder, an empty suit, a warm body. They'd all partnered with him when schedules demanded it, but because of the transient nature of his assignment and his impending retirement, no one had made much effort to know the man or to take him very seriously.

Sigrid Harald was too reserved to join in squad room scuttlebutt, yet she had been annoyed by Cluett's incompetence and puzzled by the captain's tolerance. With a vague sense of guilt now that Cluett was dead, she realized that even though he'd only returned to work a few days before Cluett was transferred back to Brooklyn, Tillie had probably known Cluett as well as any of them.

Tillie and Captain McKinnon?

As conversation flowed from Cluett's death to their own load of homicides, Sigrid wondered if the captain knew.

Some twenty blocks north, in an overheated midtown photo lab, Anne Harald could feel herself beginning to lose it.

"Look, sugar, I can talk about f/stops and film speeds and graininess till we're both blue in the face and yes, you can crop and dodge and burn and flash and all those other little precious darkroom tricks but ninety-seven point nine-nine percent of a photograph happens before you ever get around to tripping the shutter: brain and eye—what's behind the lens, not what's in it. What you see is what you get and, honey lamb, you're just not seeing."

Anne pulled a pencil from the tangle of curls behind her ear, dark curls that betrayed her true age with a dusting of silver, and thumped a particularly mawkish photo with the pencil's eraser. "Where's your eye here? Where's your brain?"

The sting of her critique was suddenly softened by the smile that danced in her hazel-gray eyes as she regarded the bearded youth whose weedy thinness topped her own five two by at least a foot. She shook her head and lapsed into exaggerated Southern dubiousness. "You do got brains, don't you, shug?"

Mid-fifties or not, Anne Lattimore Harald was still a beautiful woman, a beauty enhanced by the successful career she enjoyed; but before the dazzled apprentice could defend the photographs spread across the counter, a short pear-shaped man pushed through the darkroom curtains. "Telephone, Anne."

"Oh, come on, Lou," she protested.

The lab owner gave a hands-up shrug. "I told him you're busy. He wouldn't take no. What am I doing? Running a business or screening your calls? You want I should hang up on him, tell me already."

"No, I'll come." With one fluid movement, she plucked a couple of prints from the counter and handed them to the young man who'd shot them. "Take a grease pencil and circle the *real* emotional center of these two street scenes. I'll be back in a jiff."

Lou's telephone extension was located between the lab's salesroom and the darkrooms and Anne carried her pocket calendar along. A hardworking photojournalist, she expected the caller to be an editor with the final okay on one of several projects she had pitched since Christmas. There was an answering machine on her home phone, but most of her professional callers had quit trying to keep up with a number that changed at least once a year, if not twice or three times. They'd long since learned that if Anne were in town, Lou's shabby midtown lab was where she developed those award-winning photographs, and messages left there would always reach her sooner or later. It made for neater Rolodexes all over town.

"Hello?"

"Anne?"

One syllable in a voice she hadn't heard over the telephone in years and yet it was so instantly recognizable that adrenaline sent a rush of pure cold fear coursing through her veins.

"What's wrong? Has something happened to Sigrid?"

"No, no. Not her. Mickey Cluett," the male voice rumbled. "He was shot last night."

"Mickey Cluett?" Anne Harald ran a trembling hand through her hair. "You called to tell me Mickey Cluett's been shot? Why? Did you shoot him, too?"

"Christ, Anne! I thought you'd—"

She broke the connection without waiting to hear what Mac McKinnon thought.

Chapter 3

On the edge of Brooklyn, a dispirited sun half-heartedly tried to break through clouds as gray as the waters of Sheepshead Bay. Gusts of icy February air brought a not-unpleasant smell of fresh fish and brine to the knots of people watching from either end of a footbridge that spanned the bay's western end. The bridge was about eight feet wide, built of utilitarian creosoted timbers, salt-treated two-by-fours, and unpainted planks. It connected the largely residential Manhattan Beach neighborhood on the south side of the inlet with the boat piers and fish houses fronting Emmons Avenue on the north.

At the moment, the bridge was still cordoned off by yellow-and-blue sawhorses at each end and by yellow plastic ribbons to deter the public from entering a crime scene. Michael Cluett's heavy body had been found slumped in a corner of the access ramp on the Manhattan Beach side; and although a mobile lab had processed the whole bridge from one end to the other, it remained off-limits to all except police officers.

Detective Sergeant Jarvis Vaughn leaned on one of the wooden railings, stared into the cold gray water where the shape of a diver could just be discerned, and thought about the civil rights movement.

You've come a long way, baby, he told himself sourly as he inhaled a deep breath of frigid salty air through his nose and let it out slowly through his mouth.

He no longer looked for racial slurs beneath every casual or unthinking remark uttered in his presence and he knew that the movement had helped him advance about as fast as any other officer of similar intelligence and ambition, but he also knew he wouldn't feel true equality had been achieved till he could look at such a pitiful excuse for a human being as this Leviticus Jones, their only *ear* witness to Mickey Cluett's shooting, and not feel somehow personally debased simply because the wino was black.

Did Kirkwood's belly wrench when needletracks scarred a white skin? Did Fabrizio feel like apologizing to somebody every time Mafia power struggles erupted in gunfire? Hy Davidowitz had certainly never shown any sense of personal shame about the rising crime rate in Brighton Beach's Little Odessa. If his colleagues could distance themselves from the dregs of their race, why couldn't he?

Jarvis Vaughn took another deep breath. It was part of a relaxing technique that his sister had read about in one of those psychology books she was always lugging home from the library where she worked. Sometimes it helped.

Not today though. And not now.

He pulled a packet from the pocket of his overcoat and with gloved fingers clumsily freed an antacid mint. As he put it in his mouth, the bum standing beside him at the bridge railing stretched out a dirty hand. "Ain't had nothing to eat all day, bro."

Leviticus Jones was a long way from the land that had spawned him, but his slurred voice still carried the soft accents of his birth. His ragged overcoat was a travesty of Vaughn's almost dapper brown wool. The filthy garment was brown, too, but pilled and buttonless, cinched at the waist with a length of telephone cord, and miles too big for the emaciated frame it covered.

Shame and a guilty repugnance churned Vaughn's stomach. He bit down upon the mint and handed the pack to the wino, who immediately broke it open and let the paper fall to the ground as he crammed the remaining mints into his mouth.

"Pick it up!" Vaughn snarled.

"Huh?"

"You got to put more trash on the earth? Pick up the goddamned paper."

The derelict looked at him blankly and Hy Davidowitz stirred uneasily beside his partner. "Hey, lighten up, my man."

It was an old joke between them and for a moment, Jarvis Vaughn relaxed.

The wind caught the paper scraps and carried them off the bridge onto the water as the goggled diver broke through the surface, flipped back her mouthpiece and called, "Nothing here but garbage, Sarge."

"Keep looking," Vaughn called back.

Davidowitz turned to the bum. "Okay, Jones, tell us again. It was dark, it was quiet, right?"

Their only witness nodded hesitantly.

"You were cooped up under the ramp here when you heard voices and then the shot and then the splash like, maybe a gun being thrown in the water, right?"

"Yeah."

"And you're sure the splash was off to your right?" Davidowitz asked patiently.

The man's thin arm waggled inside his ragged right sleeve. "Yeah."

"Then why the hell can't we find it?" snarled Vaughn. He heard the anger in his voice and took another deep and steadying breath. "Show us exactly where you were," he said.

Leviticus Jones turned and lurched away and the two detectives followed his shambling form. He circled the handrail at the foot of the ramp, walked back to the seawall, and crawled through a narrow opening between the concrete bridge supports into a surprisingly capacious recess beneath the ramp.

Vaughn stooped to peer through the opening into the dark refuge Jones had found for himself. The plywood sheathing kept out the worst of icy winds off the water and a plastic shower curtain patterned with faded pink flamingos had been tacked over the cracks to further cut the wind. A couple of rumpled army blankets lay atop a pile of newspapers that insulated Jones from cold concrete that would otherwise drain away his body heat. There were some canned goods off to one side and three lumpy shopping bags.

"Sheepshead Hilton," grinned the derelict through stained and broken teeth. "No extra charge for sea breezes."

Vaughn had seen Manhattan efficiencies with less floor space than Leviticus Jones had staked out for himself underneath the sloping ramp. He watched as Jones curled up on the newspapers and drew the ragged blankets over his scrawny shoulders.

"You sure that's exactly how you were lying when you heard the splash?"

Davidowitz heard a muffled affirmative.

Vaughn straightened up with a look of exasperation on his thin black face. "Tell the diver to look on the other side of the goddamned bridge."

He patted his pockets until he located a fresh packet of antacid tablets.

Twenty minutes later, the diver found Cluett's sodden wallet. A few minutes after that, she emerged from the chilly water with a Browning semiautomatic pistol clutched in her gloved hand.

Chapter 4

As the subway train hurtled into the station, young Lotty Fischer gave her reddened nose a final dab, then tucked her handkerchief into an outer pocket and stood up. The train ground to a stop with an ear-wrecking shriek of brakes and a lurch that made her clutch at one of the upright steel poles to keep her balance. She had been fighting a cold all week with over-the-counter medications, and antihistamines always made her a little dizzy.

5:37 P.M.

There was a raw tickle in the back of her throat and the subway car seemed warmer than usual. Maybe her mother was right, Lotty thought. Maybe she *was* coming down with something more serious than a head cold and should've called in sick. Except that the computers at work were already understaffed and it would back everything up and make even more paperwork for her cop friends if she stayed out, too.

Crowds of homeward-bound commuters jostled each other on the platform as Lotty waited for the train doors to open.

The ending of their work day meant the beginning of hers.

Like a fish swimming upstream against the current, she let them surge past her. Another cascade of humanity flowed down the damp concrete steps from the street, but she kept to the right wall and doggedly continued upward. Once she'd gained the sidewalk, a vicious gust plastered her new red coat to her small body and tried to whip away the ends of her red wool head scarf. She shifted the strap of her shoulder bag and pulled the scarf ends tighter, grateful that she only had a few short blocks to walk in this icy wind. Spring couldn't get here too fast to suit her.

5:43.

Even though the days were getting longer, darkness had already fallen. Streetlights turned the overcast sky a pinkish orange but neon storefronts were a blaze of cheerful color.

Lotty ducked into one of the stores, a kosher Chinese deli, for a carton of eggdrop soup to go with the tuna salad she'd packed for her supper. "At least promise me you'll get something hot," her mother had said.

Lotty smiled indulgently as she paid for the soup and hurried back outside. Twenty-two years old and Mom still couldn't quit treating her like a little girl off to school with her lunch money clutched in her hand. She worried that Lotty wouldn't eat properly, wasn't dressed warmly enough, wasn't safe going back and forth alone on the subway.

To tell the truth, thought Lotty, she wasn't all that crazy about taking the subway home alone herself. That was the only drawback with this position. She liked the hours, had asked for them in fact so that her invalid mother never had to be alone except for that half-hour gap between the time she had to leave for work and the time her father got home from his own job.

It was supposed to be a four-to-midnight shift like the standard police rotation, but because the computer section was understaffed, she had been on six-to-two for the last week and a half. This meant going down into a subway station that was even more deserted than at midnight when others on the regular rotation might also be homeward bound. Certainly no rush hour crowds at two A.M. and no safety in numbers.

Once or twice, one of the guys working midnight-to-eight had walked her down and waited till the train came and then made sure she was in a car with a conductor. Usually though, she chickened out and took a bus. It was three times as slow, but felt six times safer.

She'd been promised that her four-to-midnight would be restored as soon as they hired more people. By the end of the month, for sure, Personnel had promised. Like summer, it couldn't come too soon for Lotty.

She entered the building and flashed a friendly smile at the familiar face of the uniformed officer behind the high booking desk.

5:58. She'd made it with two minutes to spare.

Across the drafty entrance hall, four blue-clad officers waited for the elevator and a couple of them teased her about cutting it close.

Lotty laughed, loosened her coat and pulled back the scarf. Her long chestnut hair gleamed in the overhead light and the delicate scent of her floral shampoo mingled with the men's after-shave and the smell of gun oil and leather. She was not beautiful. Her nose was much too big for her small face and she still struggled with acne, but her body was sweetly shaped, her smile came easily, she was younger than the other civilian clerks who worked in this building, and she had always been as friendly as a two-month-old puppy.

This was her fourth year on the job, and she still loved it. Loved the horseplay and us-against-them feeling of solidarity, the excitement of helping in ongoing investigations even if her part was mostly simple number-crunching: license checks, arrest records, the serial numbers on stolen goods.

As the elevator doors opened, an older uniformed officer emerged. "Hey, Lotty," he said. "You gonna have time to check out somebody for me tonight?"

"If it's as slow as last night, sure, Wally," she answered. "Might be after ten though."

"That's okay."

They went into the small room behind the main desk where her terminal was located; and while Lotty hung her coat and scarf on a nearby hook and put her purse and supper in the drawer of her desk, Officer Wally Abronski scribbled two names on her pad.

"This is the kid that my daughter's started seeing and this is his old man. I just want to make sure he's okay, you know?"

"No problem," she assured him, settling into her chair.

She cleared the computer screen, typed in the four digits of her personal security code number and reached for the first arrest worksheet of the night. The digital clock above her desk registered 18:00:59 and she mentally translated it into civilian time: fifty-nine seconds past six P.M.

Lotty's fingers danced upon the keyboard and no premonitions troubled her thoughts. As she entered arrests and ran mechanical checks, distanced from the dark deeds she recorded by a subconscious awareness that she sat in a warm, well-lighted building peopled by police officers who would, in theory, lay down their lives for her life, Lotty Fischer felt blissfully safe and protected.

Chapter 5

DETECTIVE SERGEANT JARVIS VAUGHN

At the academy, they tell us every life's got equal value.

Sounds nice but like so many nice-sounding things, it ain't necessarily so. A rich man's murder gets more attention than a poor man's, white gets more than black unless the newspapers and TV get into it, and when a cop gets himself killed—even if the cop's an old fart like Michael Cluett—the investigation takes precedence over every routine homicide already in the works. Labs process physical evidence quicker, FBI checks go faster, and the man's body gets posted and released to the undertaker in hours.

Before leaving my office to direct the search of the mucky bottom beneath the footbridge across Sheepshead Bay, I'd already gotten a phone call from the M.E.'s office with their preliminaries. An inch-by-inch examination of the bridge gave us nothing; but I knew that by tomorrow morning—tomorrow evening at the latest—I'd find on my desk all the printouts of any computer records the FBI had on that palm-size Browning semiautomatic we pulled from the inlet. Nothing much to tell the family yet. At least I wouldn't have to stonewall questions about when the undertaker could claim the body.

It was just past sunset—or what would've been sunset

if the sun'd ever made it through the frigid gray sky—as Hy Davidowitz and I got out of our unmarked car and walked down to the two-family house off Hampton Avenue that Cluett and his wife had shared with her brother and his family. Two blue-and-whites were double-parked in front.

"Days are getting longer," Davidowitz said. His dark droopy mustache gives his round face a vague resemblance to Fu Manchu. At thirty-seven he's built like one of those blue steel mailboxes you find on every other street corner and he's been just as solid whenever I've needed him.

"Soon be spring again," I agreed. The years keep getting shorter the older I get.

Somebody'd hung a big showy spray of white chrysanthemums and stiff white satin ribbons beside the front door just in case the neighbors couldn't guess by all the cars and steady stream of people in and out that there'd been a death in the house.

As we approached the steps, a couple of uniforms came through the doorway. Dark blue caps were pulled low against the frigid February twilight. One slim, a rookie about twenty-five; the other a middle-aged harness bull grown bulky on the job.

"Hello, Sarge," they said. "Davidowitz."

I couldn't remember the older officer's name but knew he was from an adjacent precinct. We stopped to talk a minute before ringing the bell.

"How're they doing in there?" Hy Davidowitz asked him.

" 'Bout like you'd expect," he answered. His colleague zipped his black leather jacket and pulled the collar up around his ears. "His children are doing okay, but Irene keeps breaking up. Married forty-two years—" He shook his head. "It blows a big hole in her life."

"Any leads yet?" asked the younger officer. "We heard you found the gun."

"The lab says it looks like he bought it with a .380 JHP and we got a .380 auto out of the bay," I answered. We did a shuffly version of the Texas two-step and moved past each other so that Davidowitz and I stood at the half-open door while the other two paused on the walk. "The confirm'll probably be there by the time we get back to the shop and we've already put it on the wire."

In the chilly night air, those chrysanthemums by the door smelled like every funeral I've ever been to. A sort of crisp vegetable odor like the celery and parsley at Kwan Te's grocery around the corner from my house. Not unpleasant exactly, but nothing to do with the smell of real flowers and certainly nothing to soothe or comfort a person. Not like the flowers around my granny's front porch when my sister and I were kids and our parents sent us to spend the summer down on her New Jersey truck farm. Her hard black hands'd had green fingertips and she'd grown lavender and stock, washtubs full of petunias, masses of sweet peas, lilacs and spicy carnations in the spring, followed by roses that perfumed the hot summer days and night-blooming nicotiana.

Quick takes of high school botany flicked through my head, along with muddled thoughts of ozone layers, pesticides, and genetic engineering. What's been done to flowers that they never smell sweet anymore?

Inside the house was what I expected: living room and dining room jammed with people, one or two uniforms, but mostly civilians.

And mostly women. Birth and death, it's always mostly women.

Cluett's daughter and two daughters-in-law went back and forth almost like hostesses at a reception. While we were there, they kept a steady stream of strong hot tea coming, and every few minutes they came around to check that everybody had all the cream and sugar and paper napkins they needed. Keeping busy.

I recognized Cluett's sons with a couple of men who were later introduced as his brothers. The men seemed stiff and half-embarrassed. They moved awkwardly between the crowded living room and kitchen and talked in low tones with neighbors who brought sympathy and plates of food.

Almost everyone had dirty smudges on their foreheads and at first I wondered if this was some sort of white-man's funeral ritual I'd never heard of before; eventually it hit me that today was Ash Wednesday. The whole family had been to mass and received the mark.

Took me a minute to pick out Irene Cluett. She sat on the gold velour couch supported by a pair of horsey-faced women. One of them wore the self-important look of A Member of the Family. The other had on one of those chopped-off black things that passes these days for a nun's veil. Irene Cluett sat between them with a glazed expression on her homely flat face. "Bearing up," Granny would call it.

Weird how much a husband and wife can start to look alike after years of marriage. She looked so much like Cluett she could have been his twin sister: thirty pounds overweight, slack gray hair cut short and parted on the same side, only hers was held in place by a plain blue plastic barrette. Her eyes were puffy and red-rimmed and when she recognized us, her lower lip started quivering.

I was Cluett's boss, but I'd only met his wife at official social functions, occasional summer picnics in Prospect Park or at widely spaced PAL events. She'd been civil every time, no half-hidden hostility, but none of that buttering-up that some of the younger wives use when they think it'll help their husbands' careers.

Maybe she'd always known Cluett's career was past help.

Tonight was partly an official expression of departmental sympathy and partly because Mrs. Cluett had to be questioned as a necessary part of our investigation. Two birds, one stone. I'd expected nothing more than formal politeness, and it surprised the hell out of me when she teared up at the sight of my face. She held out both hands to mine and put her broad cheek up for me to kiss it.

"Oh, Jarvis!" she sobbed and clutched my hands in hers like we were old friends. "Are you handling his case personally? You'll find who shot my poor Mickey down in cold blood, won't you?"

"You know we will, Mrs.—er, Irene," I assured her

awkwardly. To cover, I pulled Hy over. "You've met Detective Davidowitz, haven't you?"

Davidowitz took her limp hand. "Sorry for your troubles, ma'am." (He's picked up that useful, all-purpose condolence from the Irish.)

"Bless you both," she said brokenly. "This is my cousin, Sister Bernadette, and my brother's wife, Gina Callahan."

The two women nodded and murmured, then the elderly nun began to hoist herself from the gold velour cushions. "Take my place, Sergeant Vaughn," she offered.

"No, no, you stay right here," said Irene Cluett and called to her daughter, "Barbara, bring your father's friends a chair."

People sprang for some of the folding chairs the undertaker had supplied, but I waved them aside. "Please don't bother," I said. "I'm sorry, Mrs.—um, Irene, but is there someplace we can talk alone?"

The Cluett den had probably been the Cluett daughter's bedroom. There was something girly about the rosebud wallpaper and even though the daybed was heaped with green cushions on a matching slipcover, you could tell it'd started life as a single bed.

Four teenage kids, three boys and a girl, were sprawled before an expensive color television, but they jumped to their feet and edged past as their grandmother led us into the room.

In front of the television were two white vinyl recliners separated by a lamp table that held the remote control, a box of Kleenex, and the only reading material I'd yet noticed in the whole house: a current *TV Guide* and a couple of *National Enquirer*s. The wall above the television was plastered with family pictures: from turn-of-the-century photographs of stiff-faced old-timers to fat little Cluett grandbabies sitting on the laps of Easter Bunnies, Santa Clauses, and even a Saint Patrick's Day leprechaun.

The rose-sprigged wallpaper behind the two recliners was bare except for a brightly colored picture of the Sacred Heart. A pale-skinned, blond Christ, I noted, pissed at myself for noting. Jesus as Anglo-Saxon white bread instead of Semite bagel and how did that make Davidowitz feel?

The fancy gold frame had some faded frond of palm leaves sticking out of the top. Probably put up there on Palm Sunday a year ago and due to be replaced in a few weeks. Christmas didn't seem like more than just a couple of weeks back and all of a sudden here it was Ash Wednesday again. Soon be spring.

As if by habit, Irene Cluett headed straight to the first chair and patted the arm of the other white recliner. "Sit here, Jarvis," she said.

She didn't have to tell me it was Cluett's. I knew from the rumpsprung look of the seat that it had to be his favorite chair.

Felt weird to put my skinny behind where his fat ass must have wallowed just last night, but I pulled the chair around to face her as Davidowitz lowered his bulky form gingerly onto the daybed.

There was a pink crocheted afghan on the back of Irene's chair and she draped it over her legs even though the room felt warm to me. I loosened my overcoat and stuffed my gloves in a pocket. Davidowitz slid out of his coat altogether. He took out one of the four or five rolled-up yellow legal pads we all go through on a case and smoothed it flat for taking notes.

Without us asking, Irene had already started talking about Cluett's last evening—the pot roast and potato dumplings she'd made for his supper—"He likes everything I cook but I do believe that's really his favorite so I'm glad I fixed it. His last meal. He really enjoyed it, too. Only I made string beans and he always likes cabbage better even though it doesn't agree with him." She looked confidentially at Davidowitz. "Gas."

She described the television programs they'd watched, then how he'd gone out to walk the dog at eight-thirty.

"Did he always walk the dog at the same time?" I asked.

She pursed her thin lips in thought. "It depends. If he's going over to Sheepshead for a beer, he usually leaves then. If it's just to let Sheba do her duty, then he'll stay on the block and go out around bedtime, ten-thirty or so."

"How often did he walk across the bay?"

"Three or four nights a week," she sighed. Her fingers were so swollen—arthritis?—that the joints looked like links of tiny little white bratwursts as she plucked at the flowers on the afghan in her lap. "What can I tell you? He's not supposed to drink much on account of his weight pulling on his heart, but the doctor says he needs to walk and when he walks, he winds up over at the Shamrock. Most times it's only one beer and out and I figure he probably walks that off coming home so it's probably not all that bad for him, don't you think? I mean just one beer?"

"Probably not," agreed Davidowitz. He's the good-hearted one.

We let her tell it in her own words—the way she'd gone to bed mad at Cluett when he didn't come home by the usual ten-thirty, something that might happen once every three or four months. How the dog woke her up around midnight pawing at the back door, which had made her even madder.

"Cold as it was, leaving Sheba outdoors like that. No consideration for a poor dumb animal. Not that she has to wait outside the Shamrock. They let her come in with Mickey in the wintertime if nobody complains, but still— Of course I didn't know." She wiped fresh tears from her eyes. "I thought he was probably too loaded to walk home so he'd gone to Barbara's and Sheba'd gotten away from him and all the time I was mad at him, he was lying out there on the freezing sidewalk and—"

Irene fumbled for the box of tissues on the lamp table and loudly blew her nose. A minute later, her daughter pushed open the door and looked in. "You okay, Ma? Can I get you anything?"

"No, no, I'm fine. Unless—" She looked at Davidowitz and me. "Don't you want a cup of tea or something?"

We declined. The daughter gave us worried glances, but left without saying anything else.

We let Irene finish describing her night, how she'd phoned her daughter early this morning and how she'd felt when someone from the Six-Four rang her doorbell and gave her the bad news; then I asked, "Did he have any problems with anybody lately, Irene? Anybody that might have wanted to get back at him?"

She cut her eyes at me sharply, "Wasn't it a mugging?"

I shrugged. "His pockets were empty. That's why it took those rookies so long to identify him. But when we searched the bum that heard the shot, he had Mick's watch and a handful of loose change. That's all though. We found Mick's wallet in the bay, near the gun. It still had forty-three dollars in it and all his credit cards."

"Not a mugging," she repeated slowly. Her body had been a soft lump of flesh inside that shapeless dark wool dress. Now there was a hint of muscle that made her seem to sit a little straighter. "Somebody killed Mickey on purpose."

"We're not ready to go that far yet," I cautioned.

She didn't argue, just sat there thinking. I'd have said "cowlike" a minute earlier, now it felt more like those pale blue eyes were reading through a list of names, pause here, slide past whole columns there. She ticked them off on her fingers.

"The head mechanic over at the Chrysler place. The car's still under warranty but he don't want to fix the power steering. Three-ten a month car payments and the thing turns like a tank, Mickey says. They had hard words Saturday. Mickey was going to take it in again tomorrow. He says—said—he's going to give him one more chance and then he's getting some of the guys from the beat to hassle him about cars double-parked on the sidewalk in front of the garage."

Davidowitz interrupted her for the man's name.

"Frank's all I ever heard," she said; but she knew the garage's location. Davidowitz carefully listed it on the top sheet of his legal pad.

"The Gelson kid next door," Irene continued. "We think he may be dealing. He flew off the handle when Mickey and my brother asked him how come so many kids were hanging out back there in their garage."

"This Gelson kid have a first name?" asked Davidowitz.

"Edward." She watched him write it out. "He's about seventeen, but big and strong from lifting weights. Got a fresh mouth on him, too. All about how he knows his rights and Mickey's got no right to say who can come in their garage and who can't."

"Anybody else?" I asked.

She shook her head slowly, paused, then shook her head again.

I recognized the hesitation and pushed. "You sure, Irene? It might not seem like anything, but you've been a cop's wife long enough to know how people can do crazy things for stupid reasons."

"You said a true mouthful there, Jarvis," she nodded. "It doesn't really seem like it could be anything, but there's his cousin Neal. Neal O'Shea. We lent him five hundred dollars when he lost his job back at Thanksgiving so he and Marie could buy Christmas for their kids. He's working again but we still haven't seen a penny. Mickey only asked him about it once, but he took it wrong and we've heard he's been bad-mouthing Mickey to his brothers."

Davidowitz took down the cousin's name and address.

A sum total of three names. After a lifetime of opportunity to make enemies, could any man really go out with only three? On the other hand, assume for a minute that three's all, is that good, bad, or indifferent?

Mick Cluett hadn't been much of a detective. Lazy, sloppy, always behind in his paperwork. Always played catch-up with his notes and teetered on the skinny edge of perjury if he had to testify in court. Resented others' success. In short, not particularly interested in the job beyond picking up his paycheck and making his forty. We couldn't figure out why forty was the magic number for him. Certainly didn't mean a bigger pension. And it wasn't like he was getting serious respect or saving the free world from crime. Oh, he'd do what you asked, but damn if you didn't always have to *ask*. He was already in place when I transferred in and I was stuck with him, part of the job. Like the lousy coffee and the never-ending paperwork. Not so bad that you'd take the trouble to get rid of it once and for all—and even if I'd manipulated his clearance rates, getting rid of Cluett would have been a hell of a lot of trouble given all the job security mechanisms in place—no, he was just one more of those ongoing irritations life sends you to keep you from being too pleased with your lot.

Incurable, endurable, Granny used to say.

"Nobody else, then?" I asked Irene. "No trouble with work or anything?"

She looked blank and shook her head. "He never really talked about the job. Oh, maybe if it was something on the news and Barbara or one of the boys asked him about it, he'd say what he'd seen or heard. He should've retired after thirty, but he was so set on making forty. He went on the job when he was twenty-one and he said he was going to stay till he was sixty-one. Just like his uncle Michael, God rest him. It wasn't easy for him. Years ago, he used to talk more and, of course, we were proud of him when he finally made detective, but seems like it didn't mean as much to him. He said—"

Irene put her hand to her mouth, like a kid who's spoken out of turn and spilled a family secret.

"He said what?" I prodded.

She gave a what-the-hell? shrug. "He said that the only reason he made detective was because Chief Buckthorn wanted to stick it to Willie McMahon."

So he'd known about that, had he? I felt a sickly wave of shame wash over me even though that little bit of departmental politics was over and done with before I came on the job. Willie McMahon was my predecessor and he and the then chief—also gone before my time—had gone head-to-head in monumental clashes, if all the stories were true. I hadn't been in Willie McMahon's old office three days before I heard how Buckthorn had promoted Mick Cluett onto the detective squad just to spite McMahon. Whenever I got particularly pissed with Cluett, I had to remember that it really wasn't his fault for being where he was bound to screw up.

"The best time for Mickey was back when he was still riding patrol over in New York. He liked it when they'd give him a rookie to break in. But after a few years, when some of his rookies were getting promotions and making detective, he seemed to think he ought to try for detective, too. And with four kids, we could always use the money. He was never on the pad, Jarvis."

That I knew. Lazy and incompetent as Cluett was, the most I'd ever heard of him taking was an occasional pastrami sandwich to look the other way on some minor infractions. Pads exist. No point pretending they don't. The most you can do is keep breaking them up before they get too organized and entrenched. Opportunity's always knocking, but I think Cluett stayed straight because crooked was harder; too damn complicated to remember who knew what. Honesty probably wasn't Cluett's best policy, just the easiest.

Her fingers had gone back to picking at the afghan.

"You probably know better than me, Jarvis—you were his boss—but it seems to me that maybe a man's better off doing what he likes, what he's good at, than trying to get what he thinks he ought to want."

"The Peter Principle." Sometimes Davidowitz seemed to think out loud to himself.

We both looked at him.

"Some guy named Peter," he explained. "He said people always get promoted past the level of their competence."

He heard what he'd said and tried to backpedal. "Not that Mick was incompetent. I mean, that is, *Peter* meant that if a person's doing a good job, he'll usually get promoted on up the ladder till he lands in a job where he's no good. I mean where he's *not as* good. Mick was a *great* patrol cop, so he gets promoted and . . ."

His explanation of the Peter Principle petered out pretty lamely and Irene Cluett couldn't seem to decide whether to take Hy the right way or get mad about it on her late husband's behalf.

"He *was* a good patrol cop," she said huffily. "And if he was such a bad detective, why'd Captain McKinnon borrow him from you?"

She sure as hell had a point there. Why *did* McKinnon ask for Cluett by name? I hadn't paid all that much attention at the time, just been mildly tickled that Manhattan had pulled his name out of the hat. I was sure they'd mistaken him for some other, sharper detective. Now I remembered Cluett's face when I told him he was being specialed across the East River.

"Good old Mac!" he'd said, sucking in his gut and trying to look like a real cop for a change. "I broke him in, you know. Knew from the very beginning he was going to do okay."

"Yeah?" I'd asked as I initialed the temporary transfer.

"Now he's a big-time captain and he wants *me*, Mickey Cluett."

"How'd it go over there?" I asked Irene. As his boss I should know without asking, but I honestly couldn't remember. Oh, sure, I remembered the first day he was back, asking him how he'd liked Manhattan duty. He'd muttered something about things being the same all over, which it mostly is.

I heard him shoot the breeze with a couple of the guys about a homicide/suicide mixed up with drugs. Gory, but getting commonplace even down to the pile of blood-drenched money they'd confiscated. "A wad of hundreds big enough to bloat a goat," he'd bragged. And he'd worked that case where some dancer got herself killed on stage in front of an audience. That was a hair more interesting, but I'd still let it go in one ear and out the other.

Evidently, Irene had, too.

"He thought it was going to be something special," she said, "but it wound up just being a longer commute and more court hassle. He was supposed to go back over and testify on a couple of things and you know how he hated that. *And* it wasn't really working for Mac either. He had to take orders from a woman—a chit of a lieutenant who wasn't even born when Mickey first joined the force."

Hy Davidowitz half-smiled. "Yeah, I heard him say he once bounced her on his knee when she was a baby."

There was nothing nostalgic in Irene's tone. Instead, I caught an echo of Cluett's sour resentment.

"I'm a woman myself," she said, "and I'm for equal pay and all that, but I just don't think it's right for any police officer to have to take orders from a woman. In fact, I don't think women even belong on the force. Not on the street anyhow. You put a woman in the same patrol car with one of these young buckos and send them out on night duty—"

She shook her head at so much opportunity for sin and sex but before she could get going on what sounded like an old sore point, her daughter appeared at the door again.

"Sorry to interrupt, Ma, but Father Ambrose is here and he needs to talk to you about Pop's mass."

It was as good a time to leave as any. I guessed we'd probably got all we were going to get from Irene that night.

Back at the car, Hy radioed in. Everything was quiet at the station, so I let him drop me at the nearest subway stop. I'd promised Terry I'd pick up some shrimp salad for supper. I'd also promised to get home on time.

Oh well. One out of two's not too bad for a cop.

Chapter 6

⚏ Midtown was clogged with the beginning of rush hour traffic. As Lieutenant Sigrid Harald drew near Lou's Foto Finish, a van parked illegally at the top of a bus stop flashed its left rear blinker and pulled out in front of her. She automatically slid her car into the space he'd vacated.

Just as automatically, she flipped down the sun visor to display the emblem that identified this as a police officer's car even though she wasn't on duty. Taking advantage of her position to bend the law on minor things such as double-parking or parking at fire hydrants always gave Sigrid Harald a twinge of guilt. Obscurely, she'd promised herself that if she ever stopped feeling guilty, she'd stop doing it. Not that twinges of guilt made it all right, of course, but surely they proved that she didn't feel *entitled* to break the law.

As always when she found herself looping back and forth between guilt and morality, a Pavlovian reaction made her remember the moral struggles of an old school friend.

Kathie deNobriga had been a committed activist who marched and fasted and boycotted specific products on behalf of downtrodden farm laborers and sweatshop

workers the whole country over, but grapes were her
Achilles' heel. Others might be addicted to peanut butter
or chocolates; Kathie kept a bowl of grapes in her room
and nibbled on whatever was in season from September
to June. Yet, when Chavez called for a boycott on behalf
of California grapeworkers, she valiantly dumped the
grapes and refilled her bowl with apples and bananas.

Sometime later, Sigrid had spotted a little pile of
twigs and seeds among the oranges on Kathie's nightstand. "I thought you gave up grapes for the duration."

Sheepishly, Kathie had opened the lower drawer on
her nightstand and brought out a bag of luscious purple
bunches. "I've gone back to eating them, only now I
sneak and that makes me feel really guilty, so I'm not
enjoying them as much and that makes up for it, don't
you think?"

Remembering that bit of existential sophism, Sigrid
left the visor down, locked the car, and hurried past the
people waiting in frozen resignation at the bus stop.

A bell above the door tinkled as she entered the lab.
Lou Bensinger lifted his head from the proof sheet he was
examining and smiled at her through the large magnifying glass.

"Ah, New York's finest's finest! Come to sell me tickets to the Policeman's Ball, my darling?"

Lou Bensinger had teased her since she was twelve
and was one of the few people she felt at ease bantering
with.

"Only five hundred a pair, too, Lou. If I promise to
dance every horah with you, how many tickets will you
buy?"

Trudy, his wife of forty years, came in from a back
room. "Another Harald female come to flirt with my husband yet?" She circled the counter and gave Sigrid a big
hug. "Too long since I've seen you!"

She was even shorter than Lou, but she clasped the
younger woman by both arms and looked up at her critically. "Ho, now, what's this?"

At once Sigrid realized that she hadn't been in the
lab since she'd had her long dark hair cut short. She gave

a self-conscious shrug, but Trudy Bensinger was delighted.

"Turn! Turn!" she commanded and Sigrid obediently did a three-sixty. "I like! So who's the lucky man?"

"Why must a man be involved when a woman cuts her hair?" Sigrid countered. "I merely thought it was time for a change."

"It is, it is! And I know just the change you need. My cousin Selma's boy. The divorce, it wasn't his fault. A doll he is. A lawyer, too. I'll give him your number, okay?"

Remembering some of those cousins' sons (not to mention nephews, godsons, and the younger brothers of various in-laws) that Trudy had tried to foist off on her over the years, Sigrid hastily said, "No, please, Trudy. Actually, I *am* seeing someone right now."

"And when are we meeting this young man?"

"Oh, it's nothing like that."

"Then you can talk to Selma's boy."

"I'd better tell Mother I'm here," said Sigrid, retreating down the rear hall.

"Coward!" Lou called after her.

Sigrid found her mother in the lab's common workroom. Lou's Foto was a holdout against unnecessary high-tech gadgetry, and Anne was using a manual paper cutter on her last batch of photographs.

"Siga?" She frowned and turned to check the clock on the wall behind her. "You early or am I late?"

"Some of each. I was able to get away on time for a change."

She watched as Anne Harald briskly aligned the edge of a picture, then pulled down cleanly on the blade. Her mother's expertise often surprised strangers. Someone this decorative was not usually expected to be competent as well. And even in jeans and sneakers and a shaggy old gray sweater, with most of her lipstick eaten off and chemical stains on her fingers, Anne Harald remained a thoroughly decorative woman.

She examined with a critical eye the picture she'd

finished blocking, then handed it and another over to Sigrid. "You said you wanted copies. Happy birthday."

Sigrid took the top one and looked down into her own eyes. Not really, of course. Her eyes were a slate gray that could look silver under certain conditions but Leif Harald's had been a clear light blue. This black-and-white photo turned his blue eyes silver, though. Spaced as widely as hers, too, and shaped the same. Over the years, so many family friends and relatives had pulled her features apart one by one in an attempt to explain how someone so physically plain and awkward could have sprung from two such attractive parents that Sigrid knew exactly which attribute she'd inherited from each.

From Leif had come the eyes, thin nose, high cheekbones, silky straight hair, and her height, five ten in her stocking feet. From Anne came the changeable gray of her eyes, the darkness of her hair and a jutting chin. Neither side of the family claimed the mouth that was too wide, the neck that was too long, nor the crippling self-consciousness that had kept her tongue-tied with shyness even after she grew up.

The first picture was a three-quarters view of her father, dressed for patrol in what would have been winter blues, the jacket unbuttoned and half open. He had his hand in one pocket, his hat and nightstick in the other, and she could see the big handle of his holstered service revolver as he leaned against a door frame and smiled into Anne's camera—a confident young Viking, off to tame urban dragons, captured on film by his young wife. He couldn't have been much more than twenty-six or twenty-eight himself.

The next picture must have been snapped a moment or two later. The jacket was buttoned now, but she had crawled into the picture, a solemn, wide-eyed infant, who looked up into his laughing, indulgent face and reached for his hat with the shiny badge.

"You're sure five-by-seven is what you want?" asked Anne. "No problem to make them eight-by-tens."

"No, these are perfect," said Sigrid. "Thanks. But I thought you said you didn't have negatives."

"I didn't," she said shortly. "I had to copy the positives and make new negatives. That's why they're not as crisp as they should be."

They looked fine to Sigrid. When she'd flown down to North Carolina for a cousin's funeral back in October, she'd found these two wallet-size pictures among her grandmother's albums and had asked to borrow them. "I don't have any pictures of Dad," she said. "Photographers' spouses must be like shoemakers' children."

"You may have them to keep," Grandmother Lattimore had said. She seemed puzzled though. "There should be *boxes* of pictures. Anne was always taking Leif. I suppose it's all those moves. They say seven moves are equal to one fire. If that's true, it's a wonder your mother hasn't lost everything she ever owned."

Anne gave her a stiff protective envelope and gathered up her own things while Sigrid slid the photographs inside and tucked the envelope into her pocket.

"Ready?"

Anne nodded and they said goodnight to the Bensingers, then plunged out into the icy wind and hurried down the crowded sidewalk to Sigrid's car.

Inside, Anne shivered on the front seat beside her. "This is as cold as the night you were born. At least it's not snowing, though."

"Supposed to before morning," Sigrid warned, edging the car into the stream of heavy traffic.

"Really? I've been too busy to read a paper or listen to a weather report." She lapsed into silence.

The stop-and-go traffic had brought them only a short way west on Forty-third when Sigrid drew a momentary blank.

Most people didn't have to stop and think where their mothers lived, especially if it were in the same borough. But Anne Harald had lived in every Manhattan neighborhood from Inwood to the Battery and seldom stayed in one place more than six months. (Her record was a Tuesday-to-Friday sojourn in Connecticut and she'd have been back in Manhattan on Thursday if any of her photography students had been free then to help her reload the U-Haul-It.) These frequent moves had been so much a part of Sigrid's childhood that she'd never really questioned Anne's reasons; but for a split second, Sigrid couldn't remember if she still had that basement apartment in a Chelsea row house or had actually moved back to the Columbus Circle area as she'd threatened at Christmas. Then Anne said sharply, "If you're going to turn on Ninth, shouldn't you get over?" and Sigrid stopped feeling disoriented because Ninth Avenue was a one-way street heading south, which meant Chelsea and that pleasant residential block in the West Twenties.

Traffic was snarled around the Port Authority Bus Terminal, but once past that, it was only the usual rush hour anarchy: buses pulled in and out of stops in total disregard of smaller vehicles, no one paid attention to lane markings, and double-parkers and jaywalkers added the usual impediments to a smooth flow. Yet Sigrid could feel Anne getting tenser by the minute. Normally her mother was a relaxed passenger who chattered constantly, undistracted by near misses, not even when three lanes of cars and cabs were suddenly squeezed into one. Tonight she seemed edgy and short-tempered and she cut off every conversational gambit Sigrid offered.

Sigrid often felt like the older and staider of the two, but as tension mounted, she reacted like any guilty daughter and hastily examined her recent past to see if she'd done something to annoy her mother.

Nothing sprang to mind, unless . . . could it be their birthdays?

Today was Sigrid's; Anne's was still two weeks away, on the twenty-second. This wasn't one of those benchmarks that ended in a zero or five. Those usually elicited a rueful melancholy, an awareness of fugitive time. Tonight's edginess was something different.

"You're not coming down with something, are you?" she asked as she turned into Anne's block.

"Of course not. I never get sick. You know that. There! Is that a parking space?"

"Where?" Sigrid asked, distracted.

"Never mind. There's a motorcycle parked in it."

Sigrid drew up in front of the brownstone that contained Anne's basement apartment. "I'll let you out here and go park the car."

In that part of town, it was a statement easier made than accomplished, but eventually she found a legal space a block and a half away. Anne had left the door unlocked and was pouring boiling water into a large silver teapot when Sigrid returned.

Over the years, Anne Harald's furniture had reduced itself to a few easily packed basic pieces—bed, table and chairs, three chests, two trunks that doubled as occasional tables, some lamps, two new futons to replace a couch that had finally fallen apart during the last move, a bookcase, and the five indispensable file cabinets which held all her papers and photographs. There were also a half-dozen or more cardboard packing boxes full of odds and ends that often never got unpacked between moves. These were usually stacked two high along a bare wall. Covered with exotic fabrics picked up in one of the world's bazaars and topped with thin sheets of clear plexiglass, the large square cartons served where needed as sideboard or lamp tables.

Anne had an eye for color and design, and her collection of tablecloths, throws, quilts, and cushions complemented two very fine Persian rugs. These pulled her apartments together and created a sense of careless, comfortable luxury far above their actual monetary value.

The current apartment was a spacious floor-through. To counteract the basement's natural darkness, Anne had hung on the front wall a sunburst-patterned patchwork quilt inherited from her grandmother. On the opposite wall was a large blowup of one of her award-winning photographs. Three women whose strong features proclaimed them mother, daughter, and granddaughter stood with linked hands. All three were dressed in dazzling white slacks and sweaters. Spring sunlight glanced off the gleaming white Washington Monument behind them and turned the yellow sashes they wore into gold. The granddaughter's sash bulged over a baby carrier on her chest. Only the back of the baby's fuzzy dark head could be seen but a bright purple balloon tied to its carrier read "I'm a choice!"

A laminated life-sized cutout of Anne herself stood just inside the door, arms outstretched in welcome. It was a long-ago housewarming gift from a fellow photographer and Anne used it as a coat tree. Sigrid added her coat and scarf as Anne brought in tea and placed the tray on a trunk that served as a coffee table between the two futons.

Without asking how Sigrid wanted hers, Anne filled a chipped mug from the elegant teapot, added a slice of lemon, stirred in a spoonful of honey and handed it over to her daughter.

Sigrid smiled at the mismatched mugs, the silver badly in need of a good polishing, and the chipped pottery platter of wheat rolls and butter. "Grandmother would have a fit if she saw this."

"She has seen it," Anne smiled back. "And every time, she threatens to send me a gallon of silver polish and ten place settings of her Royal Doulton."

Sigrid buttered a roll and bit into it hungrily. "I'd almost forgotten you even had this tea set."

"Me, too," Anne admitted. "I came across it when I was hunting for these." She pushed two picture frames across the trunk top to Sigrid.

Like the ornate tea set, they were sterling silver and badly tarnished. The tea set had been a wedding present from Anne's paternal grandmother, a traditional Southerner who had considered silver and crystal as much a prerequisite to marriage as the license; and Sigrid suspected that the frames were also wedding gifts. They were chased with borders of delicate wildflowers and would probably polish up beautifully.

"Who gave you these?"

"Your Aunt Kirsten and Uncle Lars," Anne said, naming the two who'd been Sigrid's closest substitute for grandparents on her Harald side. "They were brought from Copenhagen around 1890. I thought you might like to have them."

"I would," said Sigrid.

She had never been sentimental about family heirlooms, especially heirlooms that had to be polished or treated gingerly, but these seemed appropriate for her father's pictures and she immediately slipped one into each frame. A perfect fit. She stood them up side by side on the trunk top. "Thanks, Mother."

Anne rose abruptly. "I'll get the box. Mind, these aren't your birthday present. You don't get that till next week."

With Sigrid's birthday on the eighth and Anne's on the twenty-second, the established ritual called for dinner together and an exchange of presents on the fifteenth if Anne were in town.

Sigrid watched her mother swathe the pictures in old Christmas tissue and put them back in a box. She was puzzled by the sudden return of Anne's edginess. "Are you sure you're not coming down with something?"

"Why do you keep asking me that?" Anne snapped.

"You just don't seem yourself tonight. Was it a rough day or something?"

"Or something." She seemed to hear the waspish tone in her voice and forced a smile. "Sorry. I guess the years are getting to me." She spooned more honey into her own mug and stirred it purposefully.

"Oh, come on, Mother. What's really bothering you?"

"I don't know. A combination of things, I suppose."

Awkwardly, because they seldom exchanged emotional confidences, Sigrid gestured to the box Anne had laid on the futon beside her. "Is it because of Dad? Does his picture stir up a lot of memories?"

Anne hesitated, then nodded. "And Mickey Cluett. Is it true he was shot?"

"How'd you hear that?"

"Wasn't it in the paper?" Anne answered vaguely. "What happened? Will you be investigating?"

Sigrid shook her head. "It happened in Brooklyn. Probably killed for crack money. All they know right now is that he was shot on his way home from a neighborhood bar, sometime before midnight last night, I think. Did you know him very well?" she asked curiously.

"Not really. In the early days when Leif and I were first married, Mickey used to stop by the apartment occasionally."

"That's right," said Sigrid. "I forgot. When Dad first joined the force, he was assigned to the old One-Six and Cluett said he worked there, too." She started to take a sip of tea and then remembered something else.

"I thought you said you were too busy today to read a paper or even listen to a weather report."

"Oh, for God's sake, Sigrid! Are you going to cross-examine everything I say?" Her spoon clattered sharply against the silver tray as she patted the pockets of her jeans and looked around the room. "What did I do with my cigarettes?" she muttered.

Sigrid set her mug down firmly. "Okay, Mother. What's going on?"

"There, you see?" Anne said illogically. "You made me forget that I gave up smoking a year ago. I still dream about cigarettes, did I tell you?"

Words spilled from her lips, becoming subtly more Southern in pacing and inflection the more she chattered. "I dream that I've rationed myself to two cigarettes a day and Lordy, Lordy, do they taste good! But at the same time, I'm sort of disappointed at my weakness, you know? Because I *did* take a vow never to light up another and I sort of *know* that in my dream and yet—"

Her words trailed off as her eyes met Sigrid's level gaze and she gave a rueful, hands-up laugh. *"Oy gevalt!"* she said. In her present mood, the Yiddish phrase sounded more like 'I give up.' "I always start babbling when you look at me like that."

"Mother—"

"It's okay, honey. I know you can't help it." She smiled brightly and felt Sigrid's cup. "It's cold. Want me to heat this up? And what about something to eat? I have cold chicken if you'd like a sandwich or—" She ran a hand through her tangled curls. "I'm doing it again, aren't I?"

"Yes," said Sigrid. She slipped off her boots and tucked her feet beneath her on the futon.

Anne took a deep breath. "Mac called me this afternoon."

"Mac? Captain *McKinnon*?"

Her mother nodded.

It was like stepping down on a step that wasn't there. "I didn't realize you and he were that connected."

"We're not," Anne said sharply. "When he showed up in your hospital room last fall, that was the first time I'd spoken to him since the day of your father's funeral. Today is the second time."

"Why?"

"I told you. He called me."

"No, I mean why have you never talked to him since Dad was killed? They worked together every day. They must have been close. Unless . . ." For the first time since learning that her father and her boss had been partners, the thought occurred to her: "Didn't they like each other?"

"Of course they did. They were best friends—David and Jonathan. Smith and Wesson."

Sigrid did not consider herself very good at picking up on nuances, but she sensed something darker beneath her mother's flippancy. She had such vague disconnected memories of her father and only one of those memories included other big tall men in uniforms like his. Yet she had grown up with no recollection of having heard McKinnon's name and she certainly hadn't recognized him when she first began working for him almost two years ago.

"A cop doesn't walk away from his best friend's wife and child the week that friend gets killed. Why did McKinnon?"

"I told him to." Anne had gone back to fiddling with the honey spoon. She scooped a viscous heap from the jar, then held the spoon above the rim so that the thick golden honey flowed back down into the jar.

"Because Dad was killed and he wasn't?"

"Something like that. It was all mixed up in my mind, honey. I honestly don't blame him anymore."

"Anymore?"

"That Leif died and he didn't," she said with an impatient twitch of her shoulder.

Last autumn Mick Cluett had tried to talk about her dad and she'd cut him off, thought Sigrid. Just as she'd cut him off at that farewell get-together last month. What would he have said?

"I pulled Dad's file last fall," she told Anne. "Did you know Mick Cluett was their backup?"

"I'm surprised you had to read it. Didn't Mickey tell you all about it himself?" Anne asked bitterly, as the last golden drops fell from the spoon. "He showed up at our apartment that evening still wearing the uniform drenched with your father's blood, roaring drunk, and telling anyone who'd listen how he'd cradled Leif's head in his arms as he died."

"Is that why Captain McKinnon called you today?"

"Probably. I didn't ask. Let it go, Siga. I don't want to talk about the past anymore." She stuck the spoon back in the honey jar and stood briskly. "Let's see what Mama sent us this year, okay?"

Sigrid knew it would be useless to push for more information tonight. Anne seldom let herself be pinned down very long and from here on would find a dozen ways to keep changing the subject. But the thought of McKinnon calling to tell Anne about Cluett's death was bewildering; and despite Anne's determined cheerfulness, Sigrid wasn't in the mood for one of Grandmother Lattimore's annual attempts to turn her into a candidate for Hymen's altar.

"What is it this year?" she said sourly, as Anne opened a large white envelope stuck with commemorative North Carolina stamps and addressed to both of them in Jane Lattimore's flowing Spencerian script. "A check for miniskirts and four-inch heels?"

Whenever Mrs. Lattimore sent money, she usually included clothing ads from the *New York Times* or *Vogue* and she expected to see the results on her next visit to the city. A dutiful granddaughter, Sigrid always spent the money as ordered—half her closet space was devoted to clothes as frivolous as peacock feathers—but she'd seldom worn them before Oscar Nauman entered her life and even now wasn't completely comfortable wearing them with him.

Anne slit open the envelope and extracted two smaller ones. A mischievous gurgle of laughter escaped her as she scanned the contents. "You're not going to like this," she grinned.

"What?" Sigrid asked apprehensively.

"She's sent us matching gift certificates. For *Imagine You!*"

"*Imagine You!*?" She didn't like the sound of the name. "What's that? A beauty salon? Dress shop?"

"A very expensive Fifth Avenue fashion consultant. We're going to have our colors done."

"Oh God!" Sigrid groaned.

Chapter
7

■■ By 9:30 P.M. on that Wednesday night, Lotty
■■ Fischer had cleared most of the work left in her
In-basket. When she returned from her supper break, she
picked up the names Wally Abronski had left for her and
logged in again. This was part of the job's fun. From her
computer terminal, she could access dozens of data banks
around the country. One of the first things she'd done
four years ago was locate everything available on all her
favorite stars. She knew where John Travolta lived, what
kind of car Tom Cruise drove in real life, how many
speeding tickets the Mets had amassed between them,
and which players had been charged with DWI.

Her fingers flashed over the board as she keyed in
the name of the boy Wally's daughter was seeing. No out-
standing warrants in his name. She tried him with DMV.
One speeding ticket last year. His Social Security number
did not begin with the 110 which indicated New York so
she checked a reference book on her desk and saw that it
must have been issued in Missouri. A few dozen more
keystrokes and she was querying Missouri's DMV.

Nothing.

She repeated the process with the father's name and
immediately scored a direct hit. At that very moment, the

man was wanted in St. Charles, Missouri for aggravated assault, a nonfamily incident involving a gun. The entry ended IMMED CONFIRM RECORD WITH ORI. In this case, the originating office was that of the St. Charles County sheriff's department.

"Oh, jeez," said Wally when she told him. "I didn't really think you'd get a hit. I was just playing safe. Oh jeez, Dee's gonna kill me. She really likes this guy and here I've fingered his old man."

He ripped off the printout and went away to set the appropriate wheels in motion.

Shortly before ten, her friend Jennifer phoned over from central data processing. They gossiped for a couple of minutes, then Jennifer said, "Oh, by the way: that cop that got shot over in Sheepshead Bay?"

"Mmm?" Lotty remembered hearing it mentioned during the supper break. She thought she might have seen him in passing, with some of the homicide detectives, but he was no one she'd formally met and she couldn't really put a face to Michael Cluett's name.

"We got in a notice tonight that you once ran a check on the gun that killed him."

"I did?" she asked, interested. "When?"

"Almost four years ago." Candace read off the date.

"What was it in connection with?"

"Doesn't say. Better check it out though. Someone'll probably be around tonight or tomorrow to ask you about it."

"Give me the serial number," said Lotty and wrote it down on her pad, along with the gun's make, a Browning .380 semiautomatic.

It took a while to reconstruct that evening, but it'd happened when she was still new at the job and conscientiously noting everything in the log. When she'd finished, Lotty stared blankly at her computer screen.

One gun check in the middle of a three-hour stint with license numbers? That meant it probably wasn't official.

It was coming back to her. Her natural friendly helpfulness coupled with who was asking. She could even remember the earlier conversation that had triggered the check.

A white patrol officer in the Bronx had run into a dark alley after a fleeing man reported to be armed. At the end of the alley, he'd turned with a menacing gesture as if to fire. The officer fired first; the man was killed.

Except that the "gun" in the man's hand turned out to be a stolen video tape and the "man" was a fourteen-year-old black youth.

Between the press and angry community leaders, the patrol officer had been suspended indefinitely.

Unfairly, many thought.

Lotty could remember some of the frustrated comments.

"In the dark, fourteen looks like twenty-five."

"Why'd he run, if he wasn't guilty of something?"

"The kid was a thief, wasn't he?"

"Just a matter of time before he upped it to armed robbery. Hell, I say Kearns probably saved the state a hundred thou."

"You don't see 'em giving him a medal, do you?" snorted one of the old-line officers. "That'll never happen to me," he added with heavy significance. "If I ever kill somebody, he's damn sure going to have a gun by the time the TV cameras get there."

There had been a moment of silence.

"Hey, now, wait a minute," a young officer objected. "That's really asking for trouble."

"Yeah? Go tell it to Kearns."

Three nights later, Lotty was asked to run a check on that serial number.

By then, they'd heard that Kearns had two small children with a third one on the way. They also heard that he hadn't drawn a sober breath since they'd suspended him and that his wife had taken the kids and gone back to her parents in Pennsylvania.

Lotty ran the number through without comment.

It had come back clean.

Now she sat at the terminal and gazed unseeingly at the blinking cursor.

Maybe the gun had been stolen since then, she thought.

Maybe it'd been lost. Or sold.

She gave a mental shrug and reached for the phone book. The simplest way to find out was to just ask. The clock above her desk read 22:36:15. Nevertheless, she looked up the number, dialed it, and was pleased when the phone was answered on the first ring.

Almost as if her call were expected.

Chapter
8

After leaving her mother's apartment, Sigrid had intended to see a new Polish film recommended by Oscar Nauman, but on the drive over to the East Side, she passed a small revival house and saw that *Rebecca*, one of her all-time favorites, was listed on the marquee. It'd been several years since she'd seen it on a big screen and she yielded to impulse. After all, she told herself, did anyone actually *need* East European profundity on one's birthday?

There were many who couldn't read Daphne du Maurier's classic novel or watch the Hitchcock film without becoming exasperated by the heroine's timidity and insecurity, but Sigrid thought that du Maurier had captured exactly the paralysis that can inhibit a self-conscious woman. God knows she'd experienced those same inhibitions enough times herself, she thought. She settled happily into one of the theater's dusty velour seats with a box of popcorn and watched an odious Mrs. Van Hopper bully Joan Fontaine around Monte Carlo.

After the film, she browsed in a bookstore down the street till it closed at ten, treating herself to paperback reprints of two books she'd been meaning to read for some time, Carolyn Heilbrun's *Writing a Woman's Life* and a favorably reviewed Isak Dinesen biography. Even so, it was only twenty minutes past ten when she handed her car keys to the parking attendant at the garage near her apartment.

A derelict had been sprawled on a steaming grate in front of the garage as she drove in. As she left, she saw a uniformed officer helping him into his patrol car. With the mercury hovering in the teens tonight, police all over the city would be hustling as many of the homeless as they could into the public shelters.

The walk home was bitter cold, past shuttered businesses and a failed hotel. As Sigrid hurried down Christopher Street, hugging her books and the picture frames to her chest like a small shield, a frigid wind blew straight off the river and needled her face like slivers of Arctic ice. She was glad to turn the corner of her own nondescript street and reach the gate to Number 42½, a sturdy green wooden door set in a high brick wall.

The lock was so stiff from the cold that her key would not turn at first; and for a moment, she feared she'd have to ring for Roman Tramegra, her housemate, to buzz her in. Fortunately, the key turned on her next try. She stepped inside the tiny courtyard and let the gate swing to behind her.

Here, everything was frozen as stiffly as the lock: a dormant dogwood rose from a bed of dead herbs and flowers, a young pear tree that Roman had espaliered against a wall seemed lifeless, and brittle ivy leaves growing over the front of the house rustled with metallic whispers as she passed. The little marble Eros which Roman had lugged home last summer looked utterly forlorn and abandoned. It made Sigrid think of all the homeless who would not find shelter tonight and she shivered despondently. This was no night for anyone not made of marble to spend outside, and she felt incredibly fortunate that she could turn a key in her own door and find warmth and comfort on the other side.

Roman had left a light on over the stove in the kitchen, a sure sign that he'd also left her a plate in the refrigerator, but Roman himself did not appear.

Their apartment had been added to the rear of a commercial building that fronted the next street over and it formed a chunky L around the small courtyard. The short arm of the L held the kitchen and what had been the maid's quarters when the owner, a sister to Roman's elderly godmother, had lived here between her many marriages. Since Sigrid had no interest in cooking, Roman had taken that part of the house for his own and was honestly convinced that his being there made no difference, that he certainly didn't impinge on her life.

In truth, after so many years alone, it was a little like finding herself saddled with a combination of bachelor uncle and some sort of large furry pet. He offered unsolicited advice, hot meals which she could accept or ignore without his taking it personally, and an aura of comfort which she rather welcomed but had never created for herself. Although she had been solitary by choice until accident threw them together last summer, it was pleasant to come home and find Roman puttering in the kitchen, experimenting with the herbs and spices he couldn't resist buying. (His results weren't always edible but hope sprang eternal in his heart.)

Not tonight though.

She had not told Roman of her birthday, so the door between the kitchen and his rooms was closed. A sliver of light shone from beneath it and Sigrid heard the muted tap of his typewriter. Since Christmas he'd been doggedly trying to write a mystery novel and every morning he had questions about the technicalities of a homicide investigation. Fortunately, he did not ask her opinion of his plot's plausibility and Sigrid had no intention of giving it even if solicited. She knew quite well the relative fragility of the human body compared to bullets, tempered steel, or even blunt instruments wielded with determination; but daggers made of brittle icicles struck her as highly preposterous.

She hung her coat on the halltree, then paused in the living room to pour a glass of cassis, which she took to her bedroom to drink in private celebration of another birthday.

The message light was blinking on the answering machine beside her bed and when she pressed the play button, Oscar Nauman's warm voice filled the room. Only yesterday she'd dropped him off at the airport, where he'd met Elliott Buntrock, one of the hottest free-lance curators in the art world, and caught a plane to the West Coast. Nauman knew that her machine held a sixty-minute tape and he wasn't a bit self-conscious about speaking as if she were there with him. And not just speaking but fulminating at length about the idiocy of holding the College Art Association's (or any other association's, for that matter) winter meeting in Los Angeles so that you had to keep remembering what time it was where sensible people lived and what kind of ersatz city was this anyhow and why the hell had he let Buntrock talk him into going in the first place?

Monologues came easily to Nauman. As chairman of the Art Department at Vanderlyn College, he was used to lecturing dazzled students; and his reputation as one of the leading abstract artists of the postwar years had made him confident and forthright, occasionally even careless, in his sweeping pronouncements.

Sigrid sipped her cassis and smiled. She had heard his opinions of Buntrock before. Elliott Buntrock fancied himself on the cutting edge of the art world and was already looking for a book editor to publish the first volume of his collected writings. As Nauman fumed, she undressed, hung up her clothes, and put on a scarlet gown of warm brushed wool.

"—and Buntrock's got me moderating a panel called '*Wither* Postmodernism?'" His tone dripped scorn on Buntrock's mild pun. "A bunch of bozos who paint portraits of Mickey Mouse descending a staircase or have things that slither around the floor. That smart-aleck stuff seems so thin to me now. Ah, well, they said the same about us forty years ago. As you get older, you forget how—"

Abruptly he broke off with a chuckle. "Aren't you glad I called three thousand miles to tell you this? What time is it there, Siga? It's noon here and I miss you like hell."

Her machine switched off.

"I miss you like hell." That was as romantic as Nauman ever got in words, Sigrid thought, but her eyes went to the framed silverpoint that hung above her bookcase. He had drawn her portrait on fine blue-gray paper as if her angular features were a subject for Dürer or Holbein, and the portrait warmed her like cassis whenever she looked at it.

Sigrid swallowed the last of her liqueur and got ready for bed. She had planned to read herself to sleep, but her hand touched the box Anne had given her and she unwrapped the pictures of her father, looked long at them, and then set them on her nightstand.

She wished she could remember him more clearly, that she had been old enough to know him as a person, not as a shadowy figure of other people's memories and family anecdotes. So blond and handsome. And Anne so dark and beautiful. Everyone said the brief marriage between Yankee policeman and Southern belle had been a once-in-a-lifetime romantic love match; and certainly Anne had never remarried, had never seemed the least bit interested in anyone again, so far as Sigrid knew. Not that there hadn't been opportunity and plenty of men to choose from. Anne was an outrageous flirt and loved to spar and fence, but it was a game and her male friends quickly understood it had to remain a game if they wanted to keep her friendship.

Sigrid switched off the lamp and lay wide-eyed in the darkness, troubled by unanswered questions. Why had Captain McKinnon never spoken to her of his dead partner? And why hadn't she let Mick Cluett talk to her?

She fell into uneasy sleep.

The telephone rang. Sharp and insistent.

Nauman?

The blue electronic digits of her clock radio read 2:12. She brought the phone to her ear.

"Hey, Jen, wake up! Guess what?" laughed an exultant male voice. "Your brother's a father! You're an aunt! Allie had the baby! Isn't it great? Jen?"

"I'm sorry," Sigrid told him. "I'm afraid you have the wrong number."

"I do? Oh, gee, I'm really sorry. I guess I'm so excited I must have misdialed. I hope I didn't wake you?"

"That's okay."

"Anyhow," the man told her happily, "it's a *girl*! Alice Sue. Isn't that great?"

"Congratulations," Sigrid murmured.

She returned the phone to its place and lay back with a sleepy smile.

Wind hammered on the windows of her room, a night as cold and hard as the night of her birth, Anne had said. Sigrid knew she'd arrived just before midnight and they said that Leif Harald had wakened half the east coast with the news.

She hoped that someday someone would tell little Alice Sue how excited her own father had been by her birth.

Chapter
9

Two A.M. Dead of night. Wind whipped down the deserted sidewalks. It swept the gutters clean of plastic bags and foam cups, flung discarded newspapers and fast-food cartons from wire trash baskets, and sent empty beer cans rattling through the streets. With every fresh gust, traffic signs strained and creaked against the metal utility poles, signal lights swung wildly over each intersection, and the little awning over the door of the Chinese kosher deli bellied and snapped.

The deli was dark now, the newsstand shuttered, and as she hurried toward her bus stop, Lotty Fischer was alone on the street. At two A.M. on a bitter winter night, with the threat of snow in the air, even vehicular traffic dwindles to an occasional cab or private car. Two blocks away from headquarters, there was a small food store that stayed open all night. Realistically, it was too far from the bus stop for her to shelter in while waiting, but the wind cut like icy knives and she couldn't bear to wait outdoors.

She hadn't meant to take her eyes from the window, but the clerk behind the counter was friendly and bored and Lotty didn't feel she could ignore him. Not when she was using his store for a waiting room. So she had chatted about the cold and indulged his opinions of the Knicks and the Rangers. Before she knew it, her bus was barreling down the street, less than a block away.

Flinging a hasty "Goodnight!" over her shoulder, she ran from the store, dodged a cab, and cut across the street on a long diagonal.

Too late.

The bus roared past her stop without even slowing down.

Lotty Fischer seldom cursed but she felt like cutting loose as she raced after the bus. She was positive that the driver had seen her dash across the street yet he hadn't even touched his brakes. Running in these new boots was hard, but she'd catch him if he stopped for the next light and damned if she wouldn't give that s.o.b. a piece of her mind.

As if to cock a snoot at her curses and threats, the bus rolled through a yellow at the next intersection, found green lights and empty lanes as far ahead as the eye could see and soon was only a set of dirty exhaust fumes and disappearing red taillights.

A trolling taxi slowed beside her and the driver looked over inquiringly, but Lotty shook her head angrily. Almost immediately she changed her mind, but again she was too late. He was history, too.

Now that she'd decided to spring for a cab to her transfer point uptown, no more empty ones appeared. All were either taken or off-duty.

The wind rasped her nose and cheeks and Lotty pulled her scarf higher until only her eyes could be seen between the folds of red wool. The wind cut into the bridge of her nose, making her sinuses ache and forcing her to walk with her back to the wind wherever she safely could. She looked back at the warm pink-and-orange neon sign of the all-night store, nearly three blocks behind her, and hesitated.

After two A.M., the buses ran every thirty-five to forty minutes and if she missed her crosstown connection, there went another forty minutes.

It could take two hours to get home. And on a night like this.

Her best bet now was to walk back to Lexington and grab the subway. That would get her home in twenty-five minutes flat.

Okay, Lotty, she told herself. If you don't find a cab before you get to the Lexington stop, you'll take the train.

Pessimistically, she put a gloved hand in her pocket and pulled out a token just in case a train might be pulling in as she reached the turnstile.

The heels of her new winter boots clicked along the chilled sidewalk. She kept close to the curb, well away from the shadowy recesses of darkened storefronts, but even the street people seemed under cover elsewhere this arctic night. She reached the subway without seeing anyone else on foot.

And still no empty cab.

She wavered at the top of the iron steps that led underground and heard only silence below.

Lotty's personal nightmare was a roving band of teenage males. Color or race didn't matter; they all terrified her. It wasn't just their potential for physical violence that unnerved her, but their arrogant cruelty. Their glee in degrading and humiliating anyone who fell outside their definition of beauty. Too often wolf whistles from behind had turned into snickers and brutal "Is that a hose or a nose?" jokes. She always held her breath whenever more than two young men entered her train car and she never went down into a station alone if she heard loud male laughter or sounds of raucous horseplay floating up to the street.

But tonight she was so cold and tired, she decided she could put up with crude remarks if that were all she'd have to take.

And after all, she asked herself, was there really any reasonable risk of physical danger? Conventional wisdom said that street violence rose and dropped with the mercury, so an icy February night should be safer than an August noon, right?

Right, she told herself.

Nevertheless, despite the self-administered pep talk, she shifted her subway token to her left hand and closed the fingers of her right hand around her keys so that they formed a set of brass claws.

And tomorrow, she promised herself, she was going to tell Personnel that she'd had it with these hours. If they didn't put her back on four-to-midnight, starting Monday night, she'd quit.

Lying flat on his stomach, Jerry the Canary came awake through layers of wine-laced sleep. As instantly cautious as any wild bird on its nest, he lay motionless, alert to the happy female voice that floated from directly beneath him up to where he lay undetected among the shadowy gridwork of heavy steel beams that supported the thick arches above the subway platform.

"—hate to take the train after midnight by myself," the woman was saying in high, light tones. "Awful to be such a wimp."

"Then it's lucky I got called in," said the other voice. It sounded male, lower and huskier.

The rest of their words were lost as they passed away from him. The Canary heard their footsteps and voices echo hollowly against the white tiled walls, and he cautiously turned his head to watch.

A man and a woman.

She had on a bright red fuzzy coat and scarf; he wore a bulky dark jacket, dark warm-up pants, and some sort of knitted cap.

Talking easily, they walked down another few feet and paused just out of earshot. The Canary yawned and snuggled a bit deeper into his blankets. Camouflaged up here in the sooty filthy ironwork, fifteen feet above the tracks, he'd learned that small movements were usually safe. Only big ones got noticed. And even then it was usually only the very young who spotted him: babies lying in their mothers' arms or toddlers strapped into strollers. Adults didn't look up much and they didn't pay much attention when their kids did.

Even the transit cops. They periodically swept a station's toilets and tracks for drunks and skells, but he always pitched his nests high above the center of the station, near the main turnstiles, and they never noticed him.

Sleepily, he watched the man position himself at the very edge of the platform. The woman stood close to him, yet they didn't touch like lovers. Occasionally, the man leaned out over the tracks to stare down the tunnel, his eyes passing over the Canary without registering the recumbent human form.

The Canary yawned again. Soon, a soft vibration along the length of the iron beam announced the train's approach. The vibration grew to a rumble.

He felt the rush of colder air that was pushed through the tunnel ahead of the incoming train.

Saw the woman turn to watch its arrival.

Heard the shrill scream of metal against metal as the train began to brake.

Saw the man give a mighty shove.

Heard her scream rise above the train's.

Chapter 10

The trainman was taking refuge in anger. "That's it," he told any cop who would listen. "I swear to God that's *it*! They can take this cruddy job and shove it. I'll clean sewers for a living before I'll drive one of these Gee-dee trains another Gee-dee foot."

He was a skinny little white man and the more he talked, the angrier he became and the more his voice twanged with the accents of Appalachia. "Shoot fire, I'll haul my whole family back to Pochahontas County, West Virginia and dig coal with my bare hands afore I let 'em do me like this again!"

The conductor was a plump young black woman, dressed like him in a navy blue uniform and black leather jacket, and she watched him uneasily. "Come on, Hank. Nobody's trying to get you."

"You shut up!" he snarled, drawing himself into a defensive rigidity, his back pressed tightly against the white tiled wall.

The conductor turned back to the two detectives. "He doesn't mean it," she apologized for her coworker. "Not really. It's just— Well, this is the second time in two years for him and it's kinda hard on a person."

"I'm sorry, Mr. Pyle," said Detective Elaine Albee.

"But if you've been through this before, then you know we have to keep asking you questions till we get it all down."

Privately she thought that anger was probably healthier than some reactions she'd seen from people who'd unwittingly precipitated another's death. Better to get mad than go mad. Twice this had happened to him? God!

It was the second time for her, too, that she'd been called out to this kind of homicide and she hated to think it was becoming an everyday part of city life.

At least the body wasn't cut to ribbons or decapitated like that last one. The victim here had been slammed into the channel between the rails so the wheels hadn't actually cut her. Small consolation. Albee tried not to picture that other teenage youth in light summer slacks and white shirt, but images kept coming. There was still plenty of this woman's blood, on the rails, on the ties, soon to be tracked across the platform when the M.E.'s people carried her up to the ambulance that waited amid the cop cars and blue lights clustered around the entrance at street level.

Transit's detectives had wound up handling that other one. A quick in-and-outer it'd been. Two guys in a shoving match over a girl. The shover, when they caught up with him, had professed horror at what he'd done, had pleaded guilty to involuntary manslaughter, and had drawn a two-year suspended sentence.

This one sounded different.

The call for help had come at 2:35. Their official shift was long over and sensible officers would have already gone home to bed, but the paperwork had run over and supper had turned into such an animated discussion of basketball that they'd decided they might as well bunk down at the station since they were on turnaround. They were still in the squad room when the call came and because the subway stop was so close to the office, they'd arrived within minutes, even before the transit cops who were now trying to claim jurisdiction.

The crime scene techs had just finished a job in the garment district, so they'd hopped right up on it, too.

The station had been cordoned off immediately. (Sometimes it seemed to Albee that half of New York was tied up in yellow ribbons or set off-limits by blue police barriers.) Portable floodlights had been rushed in and the orderly examination and documentation begun. Strobe lights were still going off, though with lessening frequency. The print and television reporters had gotten their pictures and quotes and had now moved on to a messy three-car wreck on the Brooklyn Bridge.

Elaine Albee loosened the blue wool scarf wound around her neck and glanced at her watch. 3:05 A.M.

The eight passengers on the train had been questioned by Transit Authority cops, their names and addresses recorded, then those who wished had been vanned to the next stop. At the moment, other trains were being rerouted past this stop, but T.A. expected everything to be back to business as usual before the morning rush hour.

While Jim Lowry went down on the tracks with the Medical Examiner, Albee took the trainman, Hank Pyle, into one of the empty train cars where it was warmer, for more detailed questioning. A T.A. cop who insisted on his right to sit in on the interview had brought him coffee, and Pyle sat with his thin legs apart, the foam cup cradled in his hands between his legs as he went over the ghastly experience once more.

According to Pyle, there'd been no warning of anything out of the ordinary while entering the station.

"Weekends you might have more riders; but during the week, this is usually the deadest part of the night." He heard what he'd said and gave a sour laugh. "Deadest. Yeah."

The coffee steamed up as he unsnapped the lid. "Some stops nobody'll get on or off so it wasn't unusual to see just two people. Yeah, I saw 'em good. They were standing a lot closer to the edge than you'd want 'em to, but people do that all the time. Gee-dee jerks," he added resentfully.

Pyle lifted the coffee cup to his lips, then lowered it again between his thin legs without drinking.

"I was braking like always and just before I pulled even with 'em, she just flew off the platform right in front of me. No time to stop. No time to yell— No time to— Never again though! Hear me, Lord! I swear on the body of Christ Jesus who died for our sins I've driven my last train. It can sit here and rust to dust for all I care."

"The man who pushed her," Elaine said softly. "Close your eyes and try to see him again for us."

Pyle took a deep breath and shut his eyes.

"How tall is he?" she asked.

Pyle's brow furrowed, then he shrugged.

"Taller than the woman?" Elaine persisted. "Shorter?"

"Taller. I could see part of his face above her head."

"How much of his face?"

Eyes still closed, Pyle placed his open hand flatly between his mouth and nose. "From about here up."

"And he was standing directly behind her?"

Pyle nodded.

Elaine wrote it on her notepad: *Perp approx. 6" taller than victim.*

"What about his build, Pyle?" asked the transit cop. "Fat? Thin?"

" 'Bout average, I'd say."

"And his clothes?" Elaine asked.

Pyle's pale blue eyes flew open. "Shoot fire, lady! You think I was noticing his Gee-dee clothes when I was getting ready to smash a woman to applesauce?"

"You're the only person who got a good look at the guy," Elaine said. "You want us to get him, don't you?"

"After what he did to me? Doggone right I do!"

"Then concentrate!" she snapped. "Quit feeling sorry for yourself, and give a thought about what he did to *her.*"

Abashed, Pyle screwed his eyes tightly shut in his narrow face and Elaine could see the effort of his struggle to recall. The transit cop started to speak but she chopped him off with a quick hand gesture.

"Relax," she coaxed. "Just take it slow and easy.

Look at his head. Is he wearing anything on it? A hat or cap?''

"Hey, yeah! It's black. One of those stocking caps like my mama used to knit for me. No tassel though.''

"Look at his coat,'' said Elaine. "Long? Short?''

"In between,'' said Pyle. "Dark. Not black though. Blue maybe? And sort of puffy. Like one of them down jackets. And baggy black pants.''

"Shoes? Boots?''

Eyes still closed, he shook his head apologetically. "Sorry, ma'am. I can't seem to see 'em. But them pants—''

"Yes?''

"They musta been warm-up pants, 'cause I seem to see 'em nip in at the ankles.'' He hesitated. "Maybe he was wearing black sneakers.''

A few feet over, on the inner set of tracks, an express train thundered through the station, drowning out Elaine's next words and vibrating their own train.

"You're doing fine,'' she repeated when she could be heard again. "Just a few more questions, okay? One more time, try to remember his face. Can you see his eyes?''

"Sort of,'' the trainman said hesitantly. "They're just eyes and nose and mouth. Nothing special. The cap was pulled down over his ears so I couldn't see 'em. Or his hair.''

"Beard? Mustache?''

"Nope. I sure b'lieve he was clean-shaven, though,'' said Pyle. "I b'lieve I'd remember any hair on his face.''

When it was her turn to be interviewed, the conductor, Oletta Bass, described her impression of someone— "I'm pretty certain it was a man''—running away from the train as they jolted to a rougher than usual stop, but she hadn't seen the couple on the platform at all. Nor had she even realized that they'd hit someone till Hank Pyle had erupted from his compartment at the front of the train, praying and yelling and kicking the train, the steel I-beams, the tiled walls, anything that stood still.

"Hank's a really good motorman and most of the time he's okay to work with, but I've noticed it before," she confided to Elaine. "Those little white hillbillies can sure lose it when things screw up."

One of the passengers had been standing at the door, waiting to exit, and he'd seen a running figure, too. All that had registered were the same nondescript dark clothes—baggy pants, knitted hat, and bulky three-quarters jacket—that the others had described.

All agreed that the man was white and that he'd sprinted over the turnstile and up the steps like someone reasonably young and in good physical shape.

None of the three were sure they'd be able to pick him out of a lineup or that they'd give him a second look if they passed him in the street tomorrow.

They shouldn't be too pessimistic, Elaine told them, even though she privately shared those doubts. Maybe they'd get lucky. Maybe their description would turn out to fit the victim's husband or boyfriend. They might feel differently if they were given someone specific to identify.

They looked at her dubiously, but didn't argue as she passed them back over to Transit.

When Elaine joined Jim Lowry and the others, they'd finally found the dead woman's purse. There'd been nothing in her pockets except a few loose coins, a couple of subway tokens and some soiled tissues. A purse was indicated, but there was no sign of one and they had begun to theorize that her killer had taken it. Then someone thought to shine a light up under the train and there it was. When they'd backed the train off the body, the strap of the black corduroy shoulder bag had been snagged and pulled away from the immediate vicinity.

At last the victim had a name: Charlotte C. Fischer, age twenty-two. Height, five three. Eyes, hazel. And she carried a police department ID badge.

"Charlotte Fischer? *Lotty?*" Horror quickened Elaine Albee's words. "There's a Lotty-somebody that works in

Records. Civilian. Remember, Jim? Shorter than me, reddish brown hair?"

"Yeah, vaguely. Works the night tours, right? Cute figure but big schn—" He caught himself, feeling suddenly loutish to mention the dead woman's nose.

Her body had already been removed but the two detectives were remembering her bloody, smashed features and Elaine let out a deep breath. "Lotty," she said and this time it was a statement, not a question.

The two detectives from Transit looked at each other and the older man gave a sour grin.

"Okay," he said. "We won't fight you over this one since she's one of your people. Just keep us posted, okay?"

Chapter
11

The crime scene people had finished. Their floodlights had been unplugged and hauled upstairs to the van, leaving the subway station to its usual dimness. The yellow ribbons were taken down, most of the uniforms had departed, another motorman had arrived to move the train, and people from the Transit Authority were doing what was necessary to eradicate the remaining traces of Lotty Fischer's violent end. By the beginning of rush hour, only commuters who paid attention to all the details of the story on the morning newscasts would realize that this was the station where a young computer clerk had met her death.

Jim Lowry came back from the telephone. "We were right," he told Elaine Albee. "Lotty Fischer left work around two."

"Why so late?" Elaine asked as she pulled on gloves and wound her blue scarf tightly around the collar of her heavy coat. "Overtime?"

"No. They've been shorthanded, so she was working six-to-two tours till they could hire more clerks." He pulled on his own gloves as they passed through the turnstile and headed up to their car. "She was single. Still lived at home. They say her father's already called twice, really worried about her. They're going to send someone around to break it to her parents."

"Good," said Albee. The relief she felt was mirrored in Jim Lowry's face. Telling a victim's family was one of the hardest things about the job.

As the two detectives reached the street, a uniformed transit officer handed Albee a sheet of paper.

The wind tried to rip it from her grasp. "What's this?"

"The names and addresses of those eight passengers that were on the train," he reminded her.

"Oh, right." She gave a quick glance at the nameplate pinned to his heavy jacket. "Thanks, Magnetti."

The early morning air felt even colder than before and something between a thin sleet and powdery snow had begun. It stung their cheeks and made their eyes tear.

"Brr!" said Albee, diving for the car.

Lowry slid in beside her and immediately started the engine to get the heater and defroster going. The windshield had begun to ice over.

"Backtrack her now?" he asked.

"Might as well try," she agreed.

Driving slowly, they circled each one-way block, finding nothing open along the route Lotty Fischer probably walked till they came to Lundigren's Twenty-four Hour Delicatessen.

They double-parked in front of the lighted entrance. The door was locked, but after looking them over, the beefy middle-aged man inside buzzed them in, a procedure that was becoming more commonplace these days.

"Help you?" he asked.

They showed him their badges, explained why they were there, and described Lotty Fischer.

The clerk's eyes widened. "I heard the sirens and saw the blue lights down there at the subway, but it never dawned on me that— Red coat, red scarf? Oh jeez, yeah, sure, she was in here. A coupla minutes past two it was."

"Alone?" asked Albee.

"Yeah. She was waiting for the bus. She was in here two or three times a week. Late. Usually right after midnight when there's more people in and out; you guys changing shift, you know? Last coupla weeks, it's been later. Bad time of night for a young kid like that, but she said it was just till they hired another girl and she liked working nights. Her mother was sick or something and this way she could be home while her dad worked."

He told them how Lotty had dashed from his store at about ten past two. He'd watched from the window as she missed her bus by inches. "The scuzzbag musta seen her, but he never stopped. You know the way they are. She chased him down the street and then I couldn't see no more, but I knew the bastard wasn't going to stop."

He scratched his ample belly through a tan button-up sweater and shook his head regretfully. "Ah jeez, it's too bad. So she tried to take the train and somebody pushed her under? Christ almighty! It's getting crazy, just crazy. She was such a nice kid, too. Goddamn nuts! Who'd want to do that?"

"When she ran for the bus," said Lowry, "did you notice anybody following her?"

"Nope. A few cars on the street, of course, but nobody on foot."

As Lowry and Albee drove the short distance back to headquarters, the snow and sleet thickened and heavy yellow sanitation trucks were beginning to salt the streets.

In the cubbyhole of an office behind the front desk, Lotty Fischer's terminal screen was blank. The space was normally shared by three other Police Administrative Aides working in rotation, so it bore no marked individuality. No personal papers or photographs, nothing to get a handle on how she'd lived or why she'd died.

Personnel on the midnight-to-eight tour were perturbed by a death so close to home. All agreed that Lotty had seemed like a nice and helpful person, but none appeared to know her well enough to suggest why she'd been killed.

Temporarily at an impasse, Jim and Elaine returned to their own office on the next floor.

"You think it was someone who knew her?" asked Jim.

"Don't you? The motorman said they were standing close together. You don't stand that near a stranger on an otherwise empty platform, do you?"

Elaine had shed her heavy coat and pushed up the sleeves of her black turtleneck sweater, but the warmth of the building was making her sleepy. She leaned back in her chair and covered a wide yawn with her hands.

It was infectious and Jim found himself yawning, too. "I'll start the paperwork," he offered. "Why don't you hit the sack?"

Elaine thought longingly of the lumpy bunk down in the women's dorm, but shook her head. Their desks were placed back to back and she smiled at him across the double width so piled with papers that it was difficult to say where his desk ended and hers began. "We'll split it so we can both sack out quicker."

A suggestive grin spread across his attractive face. "My place or yours?"

"You wish!" she jeered, but a dimple lurked in her cheek as she rollered fresh paper into her typewriter and unfolded the list of passengers' names and addresses the transit officer had given her, each one neatly numbered and printed in block letters that were thoroughly legible for a change.

Too often she was forced to search back and forth through an officer's handwritten reports as if it were some sort of code, comparing an unknown squiggle to a known one elsewhere on the page: was that a 2 or the way he wrote 7s? was this a U or a sloppy O? a small R or an uncompleted N? Give Officer Magnetti A+ for penmanship, she thought, and a gold medal for making life a little easier on everyone who had to read his reports.

Jim watched as she studied the list, her blonde hair glistening under the overhead light, and he wondered if they'd ever get it together or if she would always keep him at arm's length. They'd been partners for almost a year now, yet their off-duty relationship had never progressed beyond casual after-work drinks, an occasional dinner or, more frequently, movies. Lainey was a nut about musical comedies from the thirties and forties and she wanted to see them on a full-sized screen, not on a rented video.

Or was that because she didn't want to be alone with him, in her apartment or his? The only caresses she allowed were chaste kisses and friendly hugs. The one time they'd come close to passion, she'd broken away. "Do we really want this?" she'd asked him, taking long deep breaths to steady herself.

"Yes!" he'd said, reaching out.

But she'd gathered up her coat and purse. "I like working with you, Jim," she'd said. "Let's don't wreck it."

He'd sulked for a week, but deep down, he suspected she was right. The sex would be good, damn good; but sooner or later, it would get in the way.

They'd both seen it happen to others—lovers paralyzed by fear for the beloved's safety; ex-lovers too bitter to keep functioning. Sooner or later, one of the careers went in the toilet.

Usually the woman's.

So he didn't really blame her for being cautious, but sometimes—like tonight—when her eyes had tired shadows beneath them and all the lipstick was gone from those soft lips and she absently kneaded the back of her stiff neck, he wanted to take her in his arms and just hold her gently while she slept.

Did that mean he was falling out of lust and into love?

The thought made him uneasy. He pushed it from his mind and tried to concentrate on tonight's homicide, but as he began filling in the departmental forms, Lainey suddenly interrupted.

"How many passengers were on the train?"

"I counted eight. Why?"

"I counted eight, too. And that includes—" She looked down at the name she'd scribbled on her notepad earlier. "Patrick D. Newhouse. He's the one who saw the running perp."

"So?"

"So there're eight names on Magnetti's list. We kept

Newhouse behind for further questioning, so he's not on the list. He makes nine."

"Maybe we miscounted."

She tilted her head consideringly. "Both of us? Come on, Jim. The conductor told me that she went through the train and put all the passengers together in one car. All *eight* passengers. And she didn't open the car doors till help came."

"Everyone said that the only people on the platform were Fischer and whoever pushed her," Jim mused. *"He* went over the turnstile and up the steps and I can't see him hanging around to wait for us. So what's left?"

It hit them at the same time.

"Wino!"

"Bum!"

Despite all of Transit Authority's efforts, when the temperature dropped, the homeless persistently sought shelter in subway stations and tunnels. Bums and derelicts, the mental cases, the druggies and alkies—many were drawn to the relative warmth and illusory safety of the dark tunnels. Every winter, a handful would manage to trip against the third rail and electrocute themselves or became disoriented and lie down on the tracks so that trainmen like Hank Pyle would have nightmares the rest of their lives.

"Which one's the ringer here?" Elaine wondered, scrutinizing each name. Everything looked kosher. Fortunately, Magnetti appeared to be a by-the-book officer. If those small notations in the margins meant anything, he must have asked everyone for an ID. Surely, "NYDL, SS, Con Ed" stood for New York drivers license, Social Security card and a ConEd electric bill.

She passed the list over to Jim along with her interpretation. "What do you think?"

"Sounds logical to me. And two names with no ID: Mary Smith of the Bronx and Gerald Byrd of West Forty-fourth Street. Mary Smith? Who's she kidding?" He reached for his telephone and dialed the number.

It was answered on the second ring and Elaine listened as he said, "Mrs. Smith? *Mary* Smith? Uh, this is

Detective Lowry calling about the train accident you were in earlier tonight. I'm sorry to bother you again, but would you mind going over it for me while things are fresh in your mind?"

Evidently, thought Elaine, there really was a Mary Smith and she did mind going over it again, judging by the way Jim rolled his eyes at her. But he was good at talking people around and soon he had Mrs. Smith describing as many of her fellow passengers as she could remember.

Might as well get on with it, Elaine thought, and used her own phone to call the number Magnetti had written down for Gerald Byrd.

There was one ring, a mechanical click, then an answering machine announced that she'd reached the box office of a popular, long-running Broadway hit. She immediately remembered seeing a large poster advertising that play just inside the subway station tonight, a poster with a phone number big enough to be read fifteen feet away.

Fast on his feet, Elaine thought as she waited for Jim to finish with Mary Smith and get off the phone so she could tell him. Cute, too. *Phantom of the Opera* indeed.

Not their usual skell.

So who was this Gerald Byrd?

Chapter
12

Thursday morning dawned gray and dreary and a fine sleet pinged the clerestory windows of Sigrid's bedroom when she arose.

Out in the kitchen, Roman padded back and forth between coffee maker and refrigerator, pouring coffee, pouring tumblers of crimson juice, exhilarated by the winter weather, from which he expected to draw direct inspiration for his ski lodge murder mystery.

Sigrid, who had to leave for work in less than forty minutes, was still in her robe. Roman, who would probably be staying in all day, was not only dressed like a Forties Hollywood director's idea of Working Author: baggy corduroy slacks, heavy English sweater with leather elbow patches, a paisley scarf loosely tucked into the collar. His thinning brown hair was neatly combed over the high dome of his head and his soft face was smoothly shaven.

Getting up early was always difficult for Sigrid and she seldom wanted to talk before her second cup of coffee. Usually it didn't matter. She would simply sit with her slender fingers laced around the hot mug and Roman would read snippets from the morning paper and keep adding fresh coffee. Eventually, something he read or said would provoke her to speech.

So far this morning, all that had truly penetrated her consciousness as she sat at the green-tiled breakfast counter were the thin flakes of snow falling on the brick courtyard outside their kitchen window. Soon she would have to decide whether or not to leave the car garaged and take a bus to work. It was only three short blocks over to Hudson Street and the uptown M10 connected with the crosstown bus that would take her practically to her office door and then she could—

She became aware that Roman had quit murmuring generalities and was waiting for an answer to a specific question.

"Sorry, Roman. I don't think I heard you."

"I said, which do you like best?"

"Which what do I like best?"

He sighed good naturedly. "Do drink your juice, dear child, and I'll get you more coffee. I thought you were awake."

"I *am* awake," she said, turning away so he couldn't see her yawn. "Awake enough to recognize sarcasm when I hear it. Tell me again: which what?"

"Book title. If you recall, it takes place in the dead of winter, which would be a *marvelous* title except that it's been used about five times in the last ten years. I looked it up at the library yesterday. *Fatal February,* too. That would have been my next choice. I've narrowed it down to *Winterkill, Death Thaw,* and *Warmed Each Winter.* If you saw those on a book jacket, which would you pick up first?"

"Warmed Each Winter," she murmured.

Roman frowned. "Do you really like that best?"

"Not especially. But I *would* pick it up because I'd wonder what it meant."

"It's from an Edna Millay sonnet. I wonder if that's a good idea though? In case the estate won't give permission to quote for free. Do you know that a friend of mine wanted to quote five lines from a Mel Torme song and they asked *five* thousand dollars! That's more than his whole bloody advance."

"Millay," Sigrid reminded him.

"Millay," he agreed. "I don't remember the exact

words, but it's something to the effect that if we do *not* stop killing each other, man's blood will simply keep warming the ground each winter."

She tried another sip of cranberry raspberry juice. It made a pleasant change from the orange juice Roman usually set before her, and Sigrid savored the unfamiliar blend of sweet and tart. Rather like Roman's conversation at times. She wondered if his preoccupation with scarlet blood had influenced his choice of juices this morning. "*Is* there a lot of blood in your book?"

"Oh, my, yes," he rumbled. "Not on the *ground* exactly. But the deeds are committed with icicle daggers and the first victim bleeds all over the white bearskin rug in the ski lodge. The second one—"

"You don't think the title's too poetic for a murder mystery?"

"I know, I know. It really ought to be something short and *pungent*," Roman agreed. He had a magpie mentality that gathered snippets of trivial information that he was forever trying to weave into saleable articles; and he was now off on the meaning of February, how the *Februa* were Roman festivals of general expiation and atonement.

"The Anglo-Saxons, on the other hand," he sniffed, "were always thinking of their bellies instead of their souls. They called it *Sprout-Kale*. Time to plant cabbage. But I digress. I had *hoped* that the encyclopedia entry on February would suggest a pertinent title. Alas."

"Surely a line from the book itself should trigger a title?" asked Sigrid.

"Perhaps. But a title's not even the worst of it," Roman confessed gloomily. "I've made my killer so clever that I'm not sure my sleuth will be able to figure it out. And of course, once the icicles melt, there's *no* physical evidence left. I shall have to pick your brains, my dear, for some fancy footwork."

Sigrid shook her head. "I keep telling you, Roman. It isn't fancy footwork that solves most homicides; it's just plain old-fashioned boring legwork: asking a hundred different people 'Did you see?' or 'Did you hear?' and the hundred and first says, 'Oh, gee, yeah, I guess I did.' Or someone gets tired of being pushed around and they say, 'That no-good's been on my case. He did it to me and now I'm going to do him'; and they come in and make a statement. Acting on that information, we make arrests. I'm afraid it isn't very puzzling.''

He looked so disappointed that Sigrid took pity on him and gave him an encapsulated version of Locard's Theory of Transfer.

Roman was enchanted. ''So every murderer leaves something of himself at a crime scene and takes something of the crime scene away with him even if all that's transferred are a few grains of sand or some fabric fibers? Hmm-mm. Grains of sand may be difficult in a snowstorm.''

''I'm sure you'll think of something,'' Sigrid said.

''Maybe if I combine it with the ransom money,'' he mused. ''I looked that up, too. In so many *sloppily* written mysteries, a husband or wife will be told to put a half-million in small bills in a plain paper bag and leave it under the third park bench past the Civil War monument.''

''So?''

''My *dear* child, do you *know* how much a half-million in fives and tens would *weigh*? About a hundred and fifty *pounds*. That's seventy-five thousand pieces of paper! And you have to hope that fives and tens are small enough because if you tried to do it in ones—''

Sigrid left him punching numbers on his pocket calculator and went in to dress.

Before signing into their separate dorms in the wee hours of the morning, Elaine Albee and Jim Lowry had agreed that the first thing on their agenda would be locating Gerald Byrd. The second would be the bus driver who had roared past Lotty Fischer last night.

There were a million *if onlys* attached to every violent death, a thousand branching choices that might have led away from death or missed it by inches; and there was nothing yet to tell them that Lotty's killer might not have stalked her down anyhow at another time and place. At this moment, however, gazing bleary-eyed at each other over their take-out breakfast in the squad room, Elaine and Jim were convinced that Lotty Fischer would still be alive if the driver of that bus had only stopped, and they were looking forward to finding the bastard.

Bernie Peters and Matt Eberstadt weren't due in till four, and Lieutenant Harald seemed to be running late; but several of those working the morning shift had met the friendly young P.A.A. and exchanged pleasantries with her or waited while she ran a routine check on something, and there was much head-shaking over her ghastly end.

Detective Tildon offered to handle the routine in-house part of the investigation, to speak to her coworkers downstairs, see if there were any leads at this end that they might have missed last night. He also planned to contact the train passengers in case any could help them get a fix on Gerald Byrd, if that were indeed his name. In fact, Tillie had already copied their list and added it to one of the many neat, methodical piles of paper on his desk.

After a cribbage board exploded next to him during a tournament at one of Manhattan's poshest hotels, Tillie had spent nearly a month in the hospital, then another two months at home, and the files had suffered in his absence. He still wasn't back up to full physical strength, but the doctors had agreed to let him come back to work if he'd pull straight eight-to-fours and promise not to try any strenuous activity.

It was working out quite well. Tillie was a careful and conscientious worker who thrived on detail, forms, and timetables, and he had almost restored the order that had been missing since he was wounded.

Everyone liked Tillie and they welcomed his return; not because he was genuinely likeable—which he was— but because he was also the one person who got along well with Lieutenant Harald, a boss who was never going to have to worry about making responses to teary-eyed testimonials at her retirement dinner. Every detective in the squad had felt the sharp edge of her tongue while Tillie was out. Since he was back, she seemed much less uptight and considerably more tolerant of minor lapses.

Nevertheless, if there were legitimate reasons to be out and working before she arrived . . .

By the time Jim Lowry had washed down a second raspberry doughnut and Elaine Albee had eaten all her peach yogurt, Tillie had persuaded Transit to give him the name and address of the only driver who could have passed up Lotty Fischer at the pertinent time.

"He worked a midnight-to-eight," Tillie said.

"Good," said Elaine Albee as she put on her coat.

Jim Lowry gave a grim smile. "We'll check the subway station first, see if we can get a line on this Byrd bird. That should give our bus-driving bastard just enough time to get to sleep good before we land on him with both feet."

"Have fun, children," said Tillie, "and don't forget your galoshes."

Foul weather always added to the number of subway riders, but rush hour had crested by the time Jim and Elaine arrived at the fatal station. Although a steady stream of people continued to pass through the turnstiles, there were two workers inside the token booth and business had eased up enough that one put up a "Next window please" sign and came out to talk to them.

"Not that I can tell you anything that'll help. There's no one on duty here that late." The T.A. clerk was a large fat woman with fair skin that was splotched by acne. "And I don't know about Sam," she added, nodding toward her coworker who glanced out at them occasionally through the glass of the ticket kiosk, "but I don't walk onto that platform 'cept to catch my train home. The circus could camp in these tunnels for all I know. Tell you who might could help you though. Stevie Gr—"

An incoming train blanked the name and Jim Lowry had to roar to be heard above the shrill clangor.

"Stevie Greenapple," she yelled back. "One of our cops."

The train moved out of the station and her voice dropped back to normal. "I bet Stevie knows every flop hole in every tunnel from Thirty-fourth Street to South Ferry. The tunnels are a real hobby with him, 'specially the ghost stations. He's down here sometimes even when he doesn't have to be. It's an education just to hear that man talk about some of the things that've gone on down here from the time they started with the first trains. Bet he could tell you if there's anybody using this station regular."

Unfortunately, neither she nor the other worker knew Greenapple's schedule, so Elaine called Tillie and added it to his growing list of things to do. Then she and Jim caught the next downtown train, transferred to an F train, and soon emerged on the Lower East Side to find that the thin snow had thickened into soft white flakes.

Chapter
13

Even with overhead heaters hanging from the beams above each work station, the Chrysler dealer's garage in Sheepshead Bay felt like a drafty barn to Davidowitz and me.

The Chrysler mechanics wore brown twill coveralls, but their arms and chests were padded-looking, like they wore two or three layers underneath. The concrete floor was splotched with motor oil and transmission fluid. Probably never warmed up before summer, especially since the two bay doors kept opening and closing as they shuttled cars in and out.

A damn noisy place, too. Screeching power tools, banging to loosen rusted muffler clamps, the clang as a steel wrench or loose hubcap clattered to the floor, and those heavy metal bay doors rumbling up and down on their tracks.

The sleet had changed to wet snow and each car came in with a mound of icy slush on hood, roof, and trunk.

I held an antacid mint on my tongue and watched a harried-looking Charley of early middle age duck under a blue LeBaron convertible that was raised up on a hydraulic lift. He said something to the mechanic, who nodded and then reached up into the LeBaron's underside again with a power wrench.

He rounded a rolling tool chest, kicked a loose lug nut back to the young black mechanic who'd just dropped it, and walked up to us. "You wanted to see me?"

He had on coveralls, too, but a dark green tie was knotted at the neck of his plaid shirt beneath. Brown hair clipped short, thinning on top though. Wrinkles around his eyes. I put his age somewhere in the early forties.

"You Frank Ambrosini?" asked Davidowitz. He had to raise his voice to be heard over the pressurized air hose directly behind them. "The service manager here?"

"Who's asking?" Not hostile, just wary.

Davidowitz introduced us and I said, "One of your customers was shot yesterday. We'd like to—"

"You gotta speak up," said Ambrosini, tapping his ear.

"Got somewhere quieter we can talk?" Davidowitz asked loudly.

"Yeah, sure," said Ambrosini and took us across the noisy service area, past a large black luxury car that had its motor hanging by chains over the open hood. Clean drop cloths were draped over the fenders and front grill to protect the shiny finish from spills and scratches. It reminded me of TV medical documentaries. They draped patients like that so that only a small part of the body was left exposed for the surgeon's knife. Judging by the facial expressions of the two mechanics at work on the motor, this was going to be an equally expensive operation.

The service manager took us into a glass-fronted cubicle. Grimy clipboards hung beside the door. Each held a thin sheaf of grease-smudged checklists, work orders, and time sheets, all waiting to have their prices added to the final bills. Inside the cubicle, desk and shelves were piled high with more papers, parts catalogs, and service manuals. A calendar on every wall. Very educational to see how each Miss February illustrated a different socket wrench or air pressure gauge.

Only one extra chair. Davidowitz waved aside Ambrosini's offer to find another and leaned against the door frame.

It was only marginally quieter with the door closed. Engine smells fought with stale cigarette butts. Ambrosini slid into his chair behind the desk, pulled out a fresh cigarette, lit it, took a deep draw on it, and looked at us curiously. "So. What can I do for you guys?"

"One of your customers was shot and killed night before last," I said.

"Yeah, I heard about that. Too bad."

"We heard you and he'd had some words."

"So?"

"So we thought we'd come and ask you about it."

"Ask me what?"

"Michael Cluett was murdered, Mr. Ambrosini." I was trying to stay patient.

"So what's that got to do with me?" His face held a blank, open expression.

Too blank and open? Davidowitz and I looked at each other.

"Oh, hey, wait just a minute now!" Cigarette ashes went flying as Ambrosini wagged his hands in protest.

"You did have words with him, didn't you?"

Ambrosini shrugged. "Well, yeah. But hell! If I went out and shot every customer that jaws off about our service here—"

"You give bad service?" Davidowitz put in.

" 'Course not. But a guy that thinks he can throw his weight around just because he's a cop—"

"You don't like cops?" I asked, deliberately badgering him.

"I don't like cops that try to muscle me into fixing something that ain't broke just because he's a cop." Ambrosini sat up stiffly in his chair. "No sir, I don't like that one little bit. Would you?"

"How was he muscling you?"

Ambrosini gave a sour laugh. "I gotta tell a couple of detectives the hundred and one ways a cop on the beat can give grief to legitimate businesses? Give me a break."

He gave us the not-too-subtle threats he said Cluett

had made about ticketing every less-than-legally parked car on the street or sidewalk outside the garage bay doors, how Cluett had hassled them about EPA-mandated guidelines for proper oil and grease disposal, and anything else he could think of, merely because he'd thought the power steering was too stiff on his new car.

"That's just the way that car handles. All in his head, believe me. But he kept bitching till I finally told him where he could shove it. That's *all* I did though. You don't believe me, ask anybody here. I was steamed, sure, but I don't go off half-cocked. Look, this guy was around here every week with something new. He wanted a personal mechanic, like a personal banker, you know?"

Knowing Cluett, I could imagine.

"If that's true," I said, "can you tell us where you were between ten P.M. and midnight on Tuesday night?"

As it so happened, Ambrosini could. He stood up, opened the door to his office and shouted over the din, "Hey, George!"

The wiry young brother was bent over an engine at the middle work station. He straightened and looked our way.

"C'mere a minute."

He wiped his hands on a bright orange flannel and came over.

"These guys wanna know what I was doing between ten and midnight Tuesday." Ambrosini grinned as he stubbed out his cigarette in an overflowing ashtray shaped like a rubber tire.

The kid grinned back. "We were still celebrating at Gino's," he told us. "Man, you shoulda been there! I rolled a perfect game Tuesday night. Twelve goddamn strikes in a row! We *creamed* Arnie's Awnings."

While Davidowitz spoke to the other members of Coney Island Chrysler's bowling team, I wrote down Gino's address; but my heart wasn't in it.

The Shamrock was a bar and grill that faced the bay on Emmons Avenue. Nets and dried starfish on the walls;

a huge sailfish over the bar. In summer, fishermen and tourists jammed the big main dining room for fresh seafood or stood outside on the sidewalk to eat clams on the halfshell served through the open window. They closed off the big room during the week, but even on a winter day like this there was enough business to keep the bar and side grill open. Thick cigar smoke. One of the regulars had just become a grandfather for the first time and an open box lay on the bar. The pink-and-gold bands had "It's A Girl!" printed on them.

The bar had more people than I expected to see this early in the day and certainly more than had been at Gino's, where we confirmed Ambrosini's alibi. Not quite two o'clock and half the stools and several of the booths were full. The windows were steamed over and just the smell of beer and hot grease frying the shrimp made Davidowitz and me remember how long it'd been since our doughnuts and coffee.

The Shamrock was a neighborhood gathering place and even though we didn't live in this neighborhood, we'd both been in before. Talk flowed easily from one table to the next, with occasional banter addressed to the bartender and two waitresses loud enough for the whole room to hear.

None of them had been working Tuesday night. "But Roger'll be here in about twenty minutes," one of the women said.

"Roger?" asked Davidowitz.

"The night guy. He's coming in early so I can go pick up my kids before the snow gets too deep. They're saying six to eight inches if it stalls."

"They are?" Davidowitz lived in Nassau and hated driving the Sunrise Highway in snow.

"Relax," I told him. "They say that every time we get a few flakes."

We took our beers over to a booth and ordered the combination plate: fried oysters, shrimp, and flounder, with french fries and a salad on the side. Hy's mustache was soon flecked with beer foam and bits of lettuce.

That's the trouble with face hair. At mealtimes you look like a garbage pail that needs emptying.

We'd almost finished eating when a shaggy barrel of a man came through the door, stamping snow from his boots and shaking his thick black hair free of wet flakes. He looked a little familiar and gave us the high sign when one of the women nodded in our direction. A few minutes later, he came over carrying one of those red plastic baskets full of fried shrimp and a mug of draft beer. He pulled a chair up to the end of our booth, sat down and began to eat.

"Carol says you wanna ask me about Tuesday night and Mick Cluett." He looked at our empty glasses. " 'Nother round?"

"No, thanks," I said. We introduced ourselves. He was Roger Sorrell. "You knew Mick pretty well?"

"Sure." Sorrell popped a couple of shrimp in his mouth and talked as he chewed. "He was here three or four nights a week. You coulda knocked me over with one of those plastic drink stirrers when I heard he got shot."

Hefty swigs of beer alternated with mouthfuls of shrimp and french fries as Sorrell described Mick Cluett's last visit to the Shamrock. It'd been a slow Tuesday night, bitter cold, so Sheba, the dog, had come into the bar with him as a matter of course.

"She behaves herself. Goes to sleep on his foot and doesn't wake up till it's time to go. We used to kid him that she was his seeing eye dog—they're the only ones you're supposed to let in a place that serves food—but he never got blind drunk. Two beers, three at the most were all he ever had."

According to Sorrell, there was nothing out of the ordinary about the evening. Mick Cluett had arrived and departed around his usual times. "Although, come to think about it, he did look at the clock a coupla times and when he got up to leave, he said something about somebody not coming."

"Could you be more specific? Did he use a name?"

"Sorry," he said. "As near as I can remember, it was a coupla minutes past ten. He drained his glass and said—'' Sorrell closed his eyes to concentrate. ''—'Looks like he's not coming, so I might as well call it a night.' I was watching the game, not paying him much attention. He paid his tab, put on his coat and put Sheba back on the leash, and that was it.''

''Anybody leave around the same time he did?'' I asked, patting my pockets for my antacids. Seafood tastes great going down, but fried stuff always weighs heavy on my stomach.

Sorrell concentrated. ''Yeah, come to think of it, one of the nurses from the hospital.''

He turned heavily in the chair. ''Hey, Carol. What's the name of that nurse that comes in once in a while? Red hair starting to go gray, nice laugh. Kitty?''

''Kitty Jozell,'' the barmaid answered easily.

''Know where she lives?''

Both shrugged.

''Nearby though,'' said Carol. ''Probably around on Voorhies 'cause I know we're on her way home from the hospital.''

Davidowitz hoisted his burly form from the booth and went in search of the men's room and telephone. ''I'll see if she's in the book,'' he told me.

A few minutes later, he reported back. There was only one K. Jozell in the Brooklyn directory and the address was almost around the corner. He'd punched her number and a woman answered on the fifth ring.

''I could tell by her voice that I woke her up, but she was nice about it,'' said Davidowitz. ''She doesn't think she can help us much, but as long as we're at the Shamrock, she said we might as well come ahead.''

Kitty Jozell's apartment was in one of those plain buildings erected all over New York in the mid-fifties: a twelve-story brick-and-glass box sufficient for the demands of no-frills housing. No doorman, just rows of push buttons in an outer lobby. Probably unlocked every morning and evening by the super, who probably lived on the ground floor.

Davidowitz pressed the nurse's number and when her voice came through the speaker, he identified himself and the inner lobby door unlocked with a loud buzz. As we made the elevators, the doors opened to one of the cars. A young Asian woman stepped out, pulling a shopping cart with one hand and a small child with the other. Her eyes went from the damp flakes on our overcoats and hats to the glass doors beyond, where the air was white with swirling snow.

"Oh my God," she groaned.

The child was too bundled up for me to tell if it was a boy or girl, but a pleased look of anticipation lit up its blackberry eyes and I found myself smiling as the elevator took us up.

"You build snowmen when you were a kid, Hy?"

But Davidowitz was worrying about the long drive home. "I *knew* I should've put the tire chains on before I came in today."

"Will you quit that?" I told him. "It's supposed to stop before dark."

Our elevator came to a smooth stop and Kitty Jozell was waiting for us in the open doorway of 8-B.

She was a natural redhead, beginning to go gray and not fighting it. She wore a dark purple wool robe tightly cinched at her trim waist and her shoulder-length hair had been combed, but her face was bare of makeup and a slight puffiness around her green eyes confirmed that she'd been asleep when Davidowitz phoned.

"Sorry," she said, masking a yawn, "but I worked an eleven-to-seven last night."

She let us into an attractive studio apartment. The Murphy bed had been folded up but an edge of flowered coverlet had been caught in the crack; and the coffee table that doubled as a nightstand still held a water glass, a box of tissues, and a half-worked crossword puzzle. A wire hanger hooked over the kitchen doorway held her white uniform, and crumpled white panty hose lay on the kitchen counter. Otherwise, the apartment was neat and cozy, with bright chintzes and one of the healthiest looking polypody ferns I'd ever seen.

"How often do you fertilize it?" I asked her.

"Oh, do you grow ferns?" she said.

"Nothing like that one," I had to admit.

"You have to mist them twice a week, but only feed them twice a year or you'll burn the rhizomes."

Davidowitz cleared his throat. Real detectives aren't supposed to get off on hanging baskets. He started questioning Ms. Jozell.

She was a special-duty nurse at a nearby hospital over on Ocean Parkway, which explained her erratic hours. And yes, she occasionally stopped in at the Shamrock on her way home.

Night before last? Tuesday?

"I checked my calendar when you called," she said. "I probably left the hospital around nine-fifteen, nine-twenty."

"You don't keep regular hours?"

"I told you: I'm special-duty, not regular staff." She hesitated and her green eyes seemed to look inward for a minute. "My patient died. I filled out the necessary papers and then left. I'm not much for whisky, but it seems to help me sleep if I drink a stiff scotch after a shift like that."

Her slim fingers played with the fringed belt of her purple robe, curling and uncurling it. "He was only thirteen."

We gave her a moment, then I said, "About the Shamrock. Do you remember seeing Michael Cluett when you left?"

"The police officer that was shot? Old guy, fat, with a dog?"

I nodded.

"I didn't know him by name," she said, "but he was there almost every time I've stopped by for a drink. He left just ahead of me."

"Alone?"

"With the dog," she repeated. "I was about a half-block behind him and I turned the corner at Ocean Avenue about the time he was crossing Emmons toward the footbridge. It was pretty cold and I remember wondering if dogs feel it as much as humans and thinking about my patient dying so young and there was this old guy. Not to say that maybe Jeffy wouldn't have grown up to be an old boozer, too, some day. Next century.''

She gave us another apologetic smile. "Sorry. You don't want to hear this. Anyhow, just as I was turning my corner, I saw him—Cluett?—stop and look off to his right. I don't know if the guy called to him or if he was waiting for the dog to do his business or what, but he stopped down there under the light and someone crossed the street and they walked on together. I went on down Ocean and that was the last I saw of him.''

Davidowitz looked up from his notepad. "About what time would you say that was, Ms. Jozell?''

"Ten-ten,'' she answered promptly. "There was a two-hour special that came on at nine that Jeffy and I'd planned to watch together.''

Her voice wobbled slightly, but she caught herself. "I checked my watch and thought maybe I'd catch the end of it for him. Sounds silly, doesn't it?''

"Not really,'' I said. It struck me that Kitty Jozell was probably a very good nurse to have around if you were young and scared and deathly ill. "The person that met Cluett—was it a man?''

"I think so.'' She hesitated. "I don't know why I have that impression. Everybody wears pants and bulky jackets, but I don't know . . . something about the walk maybe? Honestly, I wasn't paying that much attention.''

She couldn't give us much of a description. Dark clothes, some sort of cap. "I can't even tell you if he was black or white.''

Height? Weight? Age?

A little shorter than Cluett, she thought, and not as broad. Again, though, it was hard to tell in winter clothes, wasn't it? As for age, she didn't think he walked like an old man but that was as far as she could go.

We thanked her for her help and apologized again for bothering her. I gave her my card and she promised to call if she remembered anything more.

None of us expected that she would.

.   .   .

Back at street level, snow was piling up on the side-walk, although traffic kept the street itself pretty clear. As we walked back to the car, we passed several guys already out with brooms and shovels to keep their storefronts clear.

Three-ten. Nearly another hour till our shift ended. Still time to check on the neighbor kid who'd smart-mouthed Cluett, but Davidowitz was really antsy, so I said, "Why don't you head on home, Hy? I can see the kid by myself."

"You sure?" He looked around for the nearest bus stop.

I brushed snow off the windshield and said, "Sure, go ahead," but I was talking to myself. Davidowitz was already half a block away and out in the street flagging down a bus.

I put the car in drive and cautiously headed for Man-hattan Beach.

Chapter
14

If the idea was to incovenience the bus driver who had ignored Lotty Fischer's attempt to board last night, Jim Lowry and Elaine Albee had timed it well. After two or three polite pushes on the intercom to 3-C got no response, Lowry planted his thumb on the small black button beside the name *T. Inskip* until a groggy male voice growled obscenities from the speaker.

"Police," Lowry growled back and continued to push until the man buzzed them through the locked door. The building was a remodeled tenement with no elevator and they climbed the steep steps up to the third-floor landing, where they had another lengthy ring on the doorbell.

There came the sound of several bolts and locks being turned, and a door opened across the hall to reveal an elderly man in slippers and robe. He held in his arms an enormous silky cat the color of orange marmalade, and cat and man stared at the police detectives in disapproval. "Teddy's gonna be pissed as hell wit' you two and you wake 'im up."

"Butt out, Pitkin," said the same grumpy voice they'd heard through the intercom.

He couldn't have been asleep for more than an hour.

He was barefooted, his face was sleep-swollen and in need of a shave, his dark hair was mashed flat on one side and stuck out in a dozen different directions on the other. His pajamas were warm-up pants and ratty sweatshirt, and two things were immediately obvious: Theodore Inskip thought he was God's gift to women and he hated having any woman, even a cop, see him like this. Most particularly did he hate having a female cop as blonde and cute as Detective Elaine Albee stand in his dirty studio apartment and look at him as if she thought he hadn't changed his underwear in five years.

He kept smoothing his hair, running his hand over the raspy growth on his chin, and kicking himself that he hadn't at least folded up the sleeper couch and put on his newish Who sweatshirt. Worse, he was so groggy that he couldn't zero in on what they really wanted from him.

Especially since they came at him from both sides. "How long you been driving?" asked the man.

"Three years, why?"

"You like it?" asked the woman.

"Sure, it's okay," he said, puzzled. "A pain at times. As many assholes as potholes."

They didn't laugh.

"Why?" he asked again. "What's this about?"

"We'll ask the questions," the man snarled.

"What about last night?" asked the woman. With the toe of her boot, she nudged aside an empty pizza box on the floor beside his television as if she suspected it had roaches. "Was it boring last night? Who'd you see on the streets between two and two-thirty?"

He tried to remember, but last night was only a blur of cold streets except for a couple of crackheads he wouldn't open up for down in the Bowery. They'd pounded the doors, run alongside for a half-block, and he'd heard something hit the side as he took off, but that was before two.

"Nobody," he said. "Just the usual. Not many riding that late."

"But you picked up everybody that wanted on?"

Their badgering was beginning to get to him and

made him uneasy. His mouth felt like the underside of a carpet.

"Sure," he said cautiously. "If they were at the stop. If they had the change. This isn't about those bums on the Bowery, is it? They were stoned and—"

Forget about the Bowery, the man told him, and concentrate on a stop farther north. They even told him which intersection along Third Avenue. "You sure you didn't see anybody try to flag you down? Fuzzy red coat?"

Now he had a fix on it. Oh, crap! The dame who'd chased after him was probably this guy's sister or something and they were going to lean on him because he hadn't stopped in the middle of the block? Well, screw her, he thought resentfully. And screw them for waking him up.

"Look, I was making up time; I didn't see nobody! Anyhow, if nobody's waiting *at* the designated stop, then I don't stop there; and I can't stop just because somebody tries to wave me down. It's against rules. Anyhow, it's her word against mine!"

As soon as the words were out, he knew he'd blown it.

"Who said it was a woman?" the man asked quietly.

Inskip cursed, but it was purely from habit. Sullenly, he admitted that he'd seen the woman, but the rules said he wasn't supposed to stop for people in the middle of the block, tie up traffic.

Then he was forced to admit that at 2:10 his bus was practically the only traffic moving along that section of Third Avenue.

The blonde had gone from looking as if he needed clean shorts to looking as if he'd just crawled out of the sewer. "You *are* a piece of work, aren't you?" she said. "Gunning your bus down Third like it's your private little red sports car, and because you had to strut your one scummy piece of power, a decent human being gets pushed under a train."

"What?"

They gave him a graphic description of Lotty

Fischer's death, and he sat white-faced and sweating amid the tumbled covers of his unmade couch.

At that minute, his phone rang and he pounced on it like a lifeline.

"Yeah, this is Ted Inskip—who . . . *who*? He said *what*? . . . No. No, I didn't. *No!*"

He slammed down the phone and looked up at them with a dazed expression on his handsome face. "That was a reporter from the *Post*. Some guy at an all-night deli saw me pass her up."

The consequences of his actions last night were finally beginning to sink in on Inskip. "I could lose my job," he said.

Lotty Fischer lost her life, they reminded him coldly.

"Listen to me," he pleaded. "I didn't mean any harm. It was just a joke. People look so funny running after you. You'll have a guy chase you four blocks and you wait till he gives up and then you stop and wait for him with the door open and when he gets on, he's panting and you can say, 'Gee, guy, I almost didn't see you.' And then he doesn't know whether to be mad or grateful so half the time he'll thank you for waiting. It's just a game, see? That's all it was last night. A game. I'd have waited for her, honest. But then the lights broke for me and that's another game—seeing how many blocks you can go without stopping."

They took him back over it and over it till he was ready to freak. But no matter how much he tried, he couldn't remember anyone else on the street with the woman in the red coat.

The telephone began ringing again as they turned to go and they left him looking at it hopelessly, afraid to answer.

Back at headquarters, Tillie had caught up with Officer Steven Greenapple by telephone. Greenapple wasn't due to report to work till late afternoon, but he agreed to meet Lowry and Albee at two. When Lowry called to check in, Tillie relayed the message.

"I guess that'll give us time to see Fischer's parents?" said Jim, half hoping she could think of a reason to put it off.

"Yeah," Elaine agreed glumly.

Breaking the news of death to someone's family was one of the most difficult things a cop had to do, but interviewing a homicide victim's family the next day wasn't much easier. Elaine called to make sure the Fischers would be there and willing to talk to them.

They stopped for lunch at a corner deli crowded with other New Yorkers bundled against the snow, which had picked up considerably in the last hour. The white tile floor was slippery with dirty gray puddles and bits of slush tracked in by each new customer. A kid ran out with a mop every few minutes, but he was swabbing against the tide. The two detectives ate their sandwiches standing up, then headed back to the nearest uptown subway station.

The subway system was almost a century old now and it showed everywhere in broken tiles, accumulated trash, temporary jacks under sagging arches. The stations and platforms were like badly patched overcoats. Every train was infested with panhandlers for charities (some legitimate, most of the self-interest variety), freelance performers who sang or played every instrument from the tuba to the piccolo, and both the colorfully eccentric and the flat-out crazy; and while the graffiti blight might be on the wane, it had, over the years, taken a dark toll in human dignity and civic pride.

Nobody really enjoyed traveling in a rolling zoo; nevertheless, trains were still the most efficient way to move around Manhattan. Especially in the snow.

Flashing their badges, Albee and Lowry passed through a side gate onto the platform as the uptown local roared into the station.

Grief, palpable and unremitting, wrapped the Fischers' bright and airy apartment on the Upper West Side.

Winston Fischer opened the door for them and his

eyes were bloodshot and red-rimmed behind thick glasses. He couldn't have been much past forty, forty-five at the outside; yet there was such a look of aged grief on his face that Elaine Albee thought she could almost mark the lines that would soon be permanently etched.

His wife was confined to a wheelchair. Multiple sclerosis had wasted Amy Fischer's leg muscles and drained her arms of strength until she could barely feed herself. The loss of her only child had devastated her store of emotional strength and her thin face was haggard with hours of crying, but she insisted on staying to talk to them even though she was clearly at the end of her physical reserves.

"You knew Lotty?" she asked. Her voice was raw with weeping.

"Yes," said Elaine. "Not very well, I'm afraid. Her work was more with the patrol units than the detective squad, but yes, we certainly knew who she was."

"We're very sorry about this, Mrs. Fischer," said Jim. "She was a nice person."

"Lotty hated coming home alone after one," said Mrs. Fischer. "She tried not to show it, but she worried. And I worried, too, but you always think— And then—oh dear God! My baby! What will we do?"

Fresh tears streamed from her eyes, but her arms were too weak for her to lift to her eyes the handkerchief she twisted helplessly in her hands. A gray-haired woman, their next-door neighbor, gently daubed the tears with a tissue.

"There, there, love," she crooned.

An attractive brunette who looked closer to Lotty's age came in from the kitchen with a lunch tray. Mrs. Fischer let the young woman hold the mug of tomato soup to her lips and took a small swallow, but she pulled her head away from the sandwich.

"I can't," she said in a shaky voice. "Thank you, Marla, but I just can't. Give it to Win."

They could see that Mr. Fischer wasn't hungry either. Then his eyes met his wife's. "Right," he said with mock heartiness. "We have to keep up our strength. I'll eat this if you'll take your soup. Deal?"

"Deal," she said, and let the young woman help her with another swallow. "I'll finish it later," she promised and turned back to Albee and Lowry.

"Lotty wasn't just our daughter, you see. She was our best friend, too, and she used to share things that happened at work. Her office was right there behind the booking desk and she heard most of what went on, so I know that a lot of parents, when their kids get booked for things, they'll come to the desk sergeant and swear on a stack of Bibles that their kids never did anything wrong in their whole lives. Lotty told me that. So I do understand why police officers might get cynical when they hear parents say things like this. But I swear to you, our Lotty—"

Her voice broke and the neighbor started to wipe her eyes again, but Mrs. Fischer jerked her head back. "Our Lotty *never* did anything bad to anybody in her life. If you knew her, then you know she was always looking to help people. You ask anybody. Right, Marla? Marla will tell you."

The younger woman nodded.

"What about men?" asked Elaine Albee. "Was she seeing anyone?"

"No," said Mrs. Fischer and again Marla confirmed it. "Not since the end of the summer."

They asked for and were given the man's name, but he was described as someone six foot one and built like a football tackle. Besides, he'd met another girl and had moved to the Bronx to be near her. Since then, there'd been no one else romantically involved in Lotty's life. No torch-bearers, no disappointed lovers.

Further questioning brought no more names.

Except for the change in her schedule, Lotty had loved her job, had spoken well of all her coworkers, and had gone off to work the night before in her new red coat without a care in the world—at least none that she'd voiced to family or friends.

The two detectives rose to go and Marla went with them after promising the Fischers to come back that evening. As they waited for the elevator at the end of the hall, Elaine and Jim pressed her again on the question of male friends.

"A friendly young woman like that, you're sure there wasn't someone she was seeing, someone maybe her parents wouldn't approve of?"

"Never. Oh, there might have been a couple of guys at work that Lotty could've liked, but she wouldn't let herself get interested in anybody right now," said Marla. "See, she was really pretty except for her nose, but most guys couldn't see past it. We talked it all out in August after Sid dumped her.

"She said there was no point spending money on fancy clothes or makeup, and why go out with guys just to get dumped again as soon as a prettier face came by? She decided she wasn't going to get involved with anybody again till she'd saved up enough for a nose job, and that was going to be this summer."

New York is a collection of parallel villages and the inhabitants of each can be surprisingly parochial. Most New Yorkers rarely venture outside the parameters defined by work and home. They use the same bus or subway route to travel back and forth, they patronize particular dry cleaners, hairstylists or grocery stores in their neighborhood, they often wait till a movie opens at one of the theaters within a five- or six-block radius, they choose a park or beach as "their" park or beach, and they frequent one particular library branch instead of another that might have better hours or a larger selection. They do these things with such regularity that they keep running into the same people over and over, citizens of the same village by virtue of having made similar choices.

This is why, in a city of seven million inhabitants, New Yorkers constantly amaze their small-town friends when they walk down a teeming Manhattan street and greet as many familiar faces as would the friends themselves back home.

Every New Yorker knows his own subway line, of

course, and can ride it with his eyes closed, keeping tabs on where he is by the squeals in the curves and whether the doors open up on the left or right. Most commuters can fall asleep on the train and wake up the instant the train pulls into their stop. But when faced with the need to get from a familiar place to one unfamiliar, even New Yorkers ask for directions. Those detailed maps are not placed in every car solely for the use of tourists.

As the Seventh Avenue local rumbled along beneath Broadway, Jim Lowry, a confirmed East Sider ever since he left his parents' Pennsylvania apple farm, hung onto an upright steel pole and studied the map.

"We change at Times Square," said Elaine Albee, denizen of the West Side, as she placidly added to her notes.

"Just checking. I always get screwed up taking the shuttle."

From the car behind theirs, a slender black man entered and began to coax an oddly appealing tune from a long wooden recorder. He wore brown wool socks pulled up over his pantlegs and lashed with leather thongs. His shaggy brown jacket was tied across his thin shoulders like a cape and he wore a brown slouch hat that almost covered dark eyes dancing with mischievous merriment. An impudent child of Pan, he paused in front of Elaine and began to pipe an elusively familiar melody.

Jim had adopted the I-don't-see-a-thing blank stare of jaded New Yorkers, and the piper glanced from his stony face to Elaine's attentive smile. Elaine laughed out loud when she realized the name of the tune; and as he finished and swept off his hat, she gladly tossed in several of the loose coins she carried in her pockets for street performers who touched or amused her.

"What was he playing?" asked Jim when the musician had passed into the next car; but Elaine shook her head and laughed again as their train slid into the Times Square station.

· · ·

Despite his name, Steven Greenapple did not look like a sylvan wanderer. If anything, he appeared stolid and unimaginative when they got off the train at the subway station near their office and spotted him waiting on the platform. A stocky man, with a broad plain face, he wore the usual blue uniform of the Transit Authority police. But the T.A. clerk to whom they'd spoken earlier had described Greenapple as a serious enthusiast of the city's underground spaces—the abandoned "ghost stations" or miles of unused tunnels—and he did look disappointed when he realized they merely wanted to locate a specific person, not book a guided tour of the tunnels in this area.

"We're looking for someone who would have been in a position to see the platform," Jim explained, as Elaine walked down to the very end and peered into the darkness of the dirty black tunnel. "Aren't there ledges and niches just beyond the light?"

"Oh sure," said Greenapple. "We just discovered like a three-room apartment at the Franklin Avenue station over in Brooklyn—complete with a La-Z-Boy recliner, hibachi pot and a pile of *Wall Street Journal*s. But if your killer was standing about *here* when he pushed her—" The bloodstains down on the ties below marked the spot. "—then a witness down *there* wouldn't have been close enough to get a make on him."

He stood quite still, considering the station. "You sure he wasn't stretched out on the bench there? Sometimes people think a drunk is just a pile of papers or old rags till they go to sit down."

"Eight people plus the trainman and the conductor swear that the station was empty except for the victim and the man who pushed her," said Elaine as she rejoined them. "The only reason we know this Gerald Byrd was even—"

"Gerald Byrd?" asked Greenapple. "Now where have I heard that—"

A broad grin suddenly lit his homely face.

"You know the name?" she asked.

"Jerry the Canary!" he exclaimed. "Has to be."

He turned and seemed to examine the main entrance. "You're right about most guys flopping down in the tunnel somewhere, but Jerry's what you might call a bird of a different feather altogether. C'mon."

He strolled along slowly as he talked, looking up into the sooty girders overhead, until he halted directly in front of the turnstiles.

"I was right," he grinned. "Look!"

Jim and Elaine followed his pointing finger and saw an irregular hump among the straight edges of filthy black I-beams and cross-braces, about fifteen feet up. Unless one were looking for it, the bundle of dark rags—clothes? blankets?—was completely unnoticeable.

"Jerry's the only one I know who builds nests," said Greenapple. Proprietary pride shone in his voice.

"Jerry the Canary has a less-than-gilded cage," said Elaine, peering up at the bedding he'd abandoned in his sudden decampment last night.

"Oh, that's not how he got the name," Greenapple told her. "I doubt if many cops know that Jerry never sleeps at street level. They call him the Canary because he panhandles for money by doing bird imitations. He can sound like any bird you want to name, and he's got pictures, too. Goes over pretty good. In nice weather. People don't stand around in the winter for him, so he works the trains till we chase him. Usually he has enough to rent a flop. With all the SRO's going, though . . ."

Greenapple's voice trailed off, but it was a familiar situation and one that was getting worse. There were many complex reasons why more people became homeless and took to the streets each year, but one big factor was that scores of buildings throughout the city had converted from low-income single-room occupancy to upscale, high-priced co-ops. As a result, hundreds now occupied space that had once housed thousands.

Jim Lowry stepped off the short distance to where Lotty Fischer and her killer had stood and looked back up at Gerald Byrd's nest. They would pull a tape on it, but he'd bet it was no more than forty feet.

No wonder the homeless man had seized the opportunity to get away before someone spotted him. From that perch, he certainly could have had a clear bird's-eye view of the killer.

Chapter
15

▟▙ The concrete Cluett drive was separated from the
▜▛ Gelson blacktop by a two-foot strip of frozen grass,
and the two garages at the rear of the yards were like
Siamese twins sharing the same wall. Both garages had
been built back when cars were a lot shorter and taller.
Cluett had bumped out the front wall so he could still
garage his car, but the Gelsons had just blacktopped their
whole backyard for a car park.

As I pulled up nose-to-nose with a shiny late-model
station wagon parked at the front curb, I figured family
and friends must still be offering Irene physical support.
Three more cars lined the Cluett drive, and someone had
swept and shoveled the sidewalk.

Nobody'd laid a shovel on the Gelson drive yet,
though a car had driven in after the snow started, judging
by the fresh tread marks. A beat-up Volkswagen, oversized
tires, no fenders. A purple paint job that must have come
out of a spray can. Dozens of faded plastic flowers epox-
ied to the roof and hood. Probably looked like hot shit at
Plum Beach in August, but on this gloomy February day
under a layer of pristine snow, it just looked like shit.

I'd deliberately parked on the wrong side of the
street and I flipped down the sun visor to warn any cruis-

ing snow plows that this particular vehicle was on OFFI-CIAL POLICE BUSINESS and better not get plowed under.

Both houses were two-story detached bricks that sat back from the street in a yardful of fifty-year-old trees and shrubs. Yuppification had so far missed this half of the block. Not that these houses looked shabby—the bushes were pruned, the shutters and trim weren't yelling for paint—but they were dowdy. No structural changes had been made since the front walls were "modernized" with picture window surgery in the fifties.

No response when I pushed the Gelsons' front bell, so I trudged down the drive and around to the back door and saw that someone had recently walked from the garish little VW to the back stoop and from the stoop, back and forth to a small door cut into one of the garage's original old-fashioned double doors. I followed the footprints and rapped on the smaller door.

"Who is it?" called a male voice.

"Police."

"Police?" The voice suddenly sounded younger and I heard scrambling noises like boxes or heavy furniture were being shoved around inside the garage.

"Hey, man, you got a search warrant?" the voice demanded. Everybody knows his rights these days. Too bad they don't care as much about the responsibilities that go with rights.

"Do I need one?"

The door opened a narrow crack and one blue eye squinted at me. A warm sweetish smell went drifting past. "What do you want?"

"Edward Gelson?"

"Yeah?"

"I want to ask you a few questions about Michael Cluett."

"What if I told you to go fuck yourself?"

"Then I send a couple of officers over and they'll bring you to me at the station," I said pleasantly.

The blue eye tried to glare, couldn't hold it.

"What's it going to be, Eddie?" I was getting impatient. "I'm not here to bust you for smoking a little pot, but you keep me freezing my butt out here in this snow-storm much longer and I'm gonna haul *your* butt down to the station."

The door swung open and the mush head stepped back to let me in.

Your typical all-American asshole. From the tip of his little pug nose to his druggie little daydreams of making it as a rock star.

Not that he'd left any joints lying around; only the tattletale smell that permeated the place. His playhouse matched the VW: dingy gray carpet, lumpy green couch pushed against one wall, rock posters on the pressed fiberboard panels that provided soundproofing for the drums and guitars arranged around a synthesizer.

"Who plays?" I asked mine host.

"Me and my friends," the kid said sullenly.

Irene Cluett said Eddie Gelson was seventeen, but this guy was built like a man five years older. Nearly six feet tall and at least a seventeen-inch neck. Real biceps under a loose orange-and-black Princeton sweatshirt; muscular thighs and calves inside his tight jeans.

Beyond the couch, I saw a weight bench with a set of barbells resting across the steel support. A chinning bar hung from two heavy hooks overhead. "You and your friends work out, too?"

"Sometimes. What'd you want to ask me about Cluett?"

I circled the garage and inspected everything before I sat down on the couch in front of a small electric heater with red-hot coils. "How come your friends aren't here today? Lifting weights, beating on the drums?"

"There's a wake next door, for chrissake." He picked up an acoustic guitar, perched on an arm of the couch, and began to strum the shiny steel strings.

"Yeah, but from what I hear that shouldn't make a difference. You weren't exactly Mick Cluett's favorite neighbor."

"Tell it to my old man," Eddie Gelson muttered as idle chords filled the garage. "Look, we weren't trying to bug him, you know? We put up soundproofing, kept the amps turned down, and we didn't play after ten. What more'd he want? Don't we have rights, too? I mean, Jesus H. Christ!" His hand crashed the guitar in a burst of ear-jangling discord.

"You're a big kid," I said. "Tall as Cluett, too. Ever try to punch him out?"

"Hell, no, man!" His hand fell away from the guitar and he sounded shocked. "My dad would've killed me."

I tried to recall the last time I questioned a kid who would admit that he gave a happy damn about how his father might react.

"When did you see Cluett last?"

He shrugged. "I don't know. Monday, maybe."

"You sure you didn't see him night before last?"

"When he got it? No way, man. It was too cold to go out and my drummer has the flu. Besides, I had a history test yesterday and I stayed in to study."

"Your parents will confirm this?"

"Sure." The baby blues shone with such blatant honesty that I knew he was lying.

"When will they be home?"

"Mom doesn't get in before six, and my dad's working late this week."

"I can come back," I told him.

"Look, I really was here the whole night," Eddie said. "But out *here,* not in the house. It's more private. I study, practice my guitar, listen to my tapes—"

"—smoke a little pot?" I needled.

"—and sometimes I fall asleep out here. My folks turn in early and this way, I don't bother them. But their bedroom's on the back here and they can see my light and they'd hear if I cranked my car. It roars like a tiger."

He seemed to think this clinched his alibi.

"They sleep with the windows open these cold nights?"

"Well, no, but—"

"So they wouldn't know if you slipped out and walked over to Sheepshead Bay?"

"Walked?"

I had to laugh. This generation will jog, run, or lift weights till sweat pours from their bodies, as long as the purpose is purely exercise. If it's a matter of getting from point A to point B, however, feet don't enter into the calculation except as applied to gas pedal or brake.

"Cluett walked back and forth all the time," I said.

"Yeah, well," said Eddie Gelson, like that just proved what a jerk Mick Cluett had been.

He went back to playing chords on his guitar; and no matter how hard I pounded, he stuck to his story. Friends had dropped by for a while after dinner; otherwise, he'd been there alone the whole evening from eight till around two A.M.

"Studying for six straight hours?"

"I told you. Sometimes I fall asleep. I remember hearing the headlines at eleven and then the next thing I knew it was ten till two. I unplugged everything and went in to bed. And you *can* ask my mom about that, because she yelled at me about it yesterday morning, okay?"

For the moment, I knew it'd have to be.

Back outside in the freezing wind, I decided that as long as I was here, I might as well see Irene Cluett again. See if she knew anything about whoever it was Cluett had expected to see at the Shamrock.

I cut across both drives with snow stinging my face; but just as I raised my hand to knock on Irene's back door, it was opened by a stocky man with a broom in his hand. He wore black knitted mittens and stocking hat and seemed as startled as me, so startled that he gave a high-pitched giggle.

"Oops! Didn't know anybody was out here. I was just coming to sweep the steps. Keep it clear. Easier to sweep than to shovel and scrape, right?" He giggled again.

"Right," I said. "I'm here to see Irene. She in?"

Before the man could answer, a little boy pushed past him and began to whine, "Daddy, Tiffy won't let me play. She says I'm a baby. Make her let me play. I want to play!"

"In a minute, Shawn, all right?"

"But I want to pla-ay. Now!"

"Daddy's talking to someone, Shawn." He half-turned and called into the kitchen, "Marie, you wanna call Shawn back in there before he's up all night with an earache again? Go to Mommy, Shawn. She'll play with you."

"She will not!" said a shrill female voice that was almost drowned out by the brat yelling, "But I wanna play with the others."

I leaned against the porch railing and waited for somebody to take charge.

The door was suddenly yanked open and an annoyed young woman said, "Shawn, you get your tail in here right this minute before I—"

Then she saw me and raised an eyebrow at her husband. He giggled nervously. "Honey, this is somebody to see Irene. Mr.— I'm sorry. I didn't get the name."

"Vaughn," I said. "Detective Vaughn."

"Oh, sure," said the young woman. She picked up her whining son, settled him on her hip and said, "Irene's in the den. Come on in."

She took me past people drinking tea at the kitchen table and into the den where I'd spoken to Irene the evening before.

She was lying back in the same white vinyl recliner. Pink chenille robe, fuzzy pink bedroom slippers, and her feet up on the footrest. A teenage granddaughter was curling her flat gray hair and I remembered that tonight was the first night of the official wake at a nearby funeral home.

Again she greeted me warmly and I told her why I'd returned. She was surprised to hear that Mickey might have gone out to the Shamrock expecting to meet someone and she had no idea who it could've been.

"But I know you won't give up till you find out." She squeezed my hand hard. "And you'll be at the funeral parlor tonight, won't you? Such beautiful flowers the department sent. They let me see him this morning. He looks good, Jarvis. Dress uniform. Wait'll you see him."

Her eyes filled with tears.

They were going to wake him three nights and I
knew I'd have to put in an appearance at least once, but
the last thing I wanted to do that night was fight my way
back through a snowstorm to the funeral home to see a
stiff Mick Cluett in his dress uniform. Before I could
think up a tactful excuse, Irene was distracted by her
daughter, who came in with three dresses that looked like
army tents on coat hangers.

"Which one you want to wear tonight, Ma?"

I left with Irene deciding whether dark red, dark
green or navy blue was best for the first of three nights.

At the front door, I was waylaid by the guy with the
broom.

"I think you want to talk to me," he said. Again that
high-pitched nervous giggle.

"I do?" I pulled on my gloves and was winding
around my neck the blue cashmere muffler Terry made
me for Christmas.

"I'm Neal O'Shea, Mickey's cousin. Marie— that's my
wife—she heard that Irene told you Mickey and me were
on the outs." He gave the top steps a halfhearted swipe
with the broom.

I looked at him with more interest. About five eight, I
estimated. Probably late twenties or early thirties.

Neal O'Shea was the first person I'd yet met that
came close to Kitty Jozell's vague description of the person who'd met Cluett after he left the Shamrock Tuesday
night. A few inches shorter, stocky but still thinner than
Cluett and certainly young enough to walk across a street
vigorously. He even had the black knitted cap.

The wind was biting, but I sensed that O'Shea pre-
ferred to keep our conversation outside, away from the
ears of his relatives.

"Why don't we go warm up my car?" I suggested.

O'Shea followed me down the walk, sweeping the
snow as we went.

At the curb, the wind had begun building low drifts
that were already higher than my boot tops. The plows
hadn't hit the side streets yet and the white stuff was

nearly three inches deep on the level. No sign of letup either. If anything, it was snowing even harder.

The department-issued car was like the inside of a refrigerator and I had to jiggle the vents to get the defroster going. O'Shea swept off the windshield and back window, then he propped his broom against the fender and crawled in beside me.

"I don't know why Irene wanted to tell you that about Mickey and me," he griped. For a minute he sounded like his son the whiner.

"She only said that you resented it when Cluett asked you to repay the money he'd loaned you," I said.

"Yeah?" O'Shea looked relieved. "The way Marie heard it, she was practically accusing me of killing Mickey myself." He giggled. "Me a killer!"

"So there weren't any hard feelings?"

"Not like you're talking about. I mean, no man likes to have somebody dunning him every week, right? Mickey knew I was good for it. But I got laid off at the warehouse at Thanksgiving and we got behind in the bills. And there was Christmas, then Shawn got sick—nothing serious, just earaches, thank God—but you know what doctors and antibiotics cost, right? Always something with kids.

"So when Mickey started dunning me as soon as I started the new job, I might've said a few things out of turn, but everybody in the family knows I loved Mickey and he loved me like a brother. Look at how he lent me the money. I know it wasn't enough to bloat a goat but you don't do that with people you think are going to shoot you, right?"

"Bloat a goat" seemed to be the Cluett family's favorite term for a lot of money. I remembered how Cluett used it to describe any thick wad of bills.

"Anyhow," said O'Shea, "soon as I heard, I scraped together a hundred and brought it right over to Irene and I told her she'd have every penny before the summer."

He reached for the door handle. "Guess I better get back inside before Marie thinks you've arrested me," he giggled.

"Just a minute, Mr. O'Shea," I said. "Cluett expected to meet someone at the Shamrock Tuesday night. Was it you?"

"Not me." The nervous titter went up another notch. "Shawn was still getting over his earache. Marie'd been up with him two nights in a row, so I took over for her Tuesday night."

My ex and I never had kids so I couldn't speak from experience, but I thought I'd heard Terry talk about how quick Adam's winter ailments always reacted to antibiotics. If that bratty kid had been on medication for three days, maybe he'd actually slept through Tuesday night as soundly as I was willing to bet Marie O'Shea had.

Nearly five when I got back to the station and went up to my office to jot down notes on the interviews while they were still fresh. Several messages waited on my desk: Hy Davidowitz had made it home safely. Fabrizio had skidded into a bus as he came off the Brooklyn-Queens Expressway and expected to be a little late getting to work. Then Kirkwood came in with a funny expression on his face.

"Did you hear?"

It'd been a long day. "Hear what?"

"The gun that killed Mick. Some P.A.A. over in New York ran a check on it a couple of years ago."

"And?"

"And they don't know why."

Kirkwood has a warped sense of humor. Normally I'd let him spin it out, but reports were piled on my desk and snow was piling up outside. "Cut to the chase," I snapped.

Kirkwood hated stepping on his own punch lines. "Okay, but at least ask me why they don't just ask her."

Resigned, I rotated my hand in the universal signal to speed it up. "Consider it asked."

"They can't. Somebody pushed her under a train last night."

"What?"

"So help me, Sarge! What's really weird though is that she worked the Twelfth. The same damn precinct that borrowed Mick from us."

"The hell you say!"

I looked at Kirkwood and I didn't like what I read on his face. Damn it all, cops aren't supposed to kill other cops.

Chapter
16

"This is AM Radio! *WNYT—New York Talks!* You're on the air, Dolores. Talk to me!"

"Hello? Roddy? I just want to say that it's not just bus drivers. We've got a whole class of city employees who act like *they're* doing *us* a favor to take these high salaries *our* tax dollars provide and give back *nothing*! I'm asking you, Roddy—whatever happened to the idea of public service? There's no service to the public—it's the public be damned. These fucking—"

New York Talks was on a ten-second delay. The show's producer grinned at host Roddy Fitzwilliam through the soundproof glass and gave the throat-slashing signal that meant he'd cut the caller off in time.

"Ah-ah, Dolores. Language! Keep it clean, people. We don't want the FCC pulling our plug, do we? *WNYT— New York Talks!* What's on *your* mind, Pete?"

"Yo, Roddy! Listen, man, I was trying to get crosstown from East 116th yesterday and this M20 driver—"

WNYT's afternoon talk show had struck a metropolis-wide nerve. The topic of today's session was supposed to be how well the city's transportation system handles a snowstorm, but the first caller asked if Roddy'd heard about the girl that got pushed under a train last night and hey, maybe she'd still be alive right now if some smartass bus driver would've stopped for her.

The show's producer sensed a real story and immediately went to a commercial break. Off-mike, the caller repeated the details he'd heard a couple of hours ago in Lundigren's Twenty-four Hour Delicatessen; and by the time the first set of commercials ended, the producer had the night clerk on the phone and Roddy Fitzwilliam was cued to conduct a live interview.

At that point, the switchboard had gone nova as New Yorkers vied to tell horror stories of their own experiences with bus drivers.

"That's all we need," Bernie Peters groaned as he switched the mini-van's dial to Radio 88 ("MORE Than Just The Headlines!") to catch the headlines. Radio 88 was into Dow-Jones averages, so he lowered the volume as he negotiated the snowy Manhattan Bridge. The powerful wipers were keeping the wide windshield swept clean. The mini felt so luxurious after the cramped sedan he'd rattled back and forth in for the last three years.

"They'll start with bus drivers," he told Matt Eberstadt, "but they'll finish with cops."

"Maybe not," said Matt. "People aren't real crazy about sanitation workers either. Especially if their cars get plowed under."

"Uh-oh." The rear wheels fishtailed slightly, and Bernie gently pressed on the accelerator to bring them out of it, enjoying the confident surge of power.

Because his new family-size van had four-wheel drive, he'd swung past Ozone Park to pick up Eberstadt. Now he was beginning to wonder if they shouldn't have taken the train to work. The snow was really coming down. Traffic was keeping it pretty much churned to slush right now, but he hated to think what it was going to be like when their four-to-midnight ended.

He glanced across at Eberstadt, who seemed tired and listless this afternoon. "You catching something?"

"Naw. I never sleep too good when Frances is away."

Eberstadt's oldest child, a girl, had just been transferred to Atlanta. It was her first move and Bernie knew that Frances Eberstadt had gone down last weekend to help her settle in.

"When's she due back?"

"Tomorrow." Eberstadt stared out through the windshield. Snow was falling so heavily that he could barely make out the twin towers of the World Trade Center, and the Empire State Building was almost obliterated as well. "Really bad about the Fischer kid, isn't it?"

"Yeah."

"Only twenty-two," Eberstadt said heavily. "Not married yet."

Bernie Peters was surprised. "You knew her pretty good, huh?"

"She was a nice kid. Friendly. I used to tease her a lot when she first came because she'd turn bright red if she got rattled. Four years ago, and she was fresh outta high school. She thought detectives were all Don Johnsons."

Canal Street was thick with traffic when they came off the bridge and worked their way over to Allen. As Peters drove north on First Avenue, he discovered he was behind a sanitation truck that was spreading salt. He'd had the underside of the mini-van sealed against salt damage but he wasn't optimistic about its effectiveness, and he switched lanes just as Eberstadt flicked the dial back to WNYT.

An irate citizen of the Bronx was saying, "—so even if she'd of had a chance to dial 911, all she'd of got was a busy signal, and *I* think if they'd put the cops back walking a neighborhood beat instead of—"

"What'd I tell you?" said Peters.

In the squad room at the station, fatigue had finally caught up with Albee and Lowry.

"I shouldn't have sat down," groaned Jim Lowry. "Now I'm too tired to get up and go home."

"Tell me about it," said Elaine. She pushed away from the typewriter and stretched her arms behind her back to flex her shoulder muscles. "If I didn't need clean clothes, I'd just sleep here again tonight."

The hall door opened and Dinah Urbanska entered the squad room.

Or tried to enter. The pocket of her black ski pants caught on the doorknob and jerked her back. She stuffed her gloves in a pocket of her parka and untangled herself, but as one pocket came free, the other dumped her gloves on the floor. Unzipping her parka, she caught the amused glances of the others and looked around wildly. "What? *What?*"

Wordlessly, Sam Hentz pointed behind her.

"Oh gosh!" she breathed and went back for the gloves. As she bent, the other pants pocket snagged on the knob.

"I don't believe this," Elaine muttered to Jim.

Flustered and flushed, Dinah finally got herself and all her articles of clothing to her desk. She was cold and damp from interviewing street corner news vendors as potential witnesses to a hit-and-run. Snow had melted on her black wool watch cap and when she pulled it off, her dark blonde hair looked wet.

Hentz handed her some paper towels.

"Anybody want the last cup of coffee before I make fresh?" asked Tillie, waving the pot in their direction.

Jim shook his head. "I'm coffeed out."

"Yeah, I'll take it," said Hentz, who was seldom without a half-full cup on his desk.

"I'll get it for you, Sam," offered Dinah, bounding up with a suddenness that banged her chair against the wall.

"No," he said tightly. "Sit. Do not get up. That's an order."

"Hot chocolate," Jim said dreamily. "Dark and sweet and three marshmallows on top."

"Huh?" asked Hentz.

Jim grinned. "That's what my mom always used to make me whenever it snowed."

Tillie pawed through the clutter behind the coffee maker. "There's a packet of instant here if you want it."

"Any marshmallows?"

"Nope." Spooning fresh coffee into the basket, Tillie smiled. Marian always made their children hot chocolate when they came in from playing in the snow. "And no whipped cream either."

Matt Eberstadt and Bernie Peters arrived, red-cheeked and almost as damp from the snowstorm as Dinah Urbanska. Bernie slung his coat over the back of his chair and walked over to hurry the coffee along.

"Rough day?" he asked Elaine. "You look like hell."

"Thanks, Bernie," she scowled. "You always know how to cheer a person up."

"Speaking of cheer—" He pulled out his wallet. "Your share of last week's winnings."

"Oh, yeah," said Dinah. "I was supposed to tell you we hit."

Every week, several of them chipped in a dollar each to buy Lotto tickets. So far, their biggest jackpot had been two hundred dollars, which put them marginally ahead of their losses.

"Four dollars apiece," said Bernie, handing bills to Jim, too.

"At this rate, I'm going to be eighty before I get my Lamborghini," Elaine complained. "I still think you were crazy to buy a van instead of a sports car."

"A sports car with bucket seats," said Bernie. "Just what every father of three needs, right, Tillie?"

Tillie looked up from sorting a handful of departmental circulars that had come up with the last mail.

"I'd take your new mini-van over a Lamborghini any day," he said wistfully. "It must be great having enough space for car seats and diaper bags."

As he spoke, a door at the end of the room opened and everyone straightened unconsciously as Lieutenant Harald entered with some papers. Her eyes fell on Lowry and Albee.

"I didn't realize you two were back," she said. "Any developments with the Fischer case?"

She listened impassively as they described the possibility of an eyewitness to the murder.

"We've got an APB on the wire and Greenapple's put the word to Transit," said Elaine.

Jim added, "If this bird's still in town, we should have him by tomorrow."

"Excellent." Sigrid paused by Matt's desk. "Ah, Eberstadt. Here's something that should interest you and Peters."

She handed him an autopsy report which had come in that day on a stabbing victim. He and Bernie were handling the investigation, a particularly violent homicide. The dead man had been stabbed over a hundred times.

"What was the name of that guy you suspected?" Sigrid asked. "A bartender, wasn't he?"

"Caygill," said Eberstadt. He laid the report on the corner of the nearest desk and began to read as he unzipped his heavy jacket and unwound the heavy wool scarf from his neck. "Zach Caygill."

"Turn over to the next page," Sigrid told him. "The M.E. found a man's ring under the victim's liver. According to Cohen, it's engraved with the initials *Z.B.C.*"

"Nice," said Matt. "Very nice. I'll just make a few phone calls, confirm that he owns a ring like that. We may be able to pick him up tonight."

When Sigrid had returned to her office, Dinah Urbanska giggled and began to flap her elbows. *"Bird* imitations? That's all the guy does? Bird imitations?"

Lowry caught the reference and laughed. It had been one of his favorite *M*A*S*H* episodes, too: one of Hawkeye's corny jokes about a little man who wanted to join the circus; but when he flapped his elbows and flew around the tent, the circus manager remained singularly unimpressed.

Amid their laughter, Tillie followed Sigrid into her office with some papers that needed her signature and one of the interdepartmental flyers he thought might interest her.

"You're Swedish descent, right, Lieutenant?"

"Danish," she corrected. "Why?"

He showed her the flyer. "The Viking Association's having a membership drive."

Sigrid frowned. "Viking Association?"

"It's one of the department's benevolent associations like the Irish and Italians have, only smaller, I guess. For police officers of Scandinavian descent."

Oblivious to her raised eyebrow, he skimmed the paper and read aloud some of the phrases. "March in Norwegian Constitution Day Parade, vacation in the fjords . . . dinner   dance . . . annual   fishing   trip   in June . . ."

He had a sudden absurd picture of Lieutenant Harald equipped with rod and reel on a party boat full of tipsy Vikings. He felt her gray eyes upon him and flushed crimson.

As if she'd read his thoughts, she took the flyer from his hand and dropped it in her wastebasket.

"I don't think so," she said dryly.

As they went over the reports that she wanted pushed the next day, the private line on her telephone rang and Tillie waited while she answered.

After listening for a long moment, she reached for her desk calendar and flipped the page to the next day. "Your office? Certainly. Yes, sir, I will."

From where Tillie was sitting, he could see that she'd penciled in "McK" at the ten o'clock hour. "Something wrong, Lieutenant?"

She leaned back in her chair and wedged one knee against the desk. "I know your shift's over at four, Tillie, but I want every file on every case that Michael Cluett worked while he was here and I want them on my desk by eight-thirty tomorrow morning."

"Ma'am?"

She looked at him coldly. "Was I unclear, Tildon? Which part did you not understand?"

"Sorry, Lieutenant," he said and beat a hasty, and very puzzled, retreat.

Alone in her office, Sigrid pondered what Captain McKinnon had just told her over the phone. She thought of the warm camaraderie that existed out there in the squad room at this moment and wondered how much longer it would last.

Chapter
17

DETECTIVE SERGEANT JARVIS VAUGHN

Friday morning. Still cold, but the wind had stopped. So had the snow.

The house has three bedrooms on the second floor and mine's the middle-sized one on the back. I could stand at the window and look out across garage roofs mounded with snow. No clouds. A sky as blue as the Lady Washington hollyhocks on the cover of the new Burpee catalog that was waiting when I got home the night before. By tomorrow there'd probably be three layers of soot. At that moment, though, the sun on the snow dazzled everything till it looked like the pearly gates of heaven Granny used to sing about when she was happy.

In the yard downstairs, a scrawny gray cat slinked through the picket fence, walked across the snowdrifts to where the wind had exposed a bit of earth, and relieved itself under my Rose of Sharon tree.

My tree, my yard, my dirt. Still wasn't used to it.

Marva Lee never wanted any part of a house. Her idea of living's a hotel with twenty-four-hour room service, so the marriage'd been over almost two years when Terry came to me at Christmas and talked me into going in on this house with her. Troy Avenue in East Flatbush.

Used to be an all-white blue-collar neighborhood. Now's it's three-quarters black and getting yuppified.

It'd be an investment, she said. Security for both of us. Rental apartment on the top that she and Adam would move into if I ever married again 'cause she sure as hell never planned to again.

"It'd be good for Adam to have you around—be good for you, too," she said. "You can even quit grieving over Granny's farm and grow your own flowers and tomatoes."

Cats might be a problem. I tried to remember what Granny had done about cats.

Or maybe cats weren't a problem if you lived on a five-acre truck farm. Enough dirt for everybody.

I pulled on warm-up pants and jacket and knocked on Terry's door as I passed.

"I'm up! I'm up!" Little Miss Sunshine.

"You lie like a rug," I called back.

She hasn't changed from when she was twelve and our parents used to send me to roust her out. If she was really up, she'd be grumpy. Cheerful was to make me think she was wide awake.

I went on down to the kitchen and found Adam eating cold cereal and reading a library book Terry'd brought home for him.

"Must be a good book," I said as I started the coffee.

He grinned, those new front teeth shining. "You bet your britches, Claude!"

"You sassing me, boy?"

"Beats me, Claude!" he giggled, tickled that I was asking the right questions. He almost bounced in his chair, waiting for me to go again.

I knew there were at least two more Claude books in the series, but I couldn't remember titles. "Finish your cereal," I told him. "I've got snow to shovel."

He went into gales of laughter. "If you say so, Claude!"

The brand new snow shovel Terry had given me for Christmas was out in the furnace room. I'd never worked one before. You don't shovel much snow in a twenty-story apartment building. But it didn't strike me as something that took too much brains. I could hear some of the neighbors out there shoveling, the rasp of metal against concrete. Once I got out there and got the hang of it, it went pretty fast. Wasn't like I had to do a half-mile. Just the steps, walk, and a stretch of sidewalk as wide as the house in front. A bit longer in the back. Enough to work up a sweat though, even in the cold.

Good exercise, I thought, as I went up to shower and shave. "I could get into this home-owner schtick," I told Terry when I passed through the kitchen.

"I suppose it'll be cows and chickens next?"

"Fat chance, Claude!" Adam called to her as he left for school.

A message was waiting at the office from the captain who'd specialed Cluett over to New York. He thought we ought to meet.

His office at ten.

Davidowitz shrugged when I told him. "What'd you expect? That he was going to come over to Brooklyn? Captains do not come to sergeants, or haven't you noticed? Anyhow," he added, stroking his droopy mustache, "you know the answer to Mick's death is over there. We were going anyhow, weren't we?"

Sometimes he's too goddamn reasonable.

Cluett's desk and locker had been cleaned out and his personal effects would be sent to Irene. Davidowitz had rounded up Cluett's current notes and worksheets and they were as messy as I expected. Someone'd had to sort it all out and as his boss, I'd elected myself and done most of it the night before. Cases were still pending. If his notes were complete though, his death shouldn't affect the outcome of any pending files.

We got all the case notes on Cluett's homicide in order and Davidowitz made an extra copy in case we wound up swapping with the Twelfth, then we took the train over.

When we walked into Captain McKinnon's office, we

found three officers from the precinct detective unit with him: a skinny brunette, a good-looking blonde, and a white male about six years younger than me.

"Thanks for coming," said McKinnon, all professional courtesy. As if it'd been an invitation and not a quasi-command. Introductions. The skinny one was a Lieutenant Harald, the other two were Detectives Albee and Lowry. I gave them Davidowitz.

Handshakes all around.

There was the usual chitchat. The skinny lieutenant sat tight as the captain asked us if we wanted anything hot to drink. She had even less than me to say about the cold and snow and how many inches we'd got, all that small talk stuff while you wait for the rookie in blue to pass around the coffee and get out. I could feel her giving off tense vibes, but nobody else seemed to notice so maybe that was her normal mode.

The captain was built like Davidowitz: not fat, but plenty big and solid.

The looey was about my age. Thin face, interesting eyes. No rings on her fingers. Married to the job? No curves under the black slacks or baggy gray jacket. Almost as flat-chested as me.

Albee. Blonde. More laid-back. Sharp in black leather boots and a loose royal blue sweater. *Not* flat-chested. Rings on her fingers, though nothing on the important finger.

Lowry. About six-foot-nothing, one-seventy. No wedding band either. Something cooking with him and the blonde? I never partnered with a woman, so it's hard to judge sometimes.

Just as I was beginning to wonder what the holdup was, someone opened the door and peered in. Another white male. Easy smile, crinkly brown hair, twinkly brown eyes, expensive hand-tooled cowboy boots. Twinkly eyes always make me check my back.

The tension level immediately went up three notches.

"Come in, Rawson," said McKinnon. "I believe you know Lieutenant Harald, Detectives Lowry and Albee?"

There were mutual *Yeah, sures,* then McKinnon turned to us. "Sergeant Vaughn and Detective Davidowitz from the Six-Four, Sheepshead Bay. Sergeant Rawson, F.I.A.U."

My nerves suddenly turned into piano wires, too.

Quis custodiet ipsos custodes?

You don't take a legal course at John Jay College of Criminal Justice without getting some Latin thrown at you. Not much sticks, but this was one of those things you only have to hear once to remember forever: *Who polices the police?*

Answer: That great Internal Affairs Division in the sky.

And who is its vicar on earth?

The precinct's Field Internal Affairs Unit.

Sergeant Rawson.

No wonder the looey was so uptight.

"Tell you what," said Rawson, hitching up a chair like he was just folks. "Why don't you begin like I'm not here?"

"Fine," said McKinnon.

Everybody was stiff getting started. I suspected that Albee and Lowry weren't sure why they were there; but I knew it was you-show-me-yours-and-I'll-show-you-mine even though I had a feeling it wasn't going to belong to either of us very long. Since Cluett was killed first, McKinnon asked me to start.

I gave the captain the copy we'd made of the case and laid out what we had: Cluett's wallet recovered with everything, including cash and credit cards intact; the lack of suspects with solid motives in Cluett's personal life; the nurse's eyewitness account of seeing someone meet up with him a little after ten on Tuesday night; and finally that Browning .380 semiautomatic. The postmortem had turned up two wounds. The first shot was from behind. It'd pierced the heart, ricocheted off a rib, and torn up some abdominal organs.

"Powder burns indicate the gun was pressed up against his coat," I said. "The second shot was to the right temple, probably after he was down. Powder traces for that one show the gun approximately two feet away."

"We put it on the net for the usual check," Davido-witz said. "No record of previous owners or that it'd ever been used in a crime."

"But the Bureau keeps a record of every serial num-ber requested," McKinnon said heavily, "and they bounced it back to Central Data Wednesday night."

He looked down the table to Lowry and Albee. "Seems Lotty Fischer ran a check on the gun four years ago."

They still didn't get it. "And?"

"There's no record of *why* she checked it out. Just that she did. Lieutenant?"

She didn't make a big production out of it. "I went over to Central Data last night and spoke to the people on duty Wednesday night. The clerk that processed the Bu-reau's reply finally admitted that she was a friend of Lotty Fischer's. She says she talked with Fischer around ten that night and, in the course of the conversation, casually mentioned Fischer's connection with the murder gun."

"Did Lotty remember running the check?" asked Lowry.

The looey shook her head. "No. According to the clerk, Fischer sounded curious about that herself and planned to check her log."

"So tell us about this Lotty Fischer," I said.

"Detectives Lowry and Albee have handled the inves-tigation so far," she said, and turned it over to them.

They weren't as together as the looey and they were rattled by the whole idea of F.I.A.U. Kept interrupting each other, repeating things as they explained the Fischer girl's work situation, that she'd been assigned here just over four years, how she'd missed her bus and wound up at the subway; the trainman's description of the incident and his fleeting impression of the perp who'd pushed her. There was some foul-up at the crime scene, an extra man that they didn't tumble to till after he'd got away; but they thought they had a good lead on him—some skell called Jerry the Canary who built nests for himself up in subway girders instead of flopping in a corner or on a steam grate like everybody else.

Nests, for Christ's sake.

Getting harder to find a deserted place to do murder, we all agreed. The homeless were everywhere and some of them were getting creative about it. Davidowitz got a smile when he told them about our Leviticus Jones and his bungalow by the sea. (For one crazy minute, I found myself wondering if the troll under the bridge in Adam's bedtime story "The Three Billy Goats Gruff" could have had its beginning in some medieval Leviticus Jones.)

Fun and games to cover what wasn't being said about why F.I.A.U. was sitting in on this session.

To do her credit, Harald was the one who put it on the table. "Either the gun belonged to Lotty Fischer and her murder's an unconnected coincidence—which seems highly unlikely on the face of it—or we go with the assumption that she was killed to prevent her telling who she ran the gun check for."

Albee's baby blues got bigger as it finally sank in exactly why Rawson was there.

Even though I knew Davidowitz and I were probably going to get bounced from the case, I put to McKinnon the question that'd been bugging me ever since Cluett got shot.

"I wonder if you'd tell us, Captain," I said politely, "why you requested Cluett last fall?"

"We were shorthanded here," he answered promptly. "One of our detectives had been injured, we needed a temporary replacement, I thought you could spare him."

"All year," I said. "But why Cluett? Why not Davidowitz? Why not the luck of the draw?"

He stiffened. "If it's any of your business, Sergeant Vaughn—" he began.

Then he broke off as his eyes met the looey's, watching him across the table.

She hadn't said a word and her face showed nothing

more than polite attention, but I suddenly realized that she was pretty damn interested in hearing him answer my question.

So was Rawson.

The captain realized it, too. He climbed off his high horse and said, "It was personal, Sergeant. I knew Cluett from my rookie days, thought it might be nice to have him around awhile, for old times' sake."

Sounded pretty, but I didn't buy it. Had a feeling Harald didn't either, but she caught me watching her reaction and turned to Rawson as he asked, "What's your reading on this, Lieutenant?"

"There would seem to be three criteria the perpetrator would have to meet," she said carefully. "It has to be someone with no alibi for Cluett's death at approximately 10:15 Tuesday night, no alibi for Fischer's death at 2:20 Thursday morning, and finally, our perp was probably someone who worked in this precinct four years ago when Lotty Fischer ran the gun check."

She paused and Rawson looked around the table. "Agreed?"

Qualified murmurs of agreement.

"Very well." She turned to Rawson and damned if she didn't tackle it head on. "In bulky winter clothes, we can't be certain the killer's a man. I do not have an alibi for Fischer's death, but I was with friends when Cluett died and I had not met Fischer before I arrived in this precinct two years ago. Albee's been here less than a year, Lowry three years. Both were in the squad room when the call came in on Fischer. Sergeant?"

I shrugged. "I can prove where I was when Cluett got it, but I was home in bed alone Thursday morning. I never worked Manhattan and never heard of Lotty Fischer."

Davidowitz: "Ditto, except my wife can vouch for me all night Wednesday."

The Captain didn't like it.

"No alibis," he growled. "And yeah, I've been here five years."

He stood up and crushed his foam coffee cup in his big hands. "Okay, Rawson. It's all yours. Do what you have to."

And with that, he dropped the cup in a wastebasket by the door and walked out.

Chapter
18

⊏⊐ McKinnon's exit from his own office had been a
dramatic gesture, but symbolism didn't mean
squatters' rights. As a one-man Field Internal Affairs Unit,
Sergeant Rawson was theoretically independent, yet Mc-
Kinnon still outranked him and was still his nominal boss.
Sergeants who planned long careers in the department
didn't try to pull too many power plays on captains.

"Okay, people, I'll make this quick." Rawson nodded to Jarvis Vaughn. "How long was this Michael Cluett
over here?"

"Three months," Vaughn answered promptly.
"From mid-October to mid-January."

"And Cluett reported to you, right, Lieutenant?"

"Yes," Sigrid replied.

He gestured to the stack of file folders in front of
her. "Those the cases he worked on?"

"Yes. In most of these, though, he was—" She hesitated, as if looking for a diplomatic phrase.

Vaughn helped her out. "Just a warm body?"

She nodded.

Davidowitz grinned. She didn't have to elucidate.

"I'll take them for now," said Rawson.

"Will you be setting up a special task force?" she asked.

"Looks like it, Lieutenant." He held out his hand for the files Albee and Lowry had begun on the Lotty Fischer investigation.

"You mean that's it?" asked Elaine Albee. "We're off the case?"

"Yep," said Rawson, with another of those crinkly smiles that didn't quite make it to his penetrating eyes. "Sorry."

Albee started to protest, but Sigrid cut it off with a brisk, "That'll be all, Albee. Lowry. Unless Sergeant Rawson has further questions for you?"

"Not now," he said. "Later, of course."

Hy Davidowitz looked at Vaughn. "I'll wait for you downstairs," he said, then hoisted himself from the chair and followed Albee and Lowry from the office.

Vaughn handed over his own files reluctantly. "You already have your task force set?" he asked.

"You applying?"

"Yes."

Rawson's less-than-genuine smile faded. "Let me think about it, Sergeant. You personally may not fit two of Lieutenant Harald's three conditions, but if some of your people back at the Six-Four do, I.A.D.'d have a problem with appearances. It'd help having somebody already up to speed on this, though. You smoke?"

"No," said Vaughn, who'd quit six years ago and still missed it.

"That's a plus," said Rawson. "I hate smoke-filled rooms. Never put a smoker on my team if I can help it."

"I don't smoke," said Sigrid, even though she knew what the answer had to be.

"Sorry, Lieutenant. Appearances again. You're too wired in here." He racked the folders in his hands and aligned the edges. "Let's continue this down in my office, Vaughn. We'll be in touch, Lieutenant."

They left her sitting alone.

•   •   •

Captain McKinnon opened the door of his office and halted.

"You're still here," he grunted.

"Yes, sir." Sigrid stood as he circled the desk. "If I was out of line before, Captain—"

He cut her off with a wave of his hand. "No. You acted correctly."

McKinnon took his seat and looked up at her. His thick brown hair was frosted with gray and his broad face was seamed with lines at mouth and eyes. "Sit down, Lieutenant."

Another time and she might have argued. She had always felt awkward with this shaggy bear of a man and it didn't help to learn four months ago that he and her father had once been partners and close friends. If anything, the knowledge only deepened the stiffness between them. She had taken the job—had *earned* it, she told herself fiercely—without knowing; yet to others it would appear that she had a protected position within the department if the situation became public.

"Well," he growled, "going to ask me if I shot Mick Cluett and pushed Lotty Fischer under a train?"

"Would you tell me if you had?" she countered coolly.

He gave a sour chuckle. "Spoken like a true cop. So why are you still here?"

"I thought you'd want to know that Rawson's going to set up a special task force to investigate both homicides. Probably with Vaughn."

That was all she'd intended to say, yet she found herself adding, "I also thought you'd want to know you can trust me."

"Yeah?"

She didn't try to explain what she'd meant, she wasn't sure she knew herself, but his brown eyes almost disappeared as he narrowed them in deliberate appraisal.

"Okay," he said at last. He handed her the file Vaughn had given him earlier and sat back with a weary sigh. "I hope they don't drag it out. This kind of thing plays hell with morale."

As Sigrid left, his voice stopped her at the doorway. "Thanks, Lieutenant."

Except for Elaine Albee, Jim Lowry, and Tillie, the squad room was empty and awkwardly silent.

"In my office, Tillie," Sigrid said without breaking stride.

When he got there, she asked him to shut the door.

His round face grew solemn as he heard that a task force was forming. "I wish I could be on it."

"Got an alibi for both nights?" Sigrid smiled.

"Just Marian and the kids," he admitted.

"And you came here three years ago from the One-Nine," she mused. "Did you know the Fischer woman before then?"

Tillie shook his head, but his eyes began to gleam as he contemplated the shape of the investigation to come. "She ran that gun check four years ago? Think how many personnel have transferred in and out since then! It doesn't have to be someone who was ever actually assigned to the precinct. All we have to do is show someone who knew Lotty Fischer four years ago and Mick Cluett now. I could pull personnel records, time sheets—"

Tillie thrived on details, on taking masses of raw data and breaking it down into orderly categories. Sigrid could picture him compiling charts with every member of the whole New York City Police Department cross-referenced.

"Sorry, Tillie," she said. "I'd offer you to Rawson if I thought he'd use you, but even though you barely worked with Cluett, he's not taking anyone from this unit."

"Not even you?" he asked.

"Nobody."

Tillie's face was as easy to read as a morning report. Raw disappointment came first, then Sigrid saw disappointment shade into apprehension as the personal aspects of the case took on flesh and blood. Originally, it had struck him as a problem of dates, statistics and intersecting bar graphs. Now, for the first time, he began to put faces beside those dates and he didn't like what he was seeing.

Sigrid said, "They'll look at everybody who worked with Cluett or who was stationed here four years ago. And that includes this detective unit as well. Sam Hentz, for instance. He worked with Cluett. I haven't gone back through all the squad files yet, but it's my impression that he's been stationed here at least four years."

Dismay filled Tillie's blue eyes. "But that's true of Eberstadt and Peters and who knows who else?" he protested.

"Exactly. It isn't just the uniforms and the P.A.A.'s that are going to feel the heat on this one. Half the precinct's going to be under investigation till this case is solved. So do me a favor, Tillie, and see if you can determine how many of our people are under Rawson's gun."

By the end of their conference, Tillie was still unhappy about the situation, but he'd promised Sigrid that she could count on him to help keep up morale in their unit.

Alone in her office again, Sigrid took an apple from her desk drawer and bit into it thoughtfully. She seldom went in for deliberate and conscious self-psychoanalyzing, but she knew now that she hadn't avoided Cluett's clumsy attempts at familiarity merely because she disliked the man personally. (Which she did, she reminded herself grimly.) She was sorry he'd been shot, but his death didn't alter the facts of his life. He'd been lazy, sloppy, and nearly useless on her squad and she wasn't going to elevate him to sainthood simply because he'd been killed.

Nevertheless, that still small voice of conscience compelled her to admit—to herself, if to no one else—that she'd deliberately discouraged Cluett because he could have told her about the past, and she didn't want to deal with whatever had happened between McKinnon and her father.

Two days past her birthday though, and wasn't it about time she finished growing up?

The picture of Leif Harald lay sealed in an envelope in her desk drawer. Balancing the apple on top of her coffee mug so that sticky juices wouldn't gum up any papers, Sigrid drew the silver-framed photograph from the envelope and looked around for a place to put it.

She had done very little to personalize the small boxy office assigned to her when she arrived. The previous occupant had painted it off-white, a change from the dark and light tones of blue throughout the rest of the building, and a fluorescent light recessed behind frosted glass in the ceiling above lent an artificial brightness. There were the usual file cabinets, desk, and bookshelves; a swivel chair upholstered in black vinyl for herself, some mismated straight chairs for visitors. Except for an administrative flowchart, a map of the city, and a drawing of the five boroughs divided by precincts, the walls were bare. The window ledge behind her desk held a neat row of police manuals and bulletins, not plants or whimsical knickknacks.

The only personal items visible were a brass lamp with a green glass shade, a large brassbound magnifying glass, the blue-green pottery coffee mug, and a small glass bowl that held a tangle of brass, steel, and silver puzzle rings which often served as worry beads for her fingers when her mind was elsewhere.

She pushed aside the bowl of puzzle rings and set the picture there so that Leif Harald faced her. In uniform. He'd died in an ordinary business suit though, died a plainclothes detective. In some down-at-the-heels cheap hotel. Would he still be a blond Viking if he'd lived?

She took another bite of apple and swiveled her chair around to look out at the cold crisp day. Thanks to snowplows and shovels, dirty snowbanks three and four feet high lined the curbs.

Nothing stayed pristine in this city very long. Even things that started out pure and clean.

The apple was her lunch and when she'd finished it, she swiveled back and dropped the core into her wastebasket.

An empty wastebasket. Sometimes the cleaning crew were too damned efficient.

Didn't matter. Tillie had mentioned that the contact person for the Viking Association was a lieutenant over in the First Precinct. She pulled the phone to her. It took less than five minutes to track him down, to say, "My father might have been a member years ago. Can you give me the names of some members who would have known him?"

Chapter
19

Revving up for the turnaround shift was never easy, and Bernie Peters and Matt Eberstadt were both yawning as they checked in Saturday morning. Bernie had been up early with his infant son, and Matt's cold seemed to be settling in his chest. There were bags under the older detective's eyes and his long face looked almost haggard.

"I'm gonna use some of the comp time I've got coming and take off early," he told Bernie. "Frances's plane gets into JFK at two and I want to pick her up."

"Sure," said Bernie, riffling through the files on his desk. "Guess we'd better get statements from some of Caygill's associates, see when they last saw him wearing that ring Cohen found in Jackson's body."

Matt Eberstadt lifted a doughnut from the box, stared at it moodily, and then put it back. Usually he could have eaten the whole box by himself. Today they looked as appetizing as wet sawdust. "Bernie?" he said.

"Um?" His partner was busily jotting down names and addresses. "Yeah?" he asked as he opened another file folder.

"Ah, never mind," said Matt. "Shove some of that

stuff over here and let's see what's on the docket for this morning."

Roman Tramegra had already written another four pages of *Freeze Factor,* the title he'd finally decided on, and was in the kitchen experimenting with a kiwi omelet when Sigrid came out to the kitchen at eight-fifteen looking for coffee. Not only was she dressed, she was dressed rather well in tailored black slacks, flat-heeled black leather shoes, a slate-blue tweed jacket Anne had given her for Christmas, and a white silk shirt with squared lapels. In one hand she carried a blue scarf, in the other a silver necklace shaped like a flat collar.

Knowing how she often slept till noon when off-duty, Roman glanced first at the calendar and then at the clock. "This *is* Saturday, is it not?"

"Don't start with me, Roman," she warned. She held out the scarf and necklace. "Which one?"

"The necklace," he answered promptly; but when she'd clipped it on, he cocked his head and examined the effect with a critical eye. "It's *nice,* yet something's lacking. More color?"

She looped the blue scarf around her neck and tucked the ends inside her shirt.

"No," Roman decided. "That's not right."

"Oh God!" she said and yanked it off again.

"Wait, wait!" he said, suddenly inspired. "I have *just* the thing you need."

He hurried through the door to his quarters and soon returned with a dark wool tie. "Power red. All the TV anchors wear one."

Sigrid took it out to the hall mirror, buttoned her shirt all the way up to the top, slipped the tie under her collar, and promptly ran afoul of the knot.

"No, no, no," Roman called from the kitchen. "Leave your shirt open as it was before, with the necklace showing, and knot the tie below the vee."

Obediently, Sigrid did as she was told. It was difficult to get the square knot to come out flat and she wasn't

crazy about the way the ends drooped when she was finished. Especially since one end was wider than the other.
"This isn't working, Roman."

"Well, of *course,* it isn't," he rumbled in his deep
voice, as he came out to supervise. "You've tied it like a
Girl Scout's neckerchief when you want a regular four-in-
hand."

Her fingers were so clumsy trying to tie a four-in-
hand at that length that Roman said, "Oh, *do* let me.
Stand still now."

He unknotted her first effort and began anew. "Oh
dear. Do you know, I've never done this for someone else.
I shall have to—"

Feeling like a child, Sigrid found herself staring into
the mirror while Roman stood behind her, his arms encir-
cling her thin body, as he, too, looked in the mirror to tie
a perfect knot: over, under, around, and through, so that
the wide end fell properly over the narrow and the knot
wound up precisely at the vee of her shirt.

"There!" he said, stepping back. "You look quite
nice. What is the occasion, may I ask?"

Sigrid continued to gaze at her reflection. *"The mirror
cracked from side to side,"* she quoted gloomily. " *'The curse
has come upon me,' cried/The Lady of Shalott."*

"Ah," Roman said with instant, and sympathetic, understanding. "A dental appointment."

"Worse," she moaned. "A fashion appointment."

Clothes and cosmetics couldn't have been further
from Dinah Urbanska's mind as the young detective
jogged along the Promenade, a cantilevered esplanade
built out over the Brooklyn-Queens Expressway. Today
was warmer than yesterday even though the sun came and
went fitfully. Another cold front was supposed to roll in
after midnight, but the morning weather report predicted a high of forty-five today. After the bone-numbing
chill of the past few days, forty-five felt almost balmy.

Even with no sunlight to sparkle on the water, the
view from high above the piers was spectacular: Brooklyn

Bridge to the north, wearing its hundred years with massive grace; the towers of lower Manhattan directly across the East River; and Governors Island just to the south, with the bay and the Statue of Liberty beyond.

The Promenade was about a third of a mile long and each time she reached one end, Dinah usually stopped and jogged in place, pumping the half-pound weights on her wrists as she savored the view. Although she'd grown up in Long Island's Levittown, Dinah was as dazzled by the city as any starstruck kid who ever fled a farm. She had made it as far as a tiny studio apartment on the edge of Brooklyn Heights and hoped to find someplace affordable in Manhattan before another summer was gone, *if*— and a very big if, she warned herself—she didn't screw up again and get busted back to patrol duty.

Not that it was her fault, strictly speaking. Cluett had been the more experienced one on the case. He was the one responsible for maintaining the chain of evidence. Yet she was the one who'd had to accept the command discipline and the mark against her record.

Every time she remembered Cluett, she got angry all over again. Why'd he want to hang on for forty anyhow? Police work wasn't for stupid old men too lazy to carry their own weight.

She turned and began jogging toward the Brooklyn Bridge. Its stones were as gray as the sky above it. Snow lay melting in dirty piles on either side of the esplanade and wind stirred the bare branches of the trees beyond. More snow predicted before morning, thought Dinah. She and Sam Hentz went on duty at four. With luck, it would hold off till their tour was over.

Thinking of Sam Hentz made her warm all over, made jogging feel like dancing. Her ponytail streamed out behind her like a golden mane as her sturdy legs, sheathed in electric-pink lycra, pounded along the Promenade. Such a difference working with him. Silly the way she'd been so scared of him at first, when now—

Oh, not that Sam gave a good goddamn about her. She knew he didn't. Not yet anyhow. Nevertheless, she couldn't stop daydreaming about him, wishing he could know that she'd do anything for him.

*Any*thing.

Despite the gray skies, Sam Hentz was sorely tempted to put the top down as he tooled back across the George Washington Bridge in a sleek black Jaguar, returning from his aunt's house a few miles up the Hudson. Half the fun of driving a racy car was the feel of wind streaming across one's face. He thought of Elaine Albee, always mouthing about a Lamborghini, and wondered what she'd think of his XJS if she saw him driving it.

A *red* Lamborghini yet, he thought scornfully. Black would be miles too subtle for her. With his free hand, he stroked the soft butterscotch leather of the other seat. If Albee ever did get a Lamborghini, she'd probably have the interior reupholstered in leopard skin.

Like a cubic zirconia in a platinum setting, *Imagine You!* was tucked into a second-floor suite with floor-to-ceiling mirror glass windows that fronted onto an exclusive section of Fifth Avenue in the mid-Fifties.

At one minute before ten, Sigrid stepped out of a brass and chrome elevator that was more burnished than a piece of high-tech jewelry and pulled open a glass door etched like crystal with the image of a butterfly emerging from its chrysalis.

Sigrid considered herself above such trite and obvious symbolism—were clients really supposed to feel like lowly caterpillars whose only hope of metamorphosing into exotic butterflies lay beyond these crystal doors?—yet as soon as she stepped inside, she was immediately intimidated by the waves of high-priced glamour that seemed to radiate from the very walls.

The tiny reception area was sheathed in space-expanding mirrors, polished black marble, and chrome. The mirrors were subtly etched with fine-line impressions of more butterflies. Some drifted in solitary flight through the middle of one panel; in another, several hovered near the floor.

Every angled surface seemed engineered to reflect and multiply the receptionist's image. A strikingly beautiful redhead, she was the only color in the room but she burned with it: a flaming yellow jacket over a purple minidress belted with fire-engine red patent leather. It was an eye-jangling combination yet somehow, on her, the blazing cacophony of hot colors worked.

She smiled at Sigrid. "May I help you?"

Sigrid identified herself. "I have a ten o'clock appointment."

"Certainly, Miss Harald." She touched a button on the shiny chrome desk top. "Carina? Miss Harald is here for her makeover."

She touched another button and a section of the mirrored wall slid aside noiselessly. "Go through please, Miss Harald."

Carina was a platinum blonde clone of the receptionist, dressed in a bright red jumpsuit. She led the way down an all-white hall to a small cubicle which she unlocked before handing the key to Sigrid.

"Please remove your outer garments and all jewelry, especially any wedding or engagement rings, and put on the robe and slippers which you will find inside." She smiled and fluted in all the right places, but it was obviously a much-repeated spiel since Sigrid wore no rings of any kind. "Then please lock the door and continue down the hall to the preparation area."

This was beginning to take on the aspects of a visit to the doctor, thought Sigrid. She slipped off her top clothes, taking pains not to disturb the perfect knot of Roman's red tie, and put on the calf-length white terry robe and cotton scuffs.

The preparation area had aspects of an ordinary beauty salon: five chairs in front of a bank of sinks and mirrors. Again, everything was gleaming white except for the attendants, who wore linen jumpsuits, each in a different primary or secondary color as pure and unsophisticated as a child's crayon.

Three of the chairs were already filled, one by Anne Harald, who smiled at her in the mirror but said nothing to give away their relationship to the others, which was one of Sigrid's conditions for coming. Talking was not encouraged at this point anyhow. Carina had pinned a name tag to Sigrid's robe that gave her first name only. The other three women were introduced as Gillian, Anne, and Phyllis.

"From this point on, Berthelot insists on first names only," she explained. "He doesn't wish to be distracted by stereotypes of ancestry. And please be very careful not to mention your marital status or profession either. Only your looks count here."

As she spoke, she brushed Sigrid's fine dark hair away from her face and slipped on a white bandeau that held the hair back and framed her face like a bandage. "The first thing we do is strip your face of all makeup."

"I'm not wearing anything except lipstick," Sigrid said.

Carina merely smiled and adjusted the white vinyl chair to a reclining position. "Lean back, please."

Resigned, Sigrid lay back in the chair and closed her eyes as Carina smoothed on warm cleansing cream and then covered her face with a hot towel.

"Ah, that feels heavenly," said Phyllis from the next chair.

Faces stripped, the four women were led into a circular mirrored conference room where a small ebullient man of late middle age awaited them. Berthelot's obviously dyed jet-black hair had receded to the top of his squarish head, but what remained was thick and brushed straight back from the hairline to hang collar length at the nape of his neck. His naturally sallow skin was deeply tanned and his dark eyes swept over them with apparent delight and admiration.

"Oh marvelous!" he cried, jumping up and rushing around the table to welcome them. "A Summer, an Autumn, and *two* Winters! Come, *mes chéries*! We shall have such *fun* discovering the glorious *you* nature intended you to be!''

It was going to be an awfully long day, thought Sigrid.

In his Greenwich Village apartment, McKinnon was finally doing something about the ill-fitting sliding glass door that led to his small balcony. In summer, the breezes that wafted around his balcony could be delightful; the winter version whistling through the cracks had sent his latest heating bill over the moon.

When the rent-controlled apartment that he'd originally shared with a string of different roommates came up for sale a few years back, McKinnon had bought it. Ever since Leif Harald moved out to marry Anne Lattimore, he'd lived alone here, content with the location, the neighbors, the apartment itself, except when subjected to the annoyances of ownership.

Year before last, when he'd first noticed the drafts, the winter had been mild enough to let him ignore the problem. Last year, he'd simply taped the cracks over with masking tape. This proved effective only so long as he didn't want to use the terrace. Unfortunately, New York could string two or three warm days together even in January and bingo! There went another whole roll of masking tape.

This year, he had launched a two-prong attack: self-adhesive foam weather stripping and heavy-duty insulated drapes. Yet there was still a discernible draft.

Which was why he had spent the last hour down at the lumberyard pricing new double-glazed French doors. He could remember when a new car could be bought for what they were going to charge to take away the old door and install the new; but this time he'd closed his eyes and written a check for the down payment. It was tentatively agreed that carpenters would arrive on the first of April.

In the meantime, McKinnon had stopped off at the hardware store for another roll of masking tape and was halfway through the process of applying it when the phone rang.

"Yeah?" He tucked the phone under his chin and continued taping the door.

"McKinnon? Mac McKinnon?"

"Yeah?"

"Mac, this is Tom Oersted. Remember me?"

"Yeah, sure Tom," he said, surprised. "Been a long time."

"Ten years or more," said Oersted. "How've you been?"

"Fine, fine. What's up?"

Oersted laughed. "Always straight to the point, eh, Mac?"

"And?" He finished taping the top of the door and began on the side.

"I got a phone call yesterday afternoon."

"Don't play games with me, Tom," said Mac. He remembered now. Oersted had always been Leif's friend, not his.

"It was Leif's kid. I'd almost forgotten he had one. Little Siga. All grown up now and following in Leif's footsteps. A lieutenant, she tells me."

"Yeah, she works for me now."

"So she said. She told me about Mick Cluett, too. I missed it on the news. Damn shame. He should've done his twenty and got out like me."

McKinnon was silent, the masking tape ignored, as he waited for Oersted to say why he'd called.

"She tracked me down through the Viking Association," said Oersted. "Wants to talk to somebody who knew her old man. I told her you were his partner, but she doesn't want to ask you. How come, Mac?"

"Who knows?" he answered.

"So what'll I tell her? About you and Leif?"

"Whatever you want," McKinnon said, "so long as you limit it to the things you know for a fact."

"Listen," Oersted said hastily. "As far as I'm concerned, it's water over the dam, but I'm supposed to see her tomorrow night. I just thought you ought to know that she's asking."

"Had to happen sooner or later," said McKinnon.

But after he'd hung up, he felt as gray and bleak as the sky beyond the glass door and he wished Oersted hadn't told him.

"Your lovely skin is like skim milk," crooned Berthelot. "See how the dusty rose loves you and yet the salmon fights with the blue undertones?"

"Oooh, yes!" breathed Gillian. Despite her New England accent, the young woman had been defined as a Southern Summer. (Not to be confused with an Eastern Summer or a California Summer, Sigrid had learned.)

The white circular conference table was littered with swatches of colorful fabrics and trays of costume jewelry that ranged from Social Register restrained to Red Light gaudy as Berthelot analyzed each woman in turn and set her small problems of finding which colors and styles fit within the new parameters he had set for her.

For Sigrid, the worst part so far had been when it was her turn to stand beneath a clear white spotlight while Berthelot peered at her skin, face, and eyes through a magnifying glass and then described her physical attributes one by one.

"Such queenly height! The carriage of an empress. Marvelous facial planes. Wait till you see how we sculpt your face! Clear porcelain skin. Everyone see Sigrid's blue undertones?"

Murmured assents from the other three women.

"And the grace of your neck. Like a swan. Women would have killed for a neck like that in ages past! Wonderful legs! Never hide them in pants. You must wear full, flowing skirts that make a dramatic statement."

The man was a cheerleader. Improbable compliments fell from his lips in never-ending variety. Listening to him, thought Sigrid, one would think we're all Miss America candidates.

Gillian's young plump body had been praised for its vitality, its harmony of line; Anne's petite frame brought ecstatic murmurs of "dynamic excitement." No mention was made of the wrinkles lining Phyllis's "piquant" face, but "This white hair will have to go. You're much too young to have your autumn fires quenched. Back to red for you!"

"I was never a redhead," Phyllis protested weakly.

"Then it's time you became one," Berthelot told her airily as he flung a length of copper silk over her head and created an elegant turban.

To Sigrid's astonishment, she saw that he was right. She couldn't begin to say why, but the copper did indeed liven Phyllis's skin and eyes in a way that her white hair did not.

She reached into the pile of fabrics on the table and chose three nearly similar shades of red—one had just enough blue to lean toward purple, one had a hint of orange, the third was equally balanced—and held them against her face, one at a time, comparing them in the oval stand mirror provided for each woman. Maybe it really was like one of those color problems Nauman set for his art students each fall, a visual puzzle no more difficult or arcane than progressive permutations of an ordinary color wheel.

Of course, the names were sheer nonsense, she'd decided. Her coloring was almost exactly the same as Anne's, yet Anne had been decreed a California Winter while she was an Eastern Winter.

As they paused for lunch, Sigrid tried to imagine what she was going to look like transformed into Berthelot's idea of a New York February.

If asked to describe himself, Matt Eberstadt would have replied that he was as honest and moral as the next man. Perhaps less concerned about the state of his immortal soul than his wife Frances; but in his opinion that didn't mean much. Women always sweated the small stuff more than men anyhow. Convenient parking wasn't an infringement of the law in his eyes, merely one of the minor perks that went with the job, and he didn't give it a second thought as he pulled into the curb in front of the air terminal and flipped down his sun visor. All he cared about was making sure there was enough police ID on his car to render it immune from tickets or towing while he went inside to meet his wife.

The plane from Atlanta was on time and when Frances came through the doorway into the waiting room, he was so glad to see her that he rushed forward to take her bags and fold her in his arms.

They were not ordinarily a publicly demonstrative couple and Frances brushed his lips with hers and said, "Goodness! I believe you *did* miss me!"

She had limited herself to a couple of carry-on pieces so they didn't have to waste time standing around the baggage carousel. Frances Eberstadt was a sensible woman little given to intuition and imagination, but when they were in the car and driving away from the airport, she looked at Matt's drawn face with concern and said, "Is everything okay at home? The boys behave themselves while I was gone?"

"Oh, sure," he replied, maneuvering through the traffic patterns that surrounded JFK until he was in the correct lane. "Well, except for Tuesday night."

They had talked every day by phone, so she'd already heard about the boys staying out till nearly one in the morning while he'd driven all over Ozone Park looking for them, earlier in the week.

"I think I might have caught a cold then," he said.

Instantly, her hand was on his forehead. "You do feel a little warm."

He caught her hand and brought it to his lips. "I missed you, kid. The house always feels cold when you're not there."

Pleased, Frances patted his thigh. "As soon as we get home, I'm going to fix you a nice hot bowl of soup. And then straight to bed for you."

"What about the boys' basketball game?" Matt protested weakly. "We promised we'd go. Kenny thinks the coach might let him start tonight. You don't want to miss that."

"No," agreed Frances, who had once led her high school basketball team in field goal percentages. "But there's no need for us both to stay home if you're going to be sleeping."

To ease her conscience, she added, "I'll tell Pam to tell Bernie that you're going to call in sick tomorrow."

The moment of truth had arrived, Berthelot told the group. Analysis over, now was the time to implement their discoveries. Back to the working area of the salon they would now go. Hair would be cut and styled, stripped and dyed; and individual palettes of makeup colors would be blended to complete their total metamorphosis into the gorgeous butterflies they'd heretofore kept hidden inside cocoons of timidity.

As Berthelot pronounced final categories (Phyllis was a California Autumn), each woman's earlier attendant reappeared to take a checklist of styling instructions from Berthelot before leading her charge away.

Sigrid was willing to agree that she should perhaps go through her closet and weed out any clothes with a yellow-based color, but she'd be damned if she'd spend the afternoon having "ashy highlights" added to her hair while Anne was having the flicks of gray removed from hers and she said as much when the other three women had been led out and only she and Berthelot and Carina were left in the conference room.

Berthelot signaled the platinum blonde attendant to wait outside.

"Ah, Sigrid, Sigrid, Sigrid," he crooned, more in sorrow than in anger when they were alone. "Why do you resist me so? All morning, you have fought me. So much negativity. Why?"

"I can't do this. It feels too artificial. Too sybaritic."

"But of course it's sybaritic. Why are you here if not to enjoy this experience?"

"It wasn't my idea," Sigrid muttered. "Today's a gift. From my grandmother. I don't know how much she paid but—"

"Money!" the little man exclaimed. "You think of this day in terms of money?"

"Don't you?" Sigrid asked coldly.

Berthelot drew himself up to his full five foot five. "My fee is no secret. An all-day seminar with me, Berthelot, is six hundred and fifty dollars."

"Six hundred?" Sigrid was appalled.

"And fifty," he snapped.

"That's obscene! That much money frittered away on skin colors and makeup charts and clothing styles to fit some idiotic category? Out there on the street, hungry people are freezing, while in here—"

"Yes?" he asked dangerously.

"I'm sorry." She drew the collar of the robe up tightly around her neck. "I knew I shouldn't have come. This place makes me feel like Marie Antoinette just before the deluge. I can't stay."

"You *will* stay." Berthelot stamped his foot. "The makeup and lotions and colors are frivolous, you think? And you are Mother Teresa?"

"No, as a matter of fact, I'm a—"

"Silence! I do not wish to know. What you do is irrelevant. What you *are,* what *I* am is important. You look at me and you see a simpering old fairy, playing the fool so bored women will spend their money with me, no?"

"I'm sorry," Sigrid repeated. "I didn't mean to insult you."

"But you have!" he said huffily. "Cosmetics frivolous? Perhaps. But do they not each year send two fine young people from the projects to—"

He caught himself, shook his head, and walked away. "This you did not hear! Forget I have said this," he ordered imperiously, clearly annoyed with himself for his outburst. "What I—*how* I choose to amuse myself, to puff my ego with my money—*n'importe.* But my clients—what do you know of the suffering my clients endure before they find the courage to come to me?"

"Suffering?" Sigrid's scorn was undermined by the altruism Berthelot had almost revealed, but her skepticism remained. "Courage?"

"A matter of degree, of course, but suffering—yes, and courage, too—comes in many forms. A woman who feels herself unlovely in a world which places physical beauty above so much else, does she not suffer?" He gave a Gallic shrug. "Be honest, *ma chérie*. Your grandmama clearly loves you and has given you a gift which costs you nothing but courage to accept. And if courage is not needed, why are you so afraid to let me bring out your true beauty?"

He looked up at her, an absurd, flattering court jester of a man. And yet . . .

"No dye," she said, wavering.

"Only to bring out those glorious highlights? No? Very well," he agreed. "No dye."

"And no mousse."

"No mousse." Beaming, he opened the door and called for Carina.

"We have reached a compromise," he told her. "No dye for Sigrid. *But,*" he added, "we *will* reshape her eyebrows."

PAST IMPERFECT   168

had to start wearing the ring on his pinkie, couple of months ago.

Chapter
20

By the time his shift ended Saturday afternoon, Bernie Peters felt he'd wrapped up a solid case against Zachary Caygill, the beefy bartender soon to be formally charged with the brutal stabbing of Harold Jackson.

"It'll take one very slick lawyer to convince the jury that the signet ring Cohen took out of Jackson's body has nothing to do with Caygill," Bernie Peters told Sam Hentz as he finished up his paperwork.

Caygill was not one of those heart-of-gold bartenders beloved by customers and coworkers alike, and Bernie had found three witnesses willing to swear they'd seen Caygill wearing the ring the evening before Jackson's death. Two of the three could also testify that Caygill had not been wearing the ring the next day.

"I still think it's odd," said Dinah Urbanska. She spread her sturdy fingers, on which three rings were firmly wedged. "I've never had any of my rings fall off."

"Probably the only thing," Sam said, tossing over an earring that had gone flying when Dinah tugged off her woollen cap upon arrival a few minutes earlier.

"Yeah, well," said Bernie, "according to one of the witnesses, he's put on a lot of weight this past year and had to start wearing the ring on his pinkie a couple of months ago."

"Ever had your hand in fresh blood, kid?" asked Sam.

Dinah made a face and shook her head.

"Slippery as motor oil," he told her succinctly.

The telephone rang on the squad's line and Dinah answered automatically. "Detective Unit. Urbanska. Sorry, they're off today. Can I—?" She listened intently. "Yeah? Okay. I'll tell them."

She hung up and began to scrabble through the papers on her desk for a proper memo form. "That was Transit," she told the two men. "They spotted that witness Lowry and Albee want. Jerry the Canary. He was doing his bird imitations on one of the Grand Central Station platforms, but he got away before they could grab him."

"Which platform?" asked Sam.

"Uptown Lexington," she said, placing the memo where Albee would see it when next she checked in.

"Hardly worth bothering with," said Bernie. "Dollars to doughnuts he was passed out and didn't see a damn thing Thursday morning."

"Bet he did," said Dinah. "Why would he run if he didn't?"

The two men shared a look of vast experience; then Sam said, "Come on, kid, use your brain. Guys like him always have reasons to run. Mostly in their heads. That doesn't make him a witness. And speaking of witnesses," he continued, turning back to the work at hand, "that baby-in-the-dumpster canvass has turned up three possibles. You can check them out tonight while I—"

"I'm outta here," said Bernie. He zipped up his heavy parka and left them to it.

"Ah-h-h," sighed Anne Harald when their waiter had brought them drinks and then gone away again with their dinner orders. She leaned back against the cushioned banquette in the midtown restaurant they'd chosen. "I'd forgotten how exhausting getting beautiful could be."

Sigrid smiled and lifted her bourbon and Coke. "Here's to beauty."

"Berthelot alone has looked on Beauty bare," said Anne, raising her own drink.

"I thought that was Euclid."

"Do you suppose Euclid ever stepped inside the Greek equivalent of *Imagine You!*?"

"I doubt if the ancient Greeks had an equivalent," Sigrid said. She took a sesame breadstick from the basket and snapped it in two, sending a shower of small seeds and crumbs across the white tablecloth. Lunch had looked perfectly elegant, but the porcelain plates had held only skimpy fruit salads, and plain Perrier with slices of lime had filled the crystal goblets. Sigrid was ready for some real food and drink. She buttered the tip of the breadstick and bit it off.

"What do you want to bet there wasn't an Athenian Berthelot hawking kohl and henna around the Aegean and telling those Greek women that the gods hated naked eyes and gray hair?" Anne touched her own hair ruefully. "It's not *too* dark, is it?"

"No," Sigrid answered truthfully. "It looks right on you."

"I should have taken some Before pictures so Mama could see the difference." Her eyes swept over Sigrid. "I do like what he did with yours."

Sigrid had gone in with hair so short that there wasn't an awful lot Berthelot could do with it, but he'd managed an asymmetrical cut that gave a slightly different emphasis to the sweep of her forehead. She usually felt defensive when her mother looked at her like that, as if through a camera's range finder or close-up lens, but after a full day of being turned and prodded and hearing every physical feature objectively dissected in minute analysis, one more observation didn't bother her.

"Actually, I like it, too," she admitted, reaching for a second breadstick.

Anne passed her the butter again. "Thanks for going

through with this. For a minute there after lunch, I thought you were going to bolt or blow up."

"When did I ever bolt or blow up?"

"Shall I start with your second birthday and the red ribbon Mama wanted to tie in your hair?" Anne asked sweetly. "Or skip directly to Christmas dinner when Aunt Lucille asked you for the eight-hundredth time if you minded not having a husband and children?"

"Blasting Aunt Lucille doesn't count," Sigrid protested. "Anyhow, you didn't exactly set an example of patient fortitude when she started on all the men you could have married since I grew up and—" She lapsed into Aunt Lucille's cultivated Southern drawl. "—'left you all by your lonesome in an empty nest with not a soul to love.' "

As the waiter brought their lemon-roasted chicken and poured their wine, they smiled at each other and Sigrid felt a sudden rush of genuine affection.

The realization surprised her. She knew she'd always loved Anne, but as a child automatically loves the most important person in her life, especially if that person returns the love in whatever helter-skelter fashion. Tonight seemed different. It was as if she were for the first time seeing Anne from her own eye level instead of looking up from a child's perspective toward a being of glamour and limitless power. It could have been because they were both pleasantly tired from sharing a day mixed with frivolity and physical self-analysis; or maybe, thought Sigrid, it was because somewhere in the past six months, since Nauman came into her life, she'd almost quit comparing herself unfavorably to Anne and had gradually learned to accept her not as a mother alone, but as a friend. A rather dear friend, in fact.

And even though she'd never felt comfortable enough to initiate mother-daughter confidences, she found herself asking, "Why *didn't* you remarry? Was it because what you had with Dad was so special that you couldn't? What was he really like?"

"We've talked about this so many times, there's nothing new to tell, honey," Anne said, cutting into the crispy grilled skin of her succulent chicken.

The mouthwatering smells of lemon, sweet yellow peppers and garlic drifted up from both plates, and Sigrid lifted her own knife and fork.

"He used to take you to the park and—"

"No," Sigrid interrupted. "Not as my father. As a man. A police officer. Your husband."

"As a man?" She chewed thoughtfully. "Okay. As a man, incredibly handsome. That was the first thing anyone noticed about him. Tall and blond and the bluest, bluest eyes I've ever seen. You know how blue your cousin Hilda's eyes are? Go one shade brighter and that's the color Leif's were. I could never quite catch it in the camera. And when he turned those eyes and that smile on you, you felt as if you were the only person in the whole world he'd ever really listened to. It was as if he'd been waiting all his life to hear the things you were saying. I'm here to tell you there was nobody like him in Colleton County."

A rueful smile curved her lips. "He certainly dazzled this little hick. Mama always swore he had an Irish tongue in his head the way he could charm birds off trees."

Sigrid had heard all the family tales of how Grandmother Lattimore had rushed up from North Carolina to save her innocent eighteen-year-old daughter from an unsuitable alliance and had wound up so charmed that she'd blessed the wedding on condition that the ceremony be shifted from the Lutheran chapel in Greenwich Village to the Southern Baptist church Grandmother's own grandparents had helped build near the family homeplace in central North Carolina.

"He never saw a stranger," Anne said. "There was a time when we couldn't walk through the Village without running into at least two people on every block who knew us and were glad to see us both. But if we did wander into a strange café or deli once in a while, and if they weren't real busy, your daddy'd have them talking like old friends in just minutes."

That was the easy-going father image Sigrid had

grown up with, and yet . . . "Mick Cluett, the last time I spoke to him, said Dad could freeze someone with a look if he wanted to." Sigrid topped their glasses from the bottle of white Zinfandel.

"Mickey said that?" Anne lowered her fork. "Yes," she mused. "Yes, he could do that, too, if the mood struck him . . . if he felt too hemmed in. It was like—"

She hesitated and her lovely face was earnest as she searched for the right words. "Once, when you were about eight or nine, the thermometer broke and you chased that little blob of mercury all across the tabletop. It kept breaking into smaller drops or slipping away from beneath your fingers and you were laughing but you were frustrated, too, because you couldn't pick it up. Remember, honey?"

Sigrid nodded.

"That was Leif. Quicksilver. Just as enchanting, just as elusive if you tried to make him stand still in one place. It took me a long time to realize that it was nothing to do with me, it was just the way he was made. Like mercury."

An undertone of regret shadowed her voice.

"Metaphors, Mother?"

Anne smiled warily and took a sip of wine. "You asked."

Sigrid began to feel as if she'd opened a bright familiar door into a dark and unfamiliar room, yet she took that first step across the threshold. "Didn't you love him?"

"Well, of course, I loved him!" Anne said, surprised. "In the beginning—"

"At the end, I meant."

"At the end, too, even though it was a different love. Time and marriage do that, sugar. You just can't sustain that catch-in-your-throat delirium; you'd burn up if you did. But certainly I loved him."

"Would you still be married if he hadn't died?"

Anne considered for a moment. "I don't know," she answered slowly, then she gave a little shrug. "Maybe *he* wouldn't have wanted to stay with me."

"Was he unfaithful?"

"*Sigrid!*"

"Sorry, Mother, but—"

"No, no, it's . . . I mean I . . ." She shook her head, looking annoyed with herself, and at the same time, faintly embarrassed. "I'm not as cold-bloodedly modern as I sometimes think I am. You're our daughter, Siga. I just *can't* talk about our sex life with you."

Sigrid was horrified. "That's not what I meant at all."

"Then what did you mean? Oh, honey, are you going to go from believing he was a hero ten feet tall to wondering if he had clay feet? Do you really want that?" She reached across the table and clasped Sigrid's hand. "You asked me what he was like as a person and all I can tell you is that he was just a man. A wonderful man most of the time—funny, smart, exciting, and yes, ma'am, sexy, too—but just a man. Isn't that enough?"

"Mick Cluett—"

"Mickey Cluett wanted to be your daddy's mentor," Anne said impatiently. "Not that mentor was a word anybody'd ever heard of back then. He was like a turkey buzzard trying to take a falcon under its wing. Leif never needed his protection and I think Mickey resented that."

"What about Tom Oersted?"

"Oersted?" Anne lifted the napkin over the bread basket and took out a soft roll. "I remember the name, but I can't quite recall a face. One of Leif's colleagues or yours?"

"Dad's, I guess. Retired now, but he used to belong to the Viking Association."

"The Viking Association!" Unexpectedly, Anne giggled. "Now *them* I can tell you about! What a wonderful, rowdy bunch they were. The year we were married, Leif took me to one of their weddings at the old Norwegian Hall in Brooklyn. I've got pictures somewhere. They carried the groom's Volkswagen up two flights of stairs and deposited it on the dance floor. For all I know it was still there when they tore the building down. And oh, the beer and aquavit that used to flow on Swedish Nation Day or after the Norwegian Constitution Day Parade! You should join them.''

"Right," Sigrid said dryly.

In the Village, forty blocks south, McKinnon leaned back on his couch, deep in memory. The coffee table, the floor, the cushions on either side of him—all were littered with piles of black-and-white photographs. Anne had taken dozens of rolls of film for her photography class and many of these were culls too good to throw away but not good enough to take to class.

He remembered sitting at the kitchen table with Leif, as Anne snapped picture after picture, experimenting with her cameras to learn their limits and what effects she could achieve by opening up or stopping down the lenses, by playing around with shutter speed and film types. Each click of the camera had been fully documented in her notebook.

Here they were in shirtsleeves, their uniform jackets draped over the backs of kitchen chairs. Close-ups of their faces, the badges on their hats, his gun, Leif's ear, his own hand holding a glass of beer. He'd forgotten this one of Mickey Cluett. Had Mickey Cluett ever been that young, that lean? A whole series of baby pictures: an owl-eyed Sigrid splashing in the deep laundry sink or seated on one of their laps to gnaw on a teething biscuit. He could almost smell the baby powder and gummy Zwieback, see those impossibly tiny fingers closed around one of his.

And there were pictures of Anne. Occasionally she'd leave a camera unattended and one of them would turn the lens on her and snap her with her head tilted back in laughter or with the tip of her tongue caught between her small white teeth as she concentrated on one of those complicated Danish recipes Leif's aunt had written out for her. God, how beautiful she'd been! And how young. Only nineteen.

More pictures spilled from another manila envelope: he and Leif clowning around the day they'd gotten their gold shields and hung up their uniforms. He could remember their celebration right down to the bottle of champagne Anne had bought. What he couldn't remember was the name of that redheaded reporter from the old *Journal-American* with whom Leif had celebrated the next night.

"Well," said Pam Peters, "I'm sorry Matt's got another cold and of course, we can always use the overtime, but you know what it's like, Frances, when you've got three little ones and he's never home to help."

Frances agreed that she did indeed know what it was like.

"I probably shouldn't have tried to go back to work so soon. Even though it's only three days a week, it just messes up my whole routine and—"

Frances uhmmed and oh?-ed in all the appropriate places, but her mind was on her own sons. Dressed in their colorful warm-up suits, they loomed over her and huffed impatiently for her to come on.

"Sorry, Frances, but the baby's crying and I have to go. Talk to you soon," said Pam and hung up as if it were the older woman who'd prolonged the conversation.

"One minute, guys," Frances said and hurried down the hall to the bedroom. She found Matt stretched out on their bed watching the news on their portable television. Except for his shoes, he was still fully dressed.

"Matt, you promised. Under the covers, lights out."

"As soon as the news is over," he said. "Honest."

"And no snacking," she ordered. "I know exactly how much ice cream's in the refrigerator and how many cookies are in the box."

"Ma-aaa," came her older son's plaintive cry from the back door.

"Go on," said Matt. "You're going to make the boys late."

She glanced at the clock, realized he was right, and rushed to join their sons.

Chapter 21

Above ground, defying the promise of more snow, Times Square was a gaudy blaze of Saturday night light and color. The temperature was still well above freezing, and up and down Broadway and along Forty-second Street, endlessly flashing marquees backlit the titles of raunchy XXX-rated movies. Brazenly garish neon signs spoke of everything from unfettered sex to every-thing-must-go luggage sales. Up above, more lights on enormous electronic billboards. Waves of light. Green for Japanese film, red for soda pop, blue for German cars and Colombian coffee—the colored lights washed their sales pitches across the buildings. Even higher, the buildings themselves, dark and massive blocks of granite, were jeweled with lighted windows and floodlit peaks. And down on the littered sidewalks, weaving in and out around overflowing trash baskets, panhandlers, and sex shills forcing handbills on every male who made eye contact, were the faces of all the nations on earth—the stunned, the stoned, and the starry-eyed—invincibly jay-walking through unbroken lines of shiny yellow taxis, avoiding the puddles of filthy slush melting at each corner, spilling around knots of people who stopped to laugh and talk and argue about whether to go here for drinks or there for the show. Steam rose from a hundred grates and manholes. Back and forth, in and out, swirling in chilled circles were families of wide-eyed tourists, threesomes of pink-cheeked South American sailors. Bridge-and-tunnel kids, acting out, razzed the transvestites who braved the winter night in short fur jackets and crotch-high leather miniskirts. Over it all, mingled with the yeasty aroma of money, sex, and cold plastic, floated the smell of damp cement, diesel fumes, and slightly charred hot pretzels.

Beneath Times Square, the push and jostle was fueled by the junction of three subway lines and the shuttle from Grand Central Station. Crowds of people flashed on and off the trains, dressed in everything from blue denim to black satin, ready for everything from just hanging out to hanging over a box seat at the theatre.

On an ordinary Saturday night, this was the frantic, jagged heartbeat of the other New York, the one they're always going to do something about. Heartbreaking and hopeless. The roar, the crush, the frayed connection were in the very marrow now; mechanically urban, determinedly artificial.

Suddenly, one section of the busy underground concourse was pierced by a wilderness sound straight from the deep woods: a barred owl's sharp, barking *hoohoo-hoohoo, hoohoo-hoohooaw!* Twice more came the calls, predatory and haunting, then they were followed almost immediately by squawks and chirps and the raucous shriek of a blue jay's *Thief! Thief!*

It was as if a crate of wild birds had suddenly been upended on one of the lower train platforms and people within hearing distance paused and craned to see.

As the wildly insane *oo-HA-oo* laughter of a loon floated up from a nearby stairwell, one of the aimlessly drifting figures stiffened like a bird dog that had unexpectedly caught the pheasant's scent out there in the tall grass. Checking out this Times Square station had been an impulsive hunch, nothing more. Turning now, quartering the area.

Oo-HA-oo.

Downstairs.

Good God! Was it really going to be that easy?

On the next level down, a slender sandy-haired man had backed himself against a steel girder between two sets of stairs. His overcoat was unbuttoned and the right side was pushed back so that passersby could, if they so desired, easily drop money into the slotted can that dangled from his belt. He carried in his hands a stack of bird pictures, cut from an adult coloring book, which he had accurately colored in vivid crayons, then glued to thin cardboard and covered with clear plastic wrap. Each picture was about six by eight inches and neat hand-lettering on the border identified each bird by both its common and Latin names.

So intent was the sandy-haired man on his act, that the nondescript figure walking slowly down the stairs didn't even register as an individual.

Easy does it, thought the bird dog. *No eye contact. Don't spook him. So that's Jerry the Canary. This clown really likes train stations. Platform's too crowded. Another push? Could I get away with it? Or better to follow and see where's he's nesting now?*

His audience hooked, Jerry the Canary held up his next bird card, a bright red cardinal, and burst into a mixture of clear and slurred whistles: *what-cheer-cheer-cheer.* In swift procession came a bluebird's soft gurgling notes, a wood thrush's rounded flutelike phrases, a robin's joyful whistle, and a virtuoso rendition of a horned lark's high-pitched series of irregular tinkling notes, which was so delightful that it brought a round of applause from his audience.

Experience had taught him when to stop and pat his money can and do his stork walk around the circle of onlookers. When one or two bills were dropped in along with several coins, he twittered a song sparrow's *sweet-sweet-sweet!*

Before the Canary came too near, his stalker had turned away, pretending an interest in the overhead sign that identified this as a stop for the Broadway-Seventh

Avenue Local. Like a taxi summoned by a doorman's whistle, the 9 train rushed noisily into the station and disgorged another load of Saturday night revelers.

Jerry the Canary had just begun to mimic a catbird when a policeman from the Transit Authority leaned over the railing above and spotted him.

"Hey!" the cop shouted, "Canary! I want to see you!"

Instantly, the catbird picture was replaced by an amateurish drawing of a fat yellow Tweety Bird. "Ooh, I t'ought I taw a puddy-tat!" he lisped and ducked into the 9 train just as the doors were closing.

The transit cop sprinted down the steps. "Wait!" he yelled.

But the conductor never heard and the train had already picked up speed. In frustration, the cop thwacked the nearest I-beam with his nightstick and glared at the laughing bystanders.

Across the platform, the bird dog reined in similar frustration and bitterly consigned all T.A. cops to hell.

"Beep!" went her answering machine and "Dammit all, Siga!" went Oscar Nauman's exasperated voice. "Why'd you give me your work schedule, if you're never going to be in?"

Sigrid clicked off the tape and lazily undressed. She'd had just enough wine to feel mellow as she hung up her slacks and jacket, put the rest in the laundry hamper, and slipped into a red silk negligee Nauman had given her. How amused he'd been to discover that while she didn't seem to care what her street clothes looked like, she *did* have a weakness for expensive silky, lacy lingerie.

The gown was a clear red. No orange overtones. An "Eastern Winter" red. Well, no one had ever faulted Nauman's color sense, had they? She smiled to herself and turned the tape back on.

"Anyway the panel went okay. The Mickey Mouse guy

dropped out to go to Cologne to pick up some prize or other. Buntrock took his place and did his usual tap, toe, and bubble dance about appropriations, simulacra, Foucault . . ."

As Nauman dismantled Buntrock's speech, Sigrid pulled from her closet all her earth-toned clothes: the browns, bricks, and terra-cottas. Next went the yellowy beiges and olives, even though this left her closet decimated. She was ruefully intrigued to see how many of Grandmother Lattimore's jewel-toned choices remained. Nauman was always trying to make her wear them. She thought of that museum benefit she'd promised to attend next week. Maybe she'd surprise him and wear that dramatic sapphire taffeta.

"—and the parties were better than I thought they would be. Got to see some of my pictures I hadn't seen in years. Years? Hell, decades! You never forget a one of them, Siga. Funny how they mellow. I hated to walk out of the room . . . was like I might never see them again . . . never had that feeling before."

The concert at Avery Fisher Hall had ended and the audience streamed out into Lincoln Center's broad plaza. As the floodlit central fountain gushed upward in changing colors, the pathetic falling cadences of a mourning dove attracted some of the concertgoers: *ah-love-love-love!* came the wistful call. *Ah-love-love-love.*

Despite the cold, many lingered to hear what would follow. With the music of Mozart and Haydn still echoing in their heads, the contrast between that sophisticated orchestra and this primitive maker of naive music was deliciously irresistible to certain jaded palates.

The sandy-haired man sat on the edge of the fountain and chirped and twittered to such an appreciative (and moneyed) group that by the time he saw two boys in blue approaching from Columbus Avenue, he had collected enough to buy food and a warm bed at the Paradiso for at least a week.

Melting into the crowd with his pictures tucked into a deep pocket, Jerry the Canary wondered if maybe he'd been wrong staying underground all winter. If they were gonna keep hassling him, he told himself, maybe he'd just migrate to the streets early this year.

Chapter 22

The temperature plummeted and snow began falling again well before daybreak Sunday morning. As if determined to disguise the city's filth, it draped a fresh white blanket over the unmelted piles of dirty snow which still lingered from Thursday, covered rotting piers and the stripped cars abandoned near those piers, hid all the paper trash caught in the shrubs and iron railings of vest-pocket parks around the island, and lent the twisty narrow streets of Greenwich Village the illusion of a nineteenth-century village again. The Sanitation Department fought back, of course, immediately deploying salt trucks and plows. Yet, because it was still the weekend, only the main transverse roads were cleared from the East River to the Hudson; and Washington Square began to take on a Currier and Ives beauty that promised to delight any Sunday strollers hardy enough to venture out.

West Tenth was one of the streets that hadn't yet been plowed or salted; and as Sigrid picked her way toward Hudson Street, an optimistic cross-country skier schussed past, heading for the waterfront.

Sigrid was an urban creature, never one to sing anthems to the beauties of nature. If she had a sport, it was swimming in a heated indoor pool, not skiing frigid peaks, that attracted her; yet waiting at her bus stop, she tipped her head up to let the dry, powdery flakes fall on her face and when her bus arrived, she took a window seat so that she could go on looking at the snow.

The heaters on this bus barely functioned; the other passengers' breaths came in puffs of steam; yet she was warmed by the memory of sledding with Nauman up in Connecticut, and for the first time since dropping him off at La Guardia last Tuesday, she admitted to herself that she missed him and wished he were back in town.

How much more pleasant it would be if she were on her way to meet him rather than facing up to what waited for her at work. She knew she should spend this commuting time on planning—if not for diffusing the tensions bound to arise when knowledge of the special task force leaked out, then certainly for her meeting with Tom Oersted at seven.

Instead, as the bus lurched and swayed from one stop to another, she continued to watch the snow.

Bernie Peters looked up in surprise as Matt Eberstadt entered the squad room shortly before eight.

"I thought you were going to call in sick," he said.

"Yeah, well after what Pam told Frances, I thought I'd better get in here and pull my weight," Matt said testily.

"Huh?"

"Frances says Pam thinks it's my fault you don't have time for the kids." He hung his quilted jacket next to Bernie's and headed for the coffee pot.

"Oh, jeez!" Bernie groaned. "I'm sorry, Matt. I guess I sorta let her think I was working a coupla times when I didn't go straight home."

"Thanks a lot, pal."

"I know, I know, but jeez, Matt, sometimes I hate to walk in the door, you know? The kids are always whining and Pam acts like it's my fault they tire her out. Maybe I shouldn't have let her go back to work. How'd you keep Frances home all these years?"

Matt snorted at the idea of making Frances do anything she didn't want to.

"It was her decision. She sat down and figured it out once and by the time she added everything in—fast food, baby sitters, extra clothes for her, bus fare, kicking us into a higher tax bracket—you know how much she'd have cleared at a nine-to-five job? Forty-four dollars a week. She decided it wasn't worth the aggravation."

"Wish she'd have a talk with Pam for me," said Bernie.

"It's different with the young women today, I guess," Matt said, uncomfortably. Pam Peters was fifteen years younger than Frances, prettier, and probably hell on wheels in bed; but he wouldn't trade a dozen spoiled brats like Pam for one level-headed Frances.

"It'll get better as the kids get older," he told his partner.

"I guess," Bernie said gloomily. "How'd the game go last night? Kenny start?"

"Yeah. Played sixteen minutes and scored four for six with three assists. Tip even got in for two minutes: Oh for two from the field; but he got the front end of a one-and-one, so Frances said they were both pretty excited."

"You didn't go?"

Matt shook his head. "She thought I ought to get straight to bed."

Bernie looked at him critically. "You sound a little better. How do you feel?"

"Okay," said Matt. "Nothing like a good night's sleep."

He promptly yawned.

As they began setting out the day's priorities, the hall door opened and Tillie arrived with a sheaf of computer printouts.

"What're you doing here?" asked Matt. "I thought you weren't supposed to pull shift duty for another month."

"I'm not. This is just some extra stuff the lieutenant needs, so I thought I'd better—"

At that moment, the lieutenant herself entered and promptly disappeared into her office with Tillie.

Matt and Bernie exchanged puzzled glances.

"Wonder what that's about?" said Bernie.

Matt shrugged.

"Thanks for getting this for me so promptly," Sigrid told Tillie, looking over the material he'd rooted out for her.

"No trouble, Lieutenant," he said, though Marian hadn't been all that thrilled that he'd volunteered to cut into their weekend.

As he watched the lieutenant skim through his findings, he realized there was a change in her appearance this morning. Her hair? It'd taken a little getting used to when he came back last month and found that she'd had her dark hair cut short. Till then, she'd worn it long and skinned back in an unbecoming knot at the nape of her neck. Now it feathered lightly around her face, softened it somehow. In fact, now that he considered it, her whole nature seemed softer since his return to duty. Oh, not that she couldn't still freeze like an arctic blast straight off the North Pole if somebody screwed up, but it was as if cutting her hair had cut away some of the stiffness she'd possessed since she took over this job.

Unaware of his scrutiny, Sigrid shook her head and looked up. "More than I thought we'd have, Tillie."

According to Jarvis Vaughn, a Brooklyn nurse said that Cluett, five eleven and overweight, had been met by someone slightly shorter and not as broad.

According to Lowry and Albee, the motorman thought Lotty Fischer's killer was white, of average build, and had stood somewhere between five eight and five ten.

There in the personnel records for their unit which Tillie had pulled, Sigrid was dismayed to see that not only had four of her people been stationed here four years ago, they also fit the physical parameters of the description:

Det. Matthew Eberstadt, 5' 10", 198
Det. Samuel Hentz, 5' 9", 165
Det. Bernard Peters, 5' 8", 170
Det. Dinah Urbanska, 5' 8", 140

The last name surprised her. "I thought Urbanska came from the Nine-Oh."

"She did," said Tillie. "But when she graduated from the Academy, this was her first assignment. She was here seven months before pulling duty in the Nine-Oh."

"I see." She laid her hand on the printouts. "I wish we had copies of those case records," she sighed.

Tillie cleared his throat and his cherubic face took on a slightly guilty glow.

"You didn't!" Her voice was stern but a smile twitched her lips.

Tillie turned even pinker. "I thought if we needed to refer back to something . . ." he started to explain.

"You copied all the files?"

"Just the index sheets," he confessed and went to get them.

"Your performance rating just went from Excellent to Superior," she said as Tillie put the records on her desk. "I don't suppose we can stop speculation. Hentz, Urbanska, Eberstadt, and Peters are going to be under a lot of pressure until it's cleared up."

"Want me to tell them?" he offered.

"Thanks, Tillie, but I'll do it. You go finish your weekend."

Sigrid followed him out into the squad room and when he was gone, walked over to Eberstadt and Peters.

"What's happening, Lieutenant?" asked Matt Eberstadt. Subliminally, he, too, noted a difference in her appearance this morning but had he tried to articulate it, he would merely have said she looked nice in the royal purple jacket she wore over a white turtleneck sweater and black slacks. Most of the time the lieutenant's clothes were as drab as a winter day.

"I'm afraid you two are in for some bother." As concisely as possible, she explained how Lotty Fischer's death linked to Cluett's and how both were going to be handled by a special task force under I.A.D. aegis.

Bernie looked stunned. "They think one of us killed Cluett?"

"That's not what I said. At the moment, lacking any other leads, they'll be looking at everyone who ever worked with Cluett and who was also stationed here in this precinct, however briefly, when Lotty Fischer ran the gun check four years ago."

"That's Matt and me both," said Bernie, starting to bristle.

"It's also Captain McKinnon, Hentz, Urbanska, and several others," she snapped. "Don't get paranoid, Peters. You have plenty of company and when they don't luck out in the first go-round, then I'm sure they'll extend the circle and it'll include even more."

"But they *do* think the perp's a cop," Matt said heavily.

"Not necessarily. There are a lot of civilian possibilities."

"Do Hentz and Urbanska know?" asked Bernie.

"I'll be talking with them when they check in at four. In the meantime," she said as she stood to go, "I want everyone to carry on as normally as possible under the circumstances."

"Yeah, sure," Bernie grumbled when she'd left. "What do you think, Matt?"

"I think I don't want to be here when Hentz gets in." He tossed Bernie his jacket and pulled on his own. "Let's roll."

Down the hall from Sigrid's homicide unit, Sergeant Rawson had commandeered a large room that had been used for other special task forces.

Already a computer and printer, a couple of typewriters, and a copier had been moved in to go with the chairs, tables, and empty file cabinets kept in the room. The clerical aide Rawson had flown in from another precinct sat in her wheelchair before the screen, steadily inputting data gleaned from preliminary reports.

Six detectives sat at the table, four male, two female. Five white, one black.

"We're it?" asked one.

"For now," said Rawson. "If we need another pair, I could probably push for it. On the other hand, it's not like we've got a serial killer or some other high-profile type on the loose. The media haven't made the connection between the two deaths. They're still mauling that poor schmuck of a bus driver, so we don't have them breathing down our necks yet. If we're lucky, maybe we'll wrap it up good and solid before they tumble."

Rawson turned to Jarvis Vaughn. "You have the forensic report on Cluett?"

"Yeah," he said.

Chapter
23

DECTECTIVE SERGEANT JARVIS VAUGHN

Wasn't much of a report. The forensic guys had done their job; not their fault everything came up negative. Powder burns showed that one shot had been fired from behind. Through Cluett's coat. A second from above, through his right temple. No sign that Cluett had fought or struggled, so no tissue under his nails, no bruised knuckles to suggest he'd marked his assailant, no unusual fibers on his clothes, no helpful brand-name shoe tracks through his blood, no stray hairs from the beard of a redheaded man with a limp or whatever the hell a Sherlock Holmes would have discovered.

Ditto with the footbridge, a public place with the usual collection of tossed trash. Every match and cigarette butt, every gum wrapper and hotdog napkin had been bagged and tagged and maybe would link to a suspect if and when we had a suspect. By themselves, they were useless to point us in any direction.

Only the gun was of any help and even that was a question mark. A Browning .380. Standard semiautomatic. According to the company's home office in Utah, that serial number was manufactured twelve years ago, shipped to a wholesaler's in New Jersey and sold at Bwana

Braverman's, a sporting goods store "For Discriminating Sportsmen" in Perth Amboy.

Bwana Braverman's got smiles around the table.

"Yeah," I said. "I called down there yesterday. They still had the purchase record of the individual who bought it. One Douglas Mytster, who says the gun was stolen seven years ago. He thought at first we were calling to say we'd recovered it."

"He for real?" asked the quiet guy from Queens. Eastman.

"Who knows?" I answered. "Off the top, I buy it. We checked with the Perth Amboy police. Mytster said he reported the theft and they did have a record of it. On the other hand, it was listed 'serial number unknown' so it never made it into the computer as a stolen piece. Sometime over the last eight years it walked from Perth Amboy to Sheepshead Bay."

"With a stop-off over here," Yow interjected. Sandy Yow. Reddish brown hair, big hips, and a bigger mouth. Her partner, Kay Obler, had dark hair and a bad overbite and seemed to let Yow do most of the talking for both of them.

"Forensic doesn't say much about the gun itself except that it hadn't been taken care of," I said. "General surface rust with heavy rust buildup on the trigger guard. Barrel was fouled, the clip had a slight dent, and there were only two rounds left in it. In fact, the slide had jammed and that may be why the perp threw it in the bay before he finished emptying it in Cluett's head."

"Any partials on the magazine or cartridges?" asked Rawson.

"One print so smudged that even if we had a full set of the perp's lying beside it, you wouldn't get enough ridge characteristics to take to court. On the other hand, they did find fibers inside the magazine housing and on the clip itself."

"What sort of fibers?"

"Wool. Pure virgin lambswool."

Eastman objected. "You said Forensic thought the

gun had been neglected. That sounds like someone with sheepskin gun wipes.''

He had a point. Most of us use whatever clean soft cloth comes to hand—old cotton T-shirts are good—to oil and lubricate our pieces, but you can spend ten or twelve bucks and buy wipes of natural sheepskin if you're gung-ho enough.

"Unless he had a jacket lined with sheepskin and the piece picked up the fibers that way," the brunette suggested softly.

I didn't think so. "They were saturated with gun oil," I said, "and up inside the magazine."

"Speculation?" asked Rawson.

It had all the earmarks of a throwaway to me and that's what I told him.

Throwaways, drop guns, put-down pieces, whatever you call them, I call them dumb-ass stupid. Okay, so one of a cop's worst nightmares is blowing away an unarmed suspect; our criminal justice system is still based on the premise "What would a reasonable man have done under those circumstances?" You chase a suspect you have reason to believe could have a gun and he makes a move you interpret as putting you or a fellow citizen in deadly jeopardy, then that's a good-faith shooting and the odds are on your side that your actions will be upheld whether or not the suspect actually had a gun.

But try to cover your butt by dropping an untraceable gun near the suspect or sticking it in his cold dead hand, and you're begging for trouble.

Premeditated murder includes malice, forethought, and deliberately altering the crime scene, and every one of those is present with a drop gun. You'd think a professional would give a little forethought to the eighty different ways he'll be linked with that gun once an investigation really heats up, but sometimes cops can be as dumb as John Q. P.

"Doesn't have to be a throwaway," said Eastman. "In fact, with rust and fouling, it sounds more like a civilian's gun to me."

"Me, too," said Roy Flick. He'd been sitting beside

me like a big silent radish. A face as round and red as a radish, too. (High blood pressure?) He quit doodling handguns on his notepad and said, "We all have off-duty or backup guns, right? And don't we clean them every time we clean our duty gun? It's like polishing shoes—you don't do one pair and stop. You do 'em all. Maybe even the wife and kids' shoes, too, while you're at it. I say anybody carrying a throwaway would automatically clean it when he cleaned his other guns. He certainly wouldn't let rust build up on the trigger guard."

"Not a throwaway, but something to scare off burglars? I like it," said Sandy Yow. "A civil service type that got the gun through a friend and didn't want the hassle of registering it. Then he stuck it in a dresser drawer or something till Cluett got in his way."

We kicked it back and forth. Rawson didn't vote, just followed the talk around the table a few minutes, then put on his glasses, opened a new folder, and went over the highlights of the Charlotte Fischer case for the benefit of the four newcomers: how a friend had told the Fischer woman that she'd run a check of the weapon four years ago, how she'd missed her bus and what the trainman saw when he pulled in the station, as well as the possibility that the skell who'd been nesting there had seen it all.

He'd had a memo that T.A.'d spotted the guy a couple of times yesterday, at Grand Central and again at Times Square, but they couldn't grab him.

Rawson peered over his glasses at me. "I want you to take a personal interest in this bird, Sergeant. Keep track of the sightings. They may help us establish his pattern of movement. If he has one."

I nodded and he went on to the forensic report on Fischer.

"Forensic didn't give us much more on Lotty Fischer than they gave Vaughn on Mick Cluett." He skimmed through the highlights of the report. "They just confirm the motorman's statement—it happened too fast for her to struggle. One thing though: she was wearing a fuzzy red coat with distinctive wool and polyester fibers that shed easily. Lab says it's a strong probability that her assailant will have some of those fibers on the clothes he was wearing when he pushed her. On his pants, on his jacket, and certainly on his gloves.''

"Hell," I said. "If the coat sheds that much, those fibers could be all over the building. We could have them on our own clothes by now.''

"Maybe not," said Yow. "January wasn't all that cold. She may not have worn the coat many times this season.'' She glanced at Rawson. "Want me to check it out?''

Rawson nodded, then closed the folder and laid his glasses on top of it. "Forensic will probably nail him down for us once we have a suspect in custody, but it won't help us pick him out of the haystack. The obvious question is how big's our haystack?''

He called across the room to the P.A.A., a tiny gray-haired woman who worked the screen from her electric wheelchair. "Got anything yet, Mrs. Delbridge?''

"It's all very rough, but I can get you started.'' Her husky voice was deep as a man's. Surprising in that little body.

She scrolled long lists of names across her screen, punched at the keyboard, and suddenly the printer sprang into noisy life. As we waited, Delbridge turned her chair around and rolled over to us.

"I've done a global search and pulled the names of everybody assigned here four years ago," she said. "Then I pulled the names of everybody assigned in the same two precincts with Detective Cluett for the past two years—I made it two years because I figured that if Cluett was killed because of a case, it would likely be something still pending.''

This Delbridge was a self-important little hacker who was going to dot every I and cross every damn T. I caught myself drumming my fingers on the armrest of my chair. Been me at this point, I'd have told her to cut to the chase, but Rawson sat back like we had all day.

"Right now, I'm printing up six copies of every name that duplicated," Delbridge said.

"How many names?" Yow and Flick spoke at the same time, so I wasn't the only one getting antsy.

"This is just sworn police personnel. I can't get the rest of the civilian records till tomorrow."

"That's okay, Delly," said Rawson, giving her one of his God-you're-wonderful smiles. "How many names for starters?"

"Fifty-one."

We all perked up at that. For some reason, I'd expected hundreds. Fifty-one was nothing. We could do a quick and dirty on fifty-one in a matter of days.

The printer went silent, Delbridge wheeled over to it, ripped off the pages, then wheeled back to us and passed them around the table. I'd seen several of the names before but not counting one patrol officer from the Six-Four, McKinnon's name was the only one I could put a face to. But then I'd never worked Manhattan.

Right away, Rawson told us to cross off for now the names of six people who'd been newly assigned to the precinct *after* Fischer ran the Browning through her computer. To be safe, Delbridge had bracketed the incident with a six-months' space on either side. Made me want to check the motor on her chair, see if she was carrying a spare battery.

Rawson made a big show of thanking her for her careful thoroughness, but said we'd put on the back burner for now any personnel who'd either retired or been reassigned in the two years before their tours overlapped Cluett's October-to-January stint here. Eleven names.

The sergeant knew that one of the clerks had married one of the patrol officers last Sunday. They weren't due back from their honeymoon in the Caribbean till sometime that afternoon. Two more gone.

"That gets us down to thirty-one," said Flick.

"Thirty-two," Delbridge corrected with prissy disdain.

"Huh? Oh, yeah." Flick's radish face got a little pinker.

•   •   •

For the first rough screening, we agreed a name had to meet the two major criteria: a tour of duty in the Twelfth four years ago when Lotty Fischer ran the gun check, plus either a tour between October and January, when Cluett was here, or else assignment in Sheepshead this past year.

We narrowed the list to twenty-six names and Delbridge started pulling personnel files that had physical data.

The trainman had described the person who pushed Lotty Fischer as apparently Caucasian, average build, and approximately six inches taller than his victim. Since she'd been five three, that meant someone around five nine, give or take an inch.

The nurse, Kitty Jozell, had told Davidowitz and me that the person she'd seen join Cluett appeared slightly shorter and not as stout. Not old either, but that was at night from at least a block away and she couldn't be sure what was physical build and what was bulky winter clothing.

Even so, since Cluett had been five eleven and weighed two-twelve at the time of his death, the two descriptions were roughly similar.

Using the more detailed files Delbridge had procured, we threw out the grossly fat, the short, and the over-six-footers. Rawson knew many of the people currently assigned here by sight and he was able to personally delete three markedly black blacks, one unmistakable Chinese-American, and a property clerk with a noticeable limp.

By midafternoon, the list was down to thirteen names.

Delbridge expected to find at least a dozen civilian employees, and she could probably double it again if she added in casual social workers, various inspectors, and other supervisory types who were in and out several times a year.

But we'd start with those thirteen names. Rawson got on the horn to the desk sergeant downstairs and told him to round up the first few and send them up one at a time.

In the meantime, Sandy Yow had called Fischer's parents and came up with our first piece of luck: The night she died was the first and only time Lotty Fischer had worn her new red coat to work, so those red fibers stood to help us after all.

Chapter 24

█ Now that Field Internal Affairs had taken over the case, Sigrid knew she should leave it alone; yet as long as any of her own people were involved, she couldn't resist taking a precautionary look at the possible nature of that involvement.

Once again Tillie's penchant for detail came in good stead. Sergeant Rawson and his special task force now had physical custody of all files of the cases that Cluett had worked; but while she might not have the reports, thanks to Tillie and his backups for backups, she did have copies of all the index sheets contained in each case folder.

These listed items submitted for evidence, such as photographs, property vouchers, and lab reports. More importantly, they also listed the daily reports turned in by each investigator, so that Sigrid could reconstruct who had worked what and when. She was supposed to be off today, but if she chose to use her own time playing connect-the-dots instead of heading for the pool or working the diagramless crossword puzzle in the Sunday *Times*, it was no one else's business, she told herself, knowing she was rationalizing, knowing I.A.D. would not agree if Sergeant Rawson found out and chose to make an issue of it.

Nevertheless, she worked steadily through the sheets,

pausing here and there as certain memories surfaced between the numbered lines of jargon and abbreviations.

Here was that case back in October where a young dancer had been impaled on an iron fence during a well-attended performance. Cluett had worked that one, along with Eberstadt and Peters, although Albee and Lowry had carried most of the load there. Cluett did manage to nail down one damning bit of evidence and he'd been in at the kill, but it was nothing the rawest rookie couldn't have handled.

The accused was coming up for trial at the end of the month. She knew Cluett had been subpoenaed to testify about that one minor point because Albee had grumbled that he'd kept her on the phone almost an hour trying to refresh his memory of the case from his sketchy notes.

What a poor excuse for a detective the man had been! Sloppy paperwork, bad work habits, always looking to shave a half hour off his shift. A potentially bad influence on the others. Look how his laziness had caused Dinah Urbanska to screw up.

Sigrid knew that everyone thought she'd been too rough on the younger woman, that Cluett should have been given that command discipline, not Urbanska. It was clearly too late for a c.d. to help Cluett straighten up, but Sigrid had hoped that rapping Urbanska's knuckles so sharply at the beginning of her career as a detective might keep her on the straight and narrow, might keep her from taking an older officer's word that it was okay to risk a case just to do someone a minor favor, might teach her that every favor carried a price tag.

It must have seemed like such a little white lie to Urbanska. Cluett had developed indigestion that evening and he'd left her to do the paperwork connected with their shift so he could cut out early. As a result, Urbanska had created an official record to which she'd signed her name that she was the one who'd witnessed the suspect doing something Cluett had told her he'd seen, something really quite minor at the time.

Who could know that the case would eventually hinge on that small point?

But during discovery, when a defense lawyer asks for and is given access to all the written records, that small discrepancy had been noticed and what should have been a watertight case suddenly sprang a leak.

At least Urbanska had sensibly owned up to the lie before it went to trial. Everyone knew at least one horror story where some officer in a similar situation had perjured himself and wound up bounced from the force and serving a suspended sentence.

The perp had walked, of course.

As she read through the index lists, Sigrid couldn't help wondering if Cluett had left them any other little time bombs. That murder at the Erich Breul House, for instance. He'd been the one to search the victim's apartment and had reported finding nothing pertinent; but even though she was confident they'd charged the right person for the murder, she'd occasionally felt there was a piece missing from that particular puzzle.

Matt Eberstadt and Bernie Peters had been in on the Breul House case; and Eberstadt, Peters, and Cluett had also worked the homicide/attempted suicide where a midlevel crack dealer had shot his lover before turning the gun on himself. Unfortunately, he'd dipped into his own stash first, and even though he tried three times, none of his bullets had hit a vital organ.

There'd been blood all over that apartment, on the confetti of money that had littered the floor, on the phone with which he'd called for help, soaked into the bed where they'd found him when his rescuers smashed in the door. The index listed property vouchers for all those small bills: 1,123 ones, 702 fives, 836 tens, 872 twenties, 449 fifties, 53 hundreds.

Sigrid could still see Cluett and Peters sitting at the kitchen table sorting the pile of blood-soaked bills they'd collected into neat, if sticky, stacks. The counting had taken longer than it once would have. Since it wasn't known whether either of the principals had ever been tested for AIDS, Cluett and Peters had pulled on three pairs of rubber gloves before they touched the blood-drenched money and it'd made their fingers clumsy.

Sigrid knew that the crack dealer's trial was due to begin next month. It was such a open-and-shut case that they'd expected an automatic plea bargain. Instead the accused man had decided to waste more taxpayer dollars and to plead self-defense.

Then there was the Negus homicide Cluett and Lowry had worked with Sam Hentz and Dinah Urbanska when Albee was out with the flu immediately after Christmas.

Alfred Negus had returned from a business trip to the luxurious Gramercy Square apartment he shared with his sixteen-month-old daughter Erica and his wife Helene. Negus had found his young daughter, stiff with rigor mortis, floating facedown in their bathtub and no sign of his wife, the owner of a pricey boutique in the Village.

With no sign of a struggle and only the wife's coat and purse missing, the detectives had at first theorized that Helene Negus might have left the baby alone in the bath, returned to find it drowned, and had then fled in panic from a mixture of grief and guilt.

Negus insisted that his wife would never have left their daughter unattended; and while the detectives had heard it all before, they had handled the investigation with care and diligence. Their professionalism paid off when Cluett, Hentz, and Urbanska accompanied Negus to his wife's boutique and discovered her body stashed in one of the dressing rooms. Nearby, they found a gaping hole in the wall and scattered jewelry. (Urbanska had created another legend for klutzy behavior when she trod on a gold and amethyst earring and walked away with it embedded in the crepe sole of her shoe.)

Forensic soon helped them piece it all together. Thieves had gained entrance to the Negus apartment, abducted Mrs. Negus before she could take little Erica from the bath, and had forced her to open up her store. From there, they had proceeded to take sledgehammers and smash their way into the tightly protected jewelry store next door without setting off any of its sophisticated alarms. Even though the owner had prudently locked his most valuable gems in his small vault, the thieves had still walked away with a quarter-million in gold jewelry and lesser gems.

They hadn't meant to kill Mrs. Negus, one of them explained when he was caught pawning his share of the loot the following week; "But she wouldn't shut up about her goddamned brat, so Arnie stuffed a gag in her mouth."

While they filled their shopping bag with expensive jewelry, strewing brooches and earrings underfoot in their haste, Mrs. Negus had suffocated on the gag.

"Arnie" hadn't yet been located, but his partner had immediately pleaded guilty to grand larceny and two counts of involuntary manslaughter and was already serving time.

Lowry and Urbanska had done every line of paperwork on that case. Hentz had been in charge of the investigation and it was the only way he could be certain it'd get done right.

Hentz had grumbled about having to use Cluett the three months he was in the Twelfth, especially after Cluett's slapdash laziness had gotten Dinah in trouble.

Nevertheless, she couldn't see that there was anything here for Sergeant Rawson to fasten on. Surely Cluett's death was rooted in Brooklyn. That's where he lived, where he'd spent the last twenty years of his career.

Unless it was something from even farther back?

She closed the last set of index records and came to the copy of the duplicate file Sergeant Vaughn had given McKinnon on Friday. She'd almost forgotten she had it and Rawson hadn't thought to collect it when he took the original from Vaughn.

Sigrid often deplored the profligate use of copying machines. Even when bureaucracy had been limited by stencils and carbon paper, they had circulated too many irrelevant documents marked "For Your Information." With the arrival of a copier in every office, the bales of paper that flowed across her desk seemed to grow exponentially each year. But occasionally, she had cause to applaud their invention. Without a photocopier, she probably would not be reading such a complete file.

She rapidly scanned the accounts Vaughn and Davidowitz had written of their interviews with Cluett's widow,
the cousin—that "bloat a goat" phrase was one she'd
heard Cluett use about the hundreds and fifties of drug
money they'd confiscated—the next-door neighbor, the
car mechanics, and the regulars at the Shamrock. There
was a summation of Cluett's last few cases and even a
photocopy of the scribbled notes where he'd pestered Albee and Peters, trying to fill in missing gaps before he
had to get up and swear to them in court.

She closed the last folder and swiveled in her chair to
gaze out her window. The exterior glass hadn't been
washed since autumn and a film of gray soot made the
gray day even duller. The powdery snow fell with a steady
hypnotic persistence as Sigrid considered each member
of her unit in the hard cold light of known facts. She still
thought Cluett's killer would prove to be someone connected with the Six-Four in Brooklyn, but there was one
point that had snagged her attention, almost like a small
jagged tear in a fingernail and just as easily smoothed
away if she could put her hands on an emery board.

Unfortunately, this was Sunday. Now who—?

A friend—Anne's friend, actually—came to mind.
Cameron Stewart. Through hard work, a thick skin, re-
lentless optimism, and a genuine talent for making
friends among the secretaries and administrative assis-
tants who keep a system functioning, Cammie Stewart had
risen high in the city's bureaucracy. True, her expertise
lay in the social services, but Sigrid was confident that
Cammie would know some workaholic who could be
called on a Sunday.

She turned back to her desk and looked up the telephone number. Cammie had her answering machine
switched on, but as soon as Sigrid identified herself to the
tape, the older woman's voice cut in. "Sigrid! How ARE
you? WHERE are you? How's Anne?"

When all the who, when, what, where, how questions
subsided, Sigrid told her what she wanted to know. Cammie went silent and Sigrid could almost hear her riffling
through a mental Rolodex.

"I thought maybe a federal clerk?" she suggested.

"On Sunday?" Cammie snorted. "No, best to go right to the source. Now let me think . . . hmm. You going to be there for the next half hour? Okay, say the name again. Spelled like it sounds?"

Sigrid spelled the name.

"And the date?"

"I'm not really sure. Sometime since Christmas anyhow."

"Okay. If it can be done today, I should have an answer for you in an hour. Ninety minutes tops."

After the connection had been broken, Sigrid went back to watching the snow. If she were lucky, Cammie would soon call back and tell her that she had an overactive imagination and that the random dots she'd connected in her mind did not produce a real picture.

The telephone remained silent.

There was work she could be doing, reports to read, assignments to fill. Instead, she fished around in the bowl of puzzle rings on her desk till she found a six-circle chain of silver links that took intense concentration to stack together into a single smooth band.

And still the phone did not ring.

Eventually, a gnawing sensation in her stomach reminded Sigrid that she'd worked through lunch again; and when she realized that she'd been hearing voices in the outer office for the last half hour or so, she gratefully left her silent phone and went out.

Sam Hentz had a stony expression on his face, Urbanska looked apprehensive and Eberstadt and Peters looked guilty.

Instantly she guessed why. "You told them?" she asked curtly.

"Sorry, Lieutenant," said Bernie Peters. "We thought you already had."

She let it pass and turned to the other two. "I shouldn't have to remind you this is just standard routine," she said. "We've all been involved in enough investigations to know that the first canvass always covers everybody tangentially involved. I expect you to carry on with business as usual."

Then the door opened and Sergeant Rawson stepped into the room. His twinkly brown eyes swept over them and he consulted the clipboard he carried. "Which one of you's Eberstadt?" he asked.

Matt Eberstadt stood up warily.

"Wonder if you'd mind stepping down the hall a minute?" Rawson said genially.

And in Sigrid's office, her private telephone line began to ring.

Chapter
25

DETECTIVE SERGEANT JARVIS VAUGHN

Of the people who'd worked with Cluett between October and January, Detective Matthew Eberstadt was our first plainclothes; so when Rawson opened the door and pointed him to my end of the table, the big crowded room got quiet for a split second before everybody went back to what they were doing.

Rawson roamed around like a high school teacher grading on the curve. Eastman was pulling data from the files of cases Cluett had worked. Flick and the two women, Yow and Obler, were spread out around the room busy with the boys and girls in blue. Delbridge went back to playing with her computer. An unlit cigarette dangled from her lips. (Even though she was teacher's pet, Rawson wasn't kidding about smoke-filled rooms and about twice an hour, Delbridge motored down the hall for a cigarette break with Eastman, the only other smoker on the team.)

From the personnel sheet Delbridge had obtained, I knew that Eberstadt lived in Ozone Park, just over the Brooklyn line in the edge of Queens. Forty-five, three kids ranging from sixteen to twenty-one. Height and weight put him just inside the physical description we had of

Fischer's killer, and—most important—he'd been stationed in this house five and a half years.

He took the chair opposite me and folded his arms in front of him on the edge of the table. Probably twenty-five pounds overweight, but he carried it pretty well except for the spare tire and bags under his eyes. One of those long faces and half-bald heads where the hairline goes right back to the top of his head and then curly gray hair the rest of the way. Upfront about knowing Fischer.

"Sweet kid," he said. "A year older than my daughter. Really makes you think. I used to kid around with her when she started working downstairs, the way I'd kid with Margie. She used to turn red every time I teased her about boyfriends. The way Margie did."

"She liked you?" I asked. "Trusted you?"

"I guess."

"Would have done you favors like check out a new neighbor for priors?"

"Sure," he said, and beat me to the punch. "And she'd have run a piece's number through for me, too. If I'd asked. Which I didn't."

"You know I gotta ask you," I said.

"Yeah, I know." He leaned back in his chair. "Tuesday and Wednesday were my regular days off. I was home both nights."

"Your wife and kids can swear to that?"

"Not really." He pushed his chair back so he could cross his legs. "The boys were there, but my daughter moved to Atlanta last weekend and my wife went down to help her. She got back yesterday afternoon."

He gave off odd vibes. I mean, Terry's always leaving those pop psychology books lying around and you can't leaf through too many of them without seeing drawings of how to read body language. The way he sat there, leaning away from me with his arms and legs crossed, this was one Charley with something to hide.

Unless it was only because he'd been a cop long enough to know how wives and kids will lie for the old man? Uptight because it wasn't a stronger alibi?

I moved on to Cluett and we went over the cases

they'd worked together. All routine. No surprises. If Cluett and Eberstadt'd had any run-ins, if Cluett and *any*body'd had run-ins, Eberstadt hadn't heard about it.

Or so he said.

Oh, well, hell, I guess I'd be the same if some dude started tossing my unit.

I thanked him nicely and asked him to send in his partner.

Detective Bernie Peters. Twenty-eight. Body of a guy meant to be six foot, short legs kept him at five eight. Good build, but no bronze Adonis. Love handles and what was going to be a thick middle in another five years if he didn't watch the doughnuts and french fries.

We got the alibi or, in his case, the non-alibi out of the way at the start.

"Wish I could say I was out dancing at the V.F.W., Sarge, but I was home both nights with only my wife and kids to vouch for me."

Just like Eberstadt except that the Peters kids were too young to tell time, much less know the days of the week. Woodhaven was only a few minutes farther from Sheepshead Bay than Ozone Park.

I moved on to the murdered girl.

"Yeah, I knew Lotty Fischer," he said. "I hadn't given it much thought, but Matt Eberstadt reminded me that we came about the same time. She was always friendly, always had a good word."

He sat at ease. Legs apart. One hand on the table, the other on his lap.

"She ever do you any favors?"

"Favors? Like with the computer?"

I nodded.

"You mean the gun," he said flatly. "Not that. But she did run a check for priors on an old guy that clipped my car a couple of years back. He wanted to pay for my repairs out of his own pocket so it wouldn't go through his insurance company. Turned out he had enough moving violations that DMV probably would have pulled his license if I'd reported him. At his age he might not've got it back."

I grinned. "Guess you got a couple of extra dents ironed out while you were at it?"

He gave a sheepish shrug. "He could afford it."

"So what it boils down to is that you and Fischer were pretty tight?"

"No, not really. Just friendly. You know: 'How ya doing? How's it going?' Like with most of the P.A.A.'s. Nice bunch, most of 'em."

He didn't really want to bad-mouth Cluett or any of his colleagues, but he did mention how Cluett seemed to get on the looey's nerves.

"In fact," he said, as if he'd just noticed it, "he seemed to rub most women the wrong way. Not just the lieutenant, but Urbanska when she got the command discipline. And Albee, too. Especially since he went back to Brooklyn."

"Command discipline?"

"Oh, jeez." He looked unhappy with himself for letting that slip out. "Maybe you'd better ask Urbanska. I don't know all the details."

"Yeah, sure, you don't," I said, but let it ride. "What about the other one? Albee? How'd he bug her from Brooklyn?"

"One of their cases is going to court soon and he was on the phone a half a dozen times trying to fill in the blanks in his notepad. Same thing with one of our cases. Jeez, you'd think a guy that worried about getting in the burn box would've taken better notes to start with."

Tell me about it, I thought. Cluett hated court because any halfway sharp lawyer could make him look like a jackass, flipping back and forth in his notes, looking for stuff he hadn't bothered writing down like he should've at the scene of the crime.

"But you got along with him okay?"

"Sure. He was easy to get along with. You just told yourself that when you were paired with Cluett, you had an empty suit on the job with you. Long as you did all the work, no problem.''

A smartass, but he sure had Cluett pegged.

Detective Dinah Urbanska. Looking at those sturdy muscular calves and thighs inside dark blue slacks, you figured she had to've played field hockey in high school or been a lifeguard out at one of the beaches. Klutzy though. She banged the table leg pulling up her chair, then dropped her pencil on the floor and almost knocked over the table trying to get it. If she was the one pushed Fischer, she could probably claim it was an accident. Don't know about a jury, but *I'd* buy it. Five eight, golden brown hair pulled up in a fat knot on the top of her head, golden skin, smooth and elastic. Yeah, she fit the physical type we were looking for all right. Worse, no alibi.

"We worked the day shift on Tuesday and Wednesday," she said, which meant she was off-duty during the relevant hours.

She'd caught an early movie with a friend Tuesday evening, then headed home to Brooklyn alone around nine. She *said* she'd taken the R train at Eighth Street for Borough Hall, but there was no way to prove she hadn't changed at Canal or DeKalb for the D train to Sheepshead Bay. I made a note to check whether there'd been any unusual delays on the D train that night.

The bartender at the Shamrock had thought Cluett expected to meet somebody before ten. If Urbanska'd been with a friend till nine, the subway was the only way she could've made it to Sheepshead Bay with time to hang around waiting for him. Even a cab would've been cutting it too close.

Wednesday night?

"I stayed in and watched television," she said stonily.

No roommates, no doorman, no way to prove she did.

Or didn't.

She admitted she'd been angry when Cluett led her

PAST IMPERFECT   201

into screwing up. The command discipline had cost her
three days' vacation time plus going down in her record.
"Lieutenant Harald was right, though. I knew it was
wrong when I did it and I didn't think ahead. The perp
walked because I let myself be used to cover Cluett's ass."

Unlike Eberstadt and Peters, Urbanska claimed she
never met Lotty Fischer the first time she worked the precinct.

According to the records, she came in one short
month before Fischer did her thing with the computer.
Interesting. Fischer would have been eighteen, Urbanska
twenty-one. She wouldn't have been the first rookie that
thought she needed insurance in case she panicked and
pulled her piece at the wrong time.

"Two young women, both new to the job, and you're
gonna tell me you never talked?" I asked.

She looked me straight in the eye. "You talk to every
middle-aged black officer you come across?"

That hurt. Since when's thirty-seven middle age?

Detective Samuel Hentz. Trim and dapper in a pin-
stripe shirt and a sharp charcoal suit. Dark hair with a
touch of gray at the temples. Dinah Urbanska's *middle-
aged* partner. Forty. Divorced, no kids. Upper West Side
address. Five nine, one sixty-five. Like Urbanska, a possible fit with the physical description we had.

Admitted knowing Lotty Fischer, but claimed their
dealings had been strictly professional and that he'd
never asked for or gotten special electronic favors.

Contempt for Cluett's unprofessionalism. Didn't say
it, but I read contempt for me, too, maybe because I'm
black, maybe because I didn't get rid of Cluett as soon as I
hit the Six-Four. Hard to tell. One uptight dude.

No alibi for either night.

As we finished the interview, the telephone rang
across the room and Yow called over to me, "A patrol unit
spotted the Canary in Union Square, but he ran as soon
as they got out of the car."

"That your witness?" asked Hentz.

I didn't answer and he gave a sour laugh. "Oh, right. I keep forgetting I'm a suspect now."

While I'd interviewed the plain brown wrappers, the others had tentatively cleared five or six blue bags who claimed to have checkable alibis.

I added Eberstadt and Peters's wives to their follow-up checklist.

"What about Captain McKinnon?" I asked Rawson. "You want to interview him or me?"

"I'd better do it," he groaned.

Chapter 26

Located around the corner and half a block down from her office, the Urban Renewal Society was not as private as Sigrid might have wished, but snow was beginning to pile up; and as her boots crunched through the white ankle-deep powder, she was glad Tom Oersted had suggested they meet there. He hadn't called to cancel, so she assumed their meeting was still on.

On this snowy Sunday evening, the crowds seemed thinner. She recognized several faces scattered through the dim smoke-filled bar, but none that obligated her to anything beyond a nod as she crossed the main room to a side booth out of the flow of traffic yet in view of the door. An unfamiliar version of *Mood Indigo* was playing in the background. Sultry, but uninsistent.

No sooner had she slipped off her coat and ordered a drink than she saw a tall flaxen-haired man of late middle age enter and scan the room. When his eyes met hers, he immediately came over.

"Mr. Oersted?"

She half rose.

"No, don't get up." He took off his heavy camel hair overcoat and hung it on a hook beside their booth. Beneath the coat was a turtleneck sweater that looked like an expensive import, handknit in shades of blue and green. He stuffed gloves and scarf into the coat pockets and spoke of the blustery snowstorm, but all the while his clear blue eyes examined her with candid curiosity.

"Damn! Little Siga. All grown up and as beautiful as Anne."

Sigrid's royal purple jacket was one of the colors on Berthelot's "Eastern Winter" chart, and she had taken pains with her makeup before leaving the women's locker-room. Somehow it had seemed important, as if making a good impression on Oersted would honor her father's memory. Nevertheless, even though she knew she looked rather nice for her, that was still nowhere near her mother's level. Blatant flattery usually offended her but he probably meant well, and she was willing to concede that the years might have dimmed his memory of Anne as effectively as they had dimmed Anne's of him.

He slid into the other side of the booth. "I didn't expect to see so much of Leif in you. You're dark like Anne, but Lord, Lord! Your eyes are exactly like his. Bet you're tall, too?"

"Yes."

The waiter returned with her drink and while Oersted detailed precisely how much splash he wanted in his scotch, Sigrid studied his face.

She knew he was sixty-one and that he'd gone through the Academy with her father and McKinnon. Time had honed away the soft planes of youth and left him with deep creases beside his eyes and around a mouth that smiled easily. He was very much as she imagined Leif would be had he lived: tall, yellow hair half faded to white; still flat-bellied though, still handsome. The last Viking raid was a thousand years in the past, yet something genetic in his careless sprawl, in the reckless thrust of his jaw, recalled those seagoing marauders.

He patted his pockets and drew out a crumpled pack of cigarettes and a disposable lighter. "Smoke?"

Sigrid shook her head.

"Mind if I do?"

"No." She disliked the smell of cigarette smoke on

PAST IMPERFECT 205

her clothes and in her hair, but it was one of the givens of police work and unless the air around her was blue enough to set off smoke alarms, she tried not to let it bother her.

Tom Oersted inhaled deeply, then looked around the tavern with evident enjoyment. "This place takes me back. There's at least one cop bar in every precinct, isn't there? And Leif and I must have hit every single one of them in our day."

"Really?" That surprised her somehow. Even though she knew her father had been friendly and outgoing, no one had ever described him as a barfly.

Oersted's scotch arrived. He tasted it and gave the waiter a thumbs-up sign of approval before turning back to Sigrid. "How's Anne?" he asked. "Still living in New York or did she go back to—where was it? Georgia? Virginia?"

"North Carolina. No, she travels a lot, but New York's still her home base. She's a free-lance photojournalist."

"That's right. I remember Leif talking about her studying photography." He moved the ashtray so his smoke wouldn't hit her. "She never remarried then?"

"No." This man was supposed to be Leif's close friend, yet it sounded as if he'd barely known Anne. So many questions ran through her head. "I mentioned your name to her."

"And she didn't remember me?" He crushed the butt in the large glass ashtray. "Shouldn't surprise you. Your mother was a nice girl and I was one of the big bad wolves."

"What does that mean?"

"You married?"

Sigrid shook her head.

"Doesn't matter. Maybe it doesn't happen with women, but you must have seen it with some of your male colleagues. There's the groupies." He gestured toward the main bar with his glass of scotch.

Sigrid didn't bother to turn and look. She knew that places like this attracted unattached women who liked to hang out with cops and listen to them talk shop, women who found it erotic to rub against a man wearing a gun. Even the terminology was sexual. His weapon. His piece. Hard iron. *Is that your gun, big guy, or are you just glad to see me?*

"Groupies are fun to play with, but you don't marry them, or have kids with them," Oersted continued. "For that you want a nice girl, someone from the neighborhood or parish, someone who wouldn't be caught dead in a cop bar unless she's with you, only you'd never bring her here where the other guys might open her eyes. Instead you marry her and try to keep your marriage in a separate compartment. It's like you make this agreement: you don't tell about the slime you walked through your last tour and she doesn't ask what truck the goodies fell off of. You talk about the kids, the house, what's on television, everything except the job."

Sigrid thought of Tillie and Marian, of Bernie Peters and his wife Pam, whom she'd never met. She'd heard both men speak of shielding their wives and children from some of the realities of the job. Hentz was divorced, like a dozen others she could name, marriages down the drain. McKinnon had never married. Only Matt Eberstadt sounded as if he and his Frances treated each other like adults.

"You're not married either?" she asked.

"Now I am. Then, I went through two wives in a hurry because I couldn't leave it at the station house like Leif could. Mac was the only one he could trust to leave it behind, too. Or some old hairbag like Cluett. I guess I was too wild. I remember you, though."

"You do?"

"I drove him home a few times when Anne was in class and he had to pick you up at the baby-sitter's. Rosie Bloomgardner. I never forgot that silly name." He smiled as he lit another cigarette. "Remember her?"

Sigrid tried, but nothing came.

"Well, you were just a baby then. And now you're a lieutenant already. Too bad you aren't black, too. You'd probably be a captain or a deputy inspector by now." He caught the waiter's eye and signaled for another scotch. "You ready?" he asked Sigrid.

Her glass was still half-full and she shook her head, tight-lipped, her hands clenched into fists beneath the table.

She didn't know which grated more, the casualness of his racist and sexist remark or the easy assumption that she shared that view. She told herself he was a dinosaur from another age, that she wouldn't change him by exploding, that she was here to learn whatever this man could tell her about her father. If she got up now and walked away from the table in anger, she knew she'd soon be asking herself if she'd left because Tom Oersted was a bigot who said no more than she'd heard a thousand times since her promotion or if it were because she really didn't want to know. She had loved her father. Everyone in the family said he'd possessed an easygoing tolerance and a knack for friendship. Why not accept that Leif had liked Oersted for reasons that had nothing to do with the man's values and attitudes?

"Is that why Mother didn't know your name? Because Dad kept everything compartmentalized?"

"Look," said Oersted. "You said on the phone you wanted to know about him. You want the truth?"

At that moment Sigrid quit trying to like him for her father's sake. "That's a loaded question, isn't it?" she asked coldly. "Obviously the only answer is yes, but it implies that the truth will hurt."

He laughed. "Ask your questions. I'll answer anything I know for sure, but not things I don't know."

"Again, that implies there are things you suspect. Bad things?"

He shrugged. "What's bad to you?"

She had to know the worst. "Was he dishonest? On the take?"

"No, nothing like that," said Oersted. Smoke curled from his nose. "Actually, he was a damn good cop. Foolhardy at times, the way he'd go wading in to break up a street fight or a barroom brawl, or worse, get between a husband and wife when one had a knife and the other a baseball bat. And smart, too. He and Mac could see patterns, make connections better than anybody I ever saw. Look how quick they got the gold shields. Took me eight years.''

"Were you ever partners?''

"Not after he made plainclothes. Before that, yeah, we pulled tours together. After, it was him and Mac all the way.'' He said it nonchalantly, but Sigrid sensed an undertone of remembered jealousy.

"Did they work as well together?''

"Better. They really were a good match.'' Oersted said it slowly, as if looking back from such a long distance were giving him new perspective. "Like pencil and paper, you know? Better together than separately. One brought out the strengths of the other.'' He gave an ironic chuckle. "Leif and I brought out each other's worst and we both knew it.''

"How?'' A burst of laughter from the bar floated above the bluesy music. Sigrid glanced over and saw a voluptuous redhead flirting with three guys from Narcotics. "Was he cheating on my mother?''

Oersted seemed amused by the chaste term. "Is the Pope Catholic?''

Sigrid suddenly felt as if she'd been kicked in the stomach.

"Hey, you really didn't know, did you?'' asked Oersted. His voice seemed to come from a long way off.

Sigrid finished her drink in two gulps and looked around for the waiter. "No.''

"I'd have thought Anne or Mac would've told you by now, especially since—but then, that's right: they didn't marry, did they?''

"What?'' The room seemed to tilt and Sigrid sat very still until it righted itself again.

"What the hell,'' said Oersted.

As he finished his own drink, Sigrid suddenly realized that he knew she found him distasteful.

"Mac told me not to tell you anything except what I knew for a fact.'' There was deliberate and satisfied malice in the glint of his eye and the curl of his lip. "This is a fact, Lieutenant: when Leif bought it, word got around that Mac had set him up so he could have Anne."

He stood up and threw some bills on the table to cover their drinks. "But they never married, so I guess it was just an ugly rumor, right?"

Chapter 27

■ ■ Once when she was eight years old and spending the summer on her grandparents' farm while Anne was on an assignment in Europe, Sigrid had run barefooted onto a clump of hard dry sandspurs. It was not the first time her soft city feet had encountered those vicious spiked burrs but this was the worst. Not one, but at least a dozen pierced the soles of her feet like tiny needles; and as she drew back from the clump, walking on her heels so as not to press them deeper, the first sharp awareness of pain gave way to anxiety over the pain to come. Each sandspur had six or eight points, each point was barbed like a tiny fishhook; and as much as they hurt going in, they hurt even worse coming out. She hobbled over to a safe patch of grass under a tree and lay down on her back to stare up into the tree, losing herself among the thousand leaves and twigs, concentrating on leaves and clouds that seemed to float on the surface of a sky as blue and limpid as a gulf reef. Her feet no longer hurt and so long as she did not touch the sandspurs, they wouldn't. She floated like a leaf on limitless blue sky, suspended between pain for almost an hour, until at last—

"Hey, Lieutenant! You okay?"

Abruptly, clouds and trees disappeared and her

senses were assaulted with the smell of cigarette smoke, toasted barley and hot pastrami, the sound of Benny Goodman's solo clarinet, and the sight of Sergeant Jarvis Vaughn's chocolate brown eyes looking down at her. Sigrid pulled herself back to the present.

"I—I— Yes, I'm fine," she stammered. But she still felt slightly disoriented, as if she should be brushing grass and leaves off the back of T-shirt and shorts instead of gesturing for Vaughn to sit down and join her in this now-crowded tavern.

"You sure?" He pushed aside the money Oersted had left on the table and set down the glass and sandwich plate he'd brought over from the bar. After another long look at her pale face, he signaled for the waiter. "Buy you another drink, Lieutenant? You look like you could use it."

"Actually," said Sigrid, "I think what I could use is some food."

"Take half of mine," Vaughn said. "It's more than I want."

In truth, sandwiches at the Urban Renewal Society were gargantuan and Sigrid felt no compunction in accepting his offer. She bit into the warm meat and savored the tang of spicy mustard against her tongue. "Just a large glass of ice water," she told the waiter.

Vaughn put some of his potato chips on the napkin she was using for a plate. "If you want to talk, I'm a pretty good listener."

Sigrid smiled. "I bet you are. No, I'm okay now. Really. You through for the day?"

"Not quite. I have a few more things to read through."

"Who'd Rawson pick for the task force?" she asked, taking another bite of the sandwich.

Vaughn gave names and postings. Sigrid had met Henry Eastman and Sandy Yow in passing, but knew none of them personally, although she'd heard of everyone. "Did you make much progress today?"

"Now, Lieutenant, you know I can't talk specifics."

"No?" She ate a salty potato chip and looked at him shrewdly. "Then why are you sitting here at this table?"

His thin brown face relaxed in laughter. "They said you were a pistol."

As he finished his half of the pastrami sandwich, he crumpled his napkin on the plate and said, "This is when I really miss cigarettes. After a meal. Relaxes everybody. Gives you something to do with your hands and eyes."

"Lets you segue into a grilling before the other person knows what's happening?" Sigrid asked sardonically.

"You got it."

"I don't like taking my unit apart person by person," she told him. "They're good officers, not—"

"Even good officers fall. You know that."

"So I'm learning." Her eyes darkened in private thought, then she shook her head impatiently. "Of course I know it. I've been on the job long enough to know it's no Sunday School choir. They know it, too. That's why it could tear us apart. So don't you ask me to start theorizing and pointing the finger at any of my people till you've cleared every civilian and uniform here in the Twelfth and at the Six-Four and even then—" She took a long steadying swallow of her ice water.

Vaughn put his elbow on the table, propped his chin on his fist and his voice was almost gentle. "It's that strong a suspicion, huh?"

She looked at him mutely and her gray eyes were sad.

He leaned across the table as if to drag it from her. "If we found the Canary tomorrow, who would you nominate for the lineup, Lieutenant?"

In the warm smoky room, her chilled glass left wet rings on the shiny pine tabletop and she moved it to form a design of interlocking circles.

"When you were a child, Sergeant, did you ever step on a sandspur with your bare foot?"

His sense of urgency suddenly diffused by what he read in her eyes, Jarvis Vaughn sat back with legs outstretched, ankles crossed, hands clasped behind his head.

"As a matter of fact, I did," he said, "only we called 'em stickers." Now that there was all the time in the world, now that he knew she would be telling him, he spoke of his granny's truck farm down on the Jersey coast, of her sweet-smelling flowers and sweet-tasting corn and luscious vine-ripened tomatoes and the treachery of New Jersey stickers.

Sigrid described the summer she was eight and then she took a deep breath as she had all those years ago. This was going to hurt worse than pulling sandspurs from her bare foot. A hell of a lot worse. But she had done it without flinching back then and she would do it now.

In a stoic's monotone, she told him what she'd suspected after reading his Brooklyn interviews and his summation of Cluett's last notes. She also told him about the wild-goose chase on which she'd sent Cameron Stewart.

"She knows someone in the main division down at the World Trade Center and he ran the name through all their computer banks without any luck, but we'll have to wait till tomorrow to query IRS."

The snitch was one of the regulars. A coward, but a braggart, too. Especially when it was as safe as this. Besides, what could a goddamned bird imitator do to him?

He fed a quarter into the phone and a few minutes later, he was saying, "Word's on the street that you guys wanna talk to Jerry the Canary. I know where he's roosting tonight. You interested? I ain't saying over the phone. I gotta have some money tonight. Meet me at the usual place."

Chapter
28

Sigrid and Jarvis Vaughn walked back through the snow together to the precinct house. Neither detective made friends easily, but sharing a pastrami sandwich and childhood memories seemed to have bridged the usual reserve.

Irrational, thought Sigrid, yet she did feel she could trust Vaughn in a way she couldn't trust Sergeant Rawson. As they parted at the elevator, he promised not to say anything to Rawson and she said she'd let him know as soon as she learned anything the next day.

The squad room was empty. Eberstadt and Peters had finished their shift before five o'clock, and Hentz and Urbanska must be out questioning witnesses or running down leads. She pulled off her heavy coat and laid it over the back of a nearby chair.

The door to her office was cracked and although she'd switched everything off when she left to meet Oersted, the green glass shade of her brass desk lamp cast a pool of light across her papers. She pushed open the door and saw Captain McKinnon standing in the shadows by the window.

Oersted's slimy insinuations had been temporarily displaced by her session with Vaughn; but at the sight of

McKinnon, they suddenly flooded back into her mind in all their ugliness.

She started to flip on the fluorescent light overhead, then let her hand drop. "Captain?"

He turned and she saw that he held the silver-framed picture of Leif Harald in his blue winter uniform. At her voice, McKinnon glanced again at the youthful face of his dead partner, then put the picture back where he'd gotten it and moved away so that she could take her usual place behind the desk.

"Tom Oersted called me yesterday," he said, sitting heavily in the other chair. The lamplight softened his rugged features, but his words came harshly.

"I know." Dreading this emotional confrontation, yet trying not to let herself be paralyzed by it, Sigrid dipped into the little pottery bowl beside the picture and began to manipulate the linked circles of the first puzzle ring her fingers touched. "He said you warned him not to tell me anything he didn't know for a fact."

When McKinnon didn't speak, she lifted her eyes from the ring to his face. "Did you set my father up to be killed?"

His face was impassive. "Is that what Oersted said?"

"He said those were the rumors at the time."

"They were lies," McKinnon said flatly.

"Was it a lie that he slept with other women?"

McKinnon shifted in the chair. "Lieutenant—"

"Was it?" she asked coldly.

"No."

"Or that you and Mother—"

The puzzle ring was clenched so tightly in her hand that the delicate circles were bent into twisted ovals and left their imprint on her palm. She heard McKinnon let out a deep breath and realized that he was as tense as she. She also realized that he was not denying it.

"Did Oersted make it sound shabby and sordid?"

Sigrid shrugged. "You mean it wasn't? She was your partner's wife and you went after her. Then you set my father up so you could have her, only Mother didn't fall into your arms afterwards."

"That's not—"

"She might make love with her husband's partner," Sigrid interrupted bitterly, "but she wouldn't marry his murderer."

"Damn it, that's not the way it was!" His fist slammed down so heavily on her desk that Leif Harald's picture fell forward onto her metal stapler and the glass shattered.

Appalled, McKinnon grabbed for it; and as he tried to set it upright, one of the shards of glass sliced the meaty pad of his right thumb. Instantly, bright red blood dripped onto the picture.

"I'm sorry," he said. "God, I'm sorry."

Rattled, Sigrid dropped the silver rings and pushed a box of tissues toward him. "Put pressure on it," she ordered and rummaged in her desk for the first-aid kit she kept there. She found a small bottle of alcohol as well and, ignoring McKinnon's protests, sloshed it over his thumb, then drew the cut edges together with a wide Band-aid. A second and third Band-aid secured the first.

"I don't think it'll need stitches," she said. "Fingers always bleed a lot."

They looked down at the picture and saw that his crimson blood had seeped into the cracked glass and stained Leif Harald's face and chest. The glass could be replaced but the photograph was ruined; and even though Anne now had a negative, Sigrid knew she would never ask her mother to make another copy.

McKinnon gave a weary sigh and sat back down. For the first time, he looked his full age.

"We should have talked months ago, but I was afraid you'd put in for a transfer if you knew; and frankly I wanted you here. After all these years, I thought if we ran into each other casually, Anne and me, maybe we could put things back together, be friends again if nothing else."

As he spoke Sigrid began to remove the bits of broken glass from her desktop to her wastebasket, piece by individual piece.

"It finally happened last October," said McKinnon. "In your hospital room. Only she wouldn't talk to me.

That's why I specialed in poor old Mickey Cluett. Stupid thing to do, but I knew he could be a motor mouth at times and I thought if he tumbled to who you were and started telling you some of the old tales, the good ones—"

He stood up and began to pace back and forth in the confined space.

"When your dad and I got out of the Academy, Mickey Cluett had charge of the rookies. He broke us in on patrol, showed us the ropes, and he was around after we got our gold shields, too. He liked Leif and he was crazy about Anne and her Southern accent. He was there the night they met. She ever tell you about it?"

"Dad thought she and another guy were robbing someone's car at one o'clock in the morning and he threatened to arrest them," said Sigrid.

"Yeah. Somebody from her photography class. They'd gotten back late from a trip up the Hudson and when the guy went to get her cameras out of the trunk, he accidentally closed the lid on his keys. For some reason, Anne thought she could pop the lock. By the time Mickey and Leif rolled up, all they'd done was dent the lid good; but Leif said they looked guilty as hell in the headlights."

An overlooked shard of glass twinkled on the desk top as she watched him pace, and she delicately transferred it to the wastebasket.

"He was always such a talker, Mickey. I was sure he'd tell you—"

"He tried," Sigrid said. "I never let him."

She tilted her head back and forth, but no more glass could be seen. "What would he have told me about Dad's death?"

"Leif and I'd been working the murder of a showgirl with mob connections. Mary-Ell Wright. At first we thought it had something to do with kickbacks the club owner was paying to one of the bosses and Mary-Ell got in the middle. Then we realized it was sexual. Pure and simple jealousy. One of the small-time mugs. Gianni Gold. Little short guy, a bagman for Benny DelVecchio. We knew him. Leif did, anyhow. He ran, we put out the word on the street, and someone fingered him. The Ambassador Hotel, one of those flop shops off Lexington these days and pretty ratty even back then.''

He looked down at the bandage on his thumb. The gauze pad showed a blur of red, but the bleeding seemed to have stopped. There was a straight-back wooden chair next to the bookcase. McKinnon pulled it out and straddled the seat, resting his arms on the back.

''Mickey was still riding patrol and he drove us over. I wanted more backup, but Leif just laughed at me and said Gianni Gold was a little mouse who'd come squeaking out of his hole as soon as he knew we were there. Mickey was all the backup we needed, he said.

''We left him watching the front and went in. The desk clerk gave us the room number but he must have called up, because as soon as Leif banged on the door and said, 'Police,' Gianni put three slugs through it. If we hadn't been standing off to the side, we'd have bought it right then and there. For some reason, Leif thought that was funny as hell. He started laughing and yelling, 'Hey, come on, Gianni! It's me, Harald.' We could hear the guy whimpering, like a little kid, and Leif kicked the door open and told Gianni to come on out.

''He was still whimpering and whining, 'Don't shoot! Don't shoot!' and we saw him come out from behind the dresser with the gun in his hand almost dragging on the floor. He wasn't much taller than the dresser and I guess it struck Leif funny 'cause he put his gun away. He just couldn't take the poor little schnook seriously.

''There was Gianni looking like a kid on his way to a licking and there stood Leif, grinning, with his hand out for the gun, and he said, 'What the hell you doing playing with guns, Gianni?' And Gianni seemed to go off his nut. Maybe it was because Leif was so tall and good-looking, like the guys Mary-Ell always went for; or maybe it was because Leif didn't give him any respect at all. Who knows? Anyhow, Gianni got red in the face and said, 'Don't laugh at me! Nobody's ever gonna laugh at me again!' and then he jerked the gun up and shot twice more just as Mickey came barreling down the hall. I got off two shots, too, but it was too late to save Leif."

For a moment, McKinnon sat with his shoulders slumped, his face buried on his arms.

"You froze?" Sigrid asked.

McKinnon straightened. "I didn't freeze. Leif was in the line and it took me too long to get clear."

"No subconscious wish fulfillment?"

"I didn't want him dead," he said evenly. "It wasn't the dark ages. Even well-bred Southern women got divorced then."

"Except that Mother still loved him."

"Yeah." His voice rasped with remembered grief. "God help us, we both did."

For some time after McKinnon stood up and walked out of her office, Sigrid sat looking at her father's picture, ruined by McKinnon's blood.

She thought about Anne, all those years of moving every few months. Had she been running away from guilt or was it her way of dealing with the loss of love?

Which love?

Sigrid reached for the phone, then jumped as it went off beneath her hand.

Automatically, she answered, "Detective unit. Lieutenant Harald."

The conversation was short and terse and a minute later, she had grabbed up her coat and was hurrying down the hall to the special operations room that the task force had taken over.

Jarvis Vaughn was the only one still there and he had just turned off the lights as she arrived, buttoning her coat and drawing on gloves. "What's up?"

"One of our informants just called. Our witness has a room at the Hotel Paradiso."

"Jerry the Canary?"

Sigrid nodded. "Want to come with me to pick him up?"

"Hey, wait a minute!" he said. "This is my case, re-member? You can come with *me*."

She glared at him hotly and then whirled away down the hall. "Are you going to stand there arguing prece-dence till he flies the coop again?

Chapter
29

DETECTIVE SERGEANT JARVIS VAUGHN

Harald had a point, but damn it all, Rawson had made the Canary *my* responsibility and techni-cally, she had no business doing anything more than pass-ing the info on to me. She kept on walking.

I followed her into the elevator and said, "You're out of line here, Lieutenant. You may outrank me, but—"

"That's right," she said. "I do." And she smiled.

Changed her whole face when she smiled like that. I've always been a pushover for sassy women.

"Okay," I said, "but I'm driving."

The car we drew had chains on it and we clanked up Third Avenue in the snow while she fiddled with the heater. It wasn't far. No need to haul out the portable blue light and stick it on the roof to expedite.

I'd spent the last half hour charting places this bird'd been sighted. Most of them were strung out along the IRT midtown stations on both the East and West Side lines. If he'd paid for a cheap hotel room, I was pretty sure he'd still be there unless Harald's snitch had spooked him.

The Hotel Paradiso was located between Third and Lex. Old and shabby, but looked like it was still struggling for respectability. Still had a faded awning over the door. Probably half welfare, half SRO. Even on this raw night, six or eight kids were huddled outside in the low stairwell, rapping.

As we passed on the opposite side of the street, Harald suddenly twisted around in her seat to get a better look at the entrance.

"What?" I eased into a place half a block down, in front of a hydrant.

"Probably my imagination," she muttered. "I didn't see the face, but the build, that walk—"

She was out of the car and running back down the snowy sidewalk before I cut the engine.

I jumped out and raced after her. As she angled across the street, dodging between cars, her heel caught an icy patch and she went down. A cab swerved in front of another car and missed her by inches. I sprinted over, hauled her to her feet and got her up on the sidewalk where she grabbed at a lamppost for support.

"You okay?"

"It's fine," she gasped, brushing snow and dirt from her trouser legs. "Really. Only a twist. Let's go."

She put her full weight on it and took off toward the entrance of the Paradiso, but I saw that she favored that ankle.

The kids out front looked us over as we threaded our way through them into a narrow shabby lobby. The walls had most of their marble slabs intact but the floor was worn linoleum and the sheetrock ceilings were stained with water marks. Directly opposite two elevators, the desk was barred and fortified with glass and metal bars like an old-fashioned bank window.

We didn't have to show our gold. The blood behind the bars made us for cops right away.

"Hey, what's shaking?" he asked when I told him we wanted Jerry Byrd's room number. "The Canary rob a bank or something? Another cop just went up."

Harald immediately leaned on the elevator buttons. The cages were the kind with a brass arrow over each door that told you what floor it was on. One arrow was at five, the other at ten. Neither budged.

"What number?" I yelled, heading for the door to the stairs.

"Five fifty-six," he yelled back. He had the house phone in his hand. Made me hope he'd warned the Canary. "When you get there, keep going left. Fifty-six is almost behind the elevator and kinda hard to find."

I slammed through the doorway and Harald followed. More kids were sitting at the top of the first flight and they scattered like Granny's chickens as we pounded up the stairs. Neither of us had our guns out yet, but these kids had enough smarts to dive for cover. The air was thick with pot and tobacco smoke, and graffiti covered the walls. Once past ground level, the stairwell was open to the elevator landings all the way up to the top. I leaned over the railing and looked up. There was a big central skylight in the roof, black now, with light bulbs around the edge, half of them broken or burned out. Made me dizzy just to look up, all those steps and railings looping back and forth, in and out of shadows. We passed the second floor. Somewhere a baby cried, and I could hear the kids scurrying around below us, foul-mouthed and excited.

Our running footsteps rolled off the walls like we were in an echo chamber. A ten-story megaphone.

"Police!" I shouted in case the other cop was in hearing distance, in case he was legit or had a twitchy finger. "Everybody stay inside!" My voice bounced off the skylight and we heard doors slam.

I rounded the fifth-floor landing and Harald was still with me. Up above came more running steps, then suddenly the goddamnedest racket filled the stairwell. Woody Woodpecker's zany cries burst upon us like automatic-rifle fire. "Eh-eh-eh-EH-oh!"

"Jerry!" Harald yelled. "Police officers! We're here to help you!"

The frantic cartoon woodpecker began again, then ended in an abrupt "Auwkp!" as a shot rang out.

Glass tinkled down from above. The slug must have hit one of the bulbs on the skylight. By the time glass quit falling, we both had our guns out, listening.

We'd paused to catch our breath and get our bearings, then Harald and I realized at the same instant that the elevator door stood open on this landing. Someone had blocked the door open with a metal ashtray.

"I'll take it to the top and work down," Harald said quietly. She kicked the ashtray out of the way and was gone before I could stop her.

Keeping close to the inner walls, I raced on up past the sixth and seventh. Still no sign of movement. The shot sounded like it came from very near the top.

I heard the elevator doors open and immediately came another burst of gunfire. Two guns this time. So he was up on the tenth floor after all.

Now I was taking the stairs two at a time, gasping for air. As I burst on to the tenth floor, the landing widened out into what must have been a nice space when the building was new. Like a big sunroom, twenty feet wide by maybe forty long. Two more skylights and tall square columns to support the roof. They probably had couches here, I thought, and pots of ferns all around. Now the walls and columns had grim black graffiti spray-painted everywhere. Instead of couches, some ugly iron benches with ratty plastic cushions were chained to the stair railings.

Even while I was thinking this, I was also looking around for bodies or movement. Both elevator doors were closed and from the mechanical hum and the arrows, both were heading down. Did Harald get shot and fall back inside with the killer?

Then I realized I was standing in a strong draft of cold air. On the other side of the room, almost camouflaged by the dim light and black spray paint was a narrow door, half open to darkness. As I rushed over, a movement on the periphery sent me diving for cover behind one of the columns.

"Come out with your hands high," I snarled.

"No," quavered a voice. "You'll shoot me."

"Canary?"

A low trill of bird whistles confirmed it.

"Hey, man, I'm a cop. We're here to save your ass, not shoot it."

"Vaughn!" The looey's voice seemed to come from far away. "Up here!"

I pushed open the door and found a set of steep iron steps that led up to the roof. Gun in hand, she was standing just outside the threshold, half shielded by the open metal fire door.

There was no light on the roof itself, but there's never real darkness in the city. We could see that kids had been up here earlier, too. A snowwoman with huge tits and fat round hips grinned at us on the other side of a skylight and there was no way to tell which of the footprints leading away from the door belonged to our killer.

"You see who it was?" I asked.

Steps sounded on the stair behind me and the Canary edged onto the landing. "You gonna get him?" he asked. "You gotta shoot him. He pushed her and he was gonna push me." Trills and whistles were all mixed in with his words as if fear had made him forget if he was a bird or a man.

"I saw him. He pushed her in front of a train. He was gonna push me over the stairs. You gotta kill him, too."

"Will you get the hell back down?" I told him. "You want to get shot?"

"Listen!" said Harald.

A metallic clatter. Fire escape.

We burst through the doorway together onto the roof. It was cluttered with air vents and chimneys, the elevator cable housing, and those three chest-high skylights. A large billboard at the far end of the roof blocked the lights of a taller building and it took us longer than it should have to locate the fire escape. Harald spotted it first, beyond the billboard scaffolding, and we rushed to peer over the edge. The bright lights of the billboard, a beer sign, made us squint, and it took a moment for our eyes to adjust. I saw nothing but inky shadows all the way down to the side street; then far below, a dark figure ran away from the building and into an alley.

"Christ! How'd he do that so fast?" I groaned.

"It's not our guy," she whispered in my ear and pointed to the undisturbed snow that still capped the fire escape rungs.

I had a feeling we'd just made a very dumb mistake.

With her gun, she waved for me to circle around while she ducked through the metal scaffold that supported the billboard. Everywhere I looked seemed to be a potential hiding place. No one crouching behind the first skylight. Across the rooftop, I saw the Canary watching me, then he glanced toward Harald and his face froze.

At that same instant, I heard her yell, "Vaughn!"

I whirled, dropped and rolled just as two slugs crashed through the skylight where I'd been standing. As I lay there at the base of the middle skylight, facedown in the snow, I realized that the metallic sound we'd thought was the fire escape was really the steel ladder up to the billboard. He'd copied the Canary's trick and gone up, not down; and if Harald hadn't yelled, I'd have been dead meat.

Carefully picking the side of the skylight in deepest shadow, I crawled around the edge and risked a look. He was lying prone on a metal ledge, his head level with hers. One hand was twined in her hair, the other held the gun pressed against the back of her skull. No sign of the Canary.

"Throw out your gun, Sergeant," he called, "or she gets it."

"Come on, Peters, this is crazy," she argued. "You know there's no way—"

He gave her hair a vicious yank that must have hurt like hell. "I mean it, Vaughn."

"Once anybody takes a hard look, it's obvious you're the one that killed Cluett," she said.

"Liar!"

"It wasn't just Albee he was bugging about court testimony; it was you, too. He told everyone there'd been a huge wad of hundred-dollar bills—enough to "bloat a goat"—but you only vouchered fifty-three, less than a quarter-inch stack, and you couldn't count on him not noticing the discrepancy if the defense la⸻

about it. There was no nineteen-thousand-dollar lottery win. They ran your name through the Lotto computers this afternoon and there's no record that you ever won anything more than that three hundred before Christmas. You skimmed it when you and Cluett had to inventory that bloody drug money."

"Shut up!" he screamed. "Vaughn!"

I lay motionless in the shadows, only the edge of my black face exposed. I had him in my sights, less than thirty feet away, but I was afraid to risk it. I do okay on a firing range, but lying flat like that, he presented almost no target; just his head next to hers. And even if I hit him, reflexive spasms were bound to jerk his trigger.

"You can't kill us all, Peters," she gasped. "Who's next? Eberstadt? Your wife? You think they never noticed you carry a drop gun? Will Pam lie when they come around to check on your alibi?"

Peters yanked her hair so hard that her body arched backward and she cried out with the pain.

"You say one more word, bitch, and I swear to God it'll be your last. Bitches and niggers fucking up the job, fucking *me*—"

In one fluid motion, he pulled her in front of him and dropped to the rooftop. She was a good two inches taller and to maintain his grasp on her short hair, he had her head tilted back till her face was almost pointed up to the heavy sky. Lights reflected off the clouds in a brownish pink glow. He pushed her toward the door and kept his body so close there wasn't a prayer in hell for me to miss her. My gun was almost quivering I was so damn frustrated.

Another few steps and he'd be inside the door and on his way down and there wouldn't be a damn thing I could do about it unless I could get a clear shot from the busted skylight, but the risk—

At that moment, Jerry the Canary popped up from behind the far skylight and gave that lunatic, "Oo-oo-oo-EH-oh! Oo-oo-oo-EH-oh! Eh-eh-eh-eh!"

Instinctively, Peters swung to fire in that direction,

and just as instinctively I squeezed off three shots at the broad target he'd given me.

They went down together as if poleaxed.

I rushed over and kicked away the gun. "Hey, Lieutenant, you okay? Lieutenant?"

She groaned. "Oh, God, my head!"

The guy's fingers were still wrapped in her hair. I pried them open and untangled her hair, and she twisted around to look at him. "Peters!"

He lay on his back. The front of his dark jacket was even darker with a wet stain as blood soaked through. His eyes opened. Focused on our faces over his. "Bitch," he gasped. "Nig—"

And that was it.

The Canary crept over to us, chirping and tweeting forlornly.

Harald sat there on the cold rooftop while I went down and called for help. And she sat there till the crime scene unit made it down from the Bronx. Someone brought a blanket and she let them drape it around her, but she didn't move away from Peters's body till they told her she was hampering their work. Even then, she wouldn't leave the roof until they carried him away. She didn't make a big scene about it. No sobs, no break in her voice when she told her version of events first to McKinnon, who arrived with the precinct boys, and again to Rawson, who'd heard it on his scanner and rushed down. But she couldn't seem to stop the tears that streamed from her eyes whenever she looked over at Peters's still form under Forensic's portable floods.

Three dead because a cop couldn't resist the temptation of grabbing some of that easy drug money. A new widow out in Woodhaven with three fatherless kids now. A partner who'd suspected and had called in sick or looked the other way because he didn't want to know for sure. And Harald and me left to spend the rest of our lives wondering if things would have turned out diff we'd thought to look up instead of down when we first went out on the roof.

No more pop psychology. They'd send us both to real psychiatrists over this. S.O.P. these days, Rawson reminded us.

"And a good thing, too," McKinnon growled. "Come on," he told Harald at last. "I'll drive you home."

"Not home." She looked as exhausted as I felt, but she handed someone the blanket and said to McKinnon, "To Mother's."

That surprised me. She hadn't struck me as anyone with a mother to run home to. Must've surprised McKinnon, too, because I heard him say, "You sure, Sigrid?"

She was already moving into the stairwell, so I didn't get her answer, but McKinnon had an odd look on his face.

Almost like he was afraid.

Which was crazy now that everything was over.

About the Author

MARGARET MARON lives with her artist husband on their family farm near Raleigh, North Carolina. She is a former president of Sisters in Crime.